JENSEN-|||

Star Trainer

FAITH IN FOOLS

HOLLYWOOD

FAITH IN FOOLS

JORDYN BARNES

THE HOLLYWOODLAND SERIES
BOOK TWO

Copyright © 2024 by Jordyn Barnes

All rights reserved.

First Published in 2024, Orlando, Florida, USA

No part of this publication may be reproduced, distributed, or transmitted in any form or by any means, including photocopying, recording, or other electronic or mechanical methods, without the prior written permission of the author, except as permitted by U.S. copyright law. For permission requests, contact jordynblainebarnes@gmail.com.

This is a work of fiction. Unless otherwise indicated, all the names, characters, businesses, places, events and incidents in this book are either the product of the author's imagination or used in a fictitious manner. Any resemblance to actual persons, living or dead, or actual events is purely coincidental. Any product or location names used in this book are trademarks, registered trademarks, or trade names of their respective holders. The author is not associated with any product or vendor in this book.

Paperback: 979-8-9905034-4-1

Ebook: 979-8-9905034-5-8

No AI tools were used in the writing of this book, its contents, or any artwork including the cover. NO AI TRAINING: Without in any way limiting the author's [and publisher's] exclusive rights under copyright, any use of this publication to "train" generative artificial intelligence (AI) technologies to generate text is expressly prohibited. The author reserves all rights to license uses of this work for generative AI training and development of machine learning language models.

Edited by: Horn & Ink

Book Cover and Illustrations by: Jordyn Barnes

LA skyline, gym equipment, and palm trees by Freepik.com and Vecteezy.com

❀ Created with Vellum

CONTENT/TRIGGER WARNINGS

This book is a romance, and it *does* end with an HEA, but there are heavy topics. I can make sure this book is right for you. Take care of your mental health and don't be ashamed to ask for help if you need it. You're not alone out there.

Homophobia (Internalized and external), Transphobia (Internalized and external), Toxic Fathers, Misogyny, Alcohol Use, Drug Use (weed and ecstasy), Anxiety, Bullying, Death of Sibling (off page), Death of Parent (off page), Cheating, Emotional Abuse, Past Physical Abuse (as a child), Misgendering, Divorce (parents, off page)

This book is intended for an adult audience. Please read responsibly. If you're not sure about the warnings, reach out to me at any of my social media platforms or my website jordynbarnes.com.

For anyone who was ever told you weren't good enough.
You're better than every person who ever said that to you.
Be who you want to be, fuck everyone else.

Also, for that coach who said I wasn't good enough

for varsity because I didn't go to church on Wednesday nights.

Thanks for cutting me, I spent the day at Disney instead.

"I have great faith in fools—
self-confidence my friends will call it."

EDGAR ALLAN POE

DICKTIONARY

Want to find (or avoid?) the open door chapters? Here is a list, and you'll find a pepper icon near the image at the start of each of these chapters as a reminder.

🌶 Chapter 3
🌶 Chapter 9
🌶 Chapter 12
🌶 Chapter 13
🌶 Chapter 17
🌶 Chapter 21
🌶 Chapter 28
🌶 Chapter 29

CONTENTS

JENSEN

Star Trainer

STEVE
+
ETHAN

HOLLYWOOD
Steve

CHAPTER 1
I'M SHIPPING UP TO BOSTON

DROPKICK MURPHYS

MY CURRENT GIRLFRIEND—OR at least that's what she calls herself—is the perfect example of why I don't believe in love. She storms into the gym like she owns it; her bleached blond hair bouncing in time with her boobs. When she gets to me, she shoves two Halloween costumes in front of me, completely ignoring the fact that I'm with a client. One costume is a white polo that's too small for me with an orange scarf thing. The other looks like a superhero getup in red and black spandex with a giant lowercase "i" in the middle of the chest.

"Pick a costume, Steve." She pouts, sticking her tits out and licking her lips. It's all for attention, and likely not even mine. At this point, several of the gym members have turned to check her out, and I don't blame them. She's got it, and she sure does love to flaunt it. "There's only two weeks before the party and people are running out of good costumes, so we have to pick one—now!"

"Seriously, cartoon characters are the best you've got?" I scrunch up my face and turn back to my client. "Do that rep again. You slacked off because you thought I wasn't watching. Come on, you got this, Robbie!"

"Steve! Focus! I've been to every damn store I could find, and these are the ones I liked."

Kennedy and I hooked up at a party after a mutual friend, Dani, introduced us. More like set us up; she likes to think she's some kind of matchmaking genius. Also, mutual friend is an overstatement and an understatement all in one. Dani and Kennedy work together and barely tolerate each other, while Dani's my friend in a kid sister kind of way. She's ruthless, so there's a devious reason she played matchmaker to Kennedy and I. Kennedy pissed her off, and I'm a serial dater, or as Dani likes to call me, a man-whore. I told her that terminology is offensive, but she had some snippy comeback about not calling me a male sex worker because that's insulting to sex workers. It was a fair point.

Staring at the costumes wrapped in clear plastic, I groan and tell Robbie to take a break before I drag Kennedy to the back of the room by the vending machines. I could take her to my office, or one of the handful of private rooms and classrooms, but we'd end up fucking around and I don't have time for that. It's the only thing we have in common: we both really love sex.

"First off, I've told you not to fucking come in here when I have clients. Second off, are you Velma or Daphne in this stupid equation? Thirdly, what the hell happened to the Adam and Eve idea?"

"You said I couldn't wear a bodysuit and had to go with the leaves stuck on. Gross. I'm not showing up naked just so you can show me off to your weirdo friends."

"Come on, baby," I coo, tilting her head back while my other hand grabs her round ass. "You know it's so I can lick that sweet—"

"Hey Steve!" my buddy, Craig, yells out from the front. "You've got company!"

"Alright!" I shout back, then consider both costumes Kennedy is holding out. "Uhm, fine. Freddie and the gang it is. Oh shit, can I go as Freddie and Fred? Like a mashup."

"Who's Freddie?"

"Nightmare on Elm Street?" She stares at me like I've just grown two new heads and they're not the fun kind. "Fuck, how do you not know Freddie? It's a classic horror film! Fucked up face, glove with blades on it, haunts dreams?"

"Jesus, Steve, that sounds so stupid. I gotta go pick up my sister." She leaves the way she came in, a raging storm of cute ass and nice tits.

"Who was that?" Craig asks as he grabs a fresh bottle of water from the cooler.

"That is the reason I need to stop dating anything below twenty-five. Dani hooked us up, and I'm pretty sure it was a punishment for something I did to offend her."

"Bro, that could be any number of things. So you're gonna break up with her?"

"Not until after the party. She's gonna look so fucking hot in that costume. I'll tap it and then drop her the next morning."

"You're a dog, you know that."

"Woof fucking woof, Craig. Besides, she's fucking some other guy already. Hey, can you finish out Robbie's set for me?" I check my watch, but I'm pretty sure I don't have any meetings on the schedule for today. I turn the corner and see my best friend's brother—soon-to-be hockey legend—Devin Cooper, standing there next to the head coach for the local pro team. I'm gonna like this. "Mini Coop! Bro! What's a loser like you doing hanging out with the best coach in the show?"

"Hi, Steve!" He says it like he's still twelve, like he still looks up to me as if I'm another brother. The kid is our team's starting goalie after only one season—he's that damn good. But he's also like family. "We just signed a new guy, and he needs a tuneup. I told Coach I don't mind splitting training sessions with him since you're busy and all, but—"

"Jensen, the owner and I talked." Coach always loves to cut to the chase. "We'd like to hire you on to make sure this kid is back in shape before he hits the ice. I wanted to come down and give you the backstory personally, since this is a big deal."

"The season already started. Why come to me now?" I'm not here to turn down pro hockey money, but I'm also not about to set myself up for failure. Failure is always the option for my dating life, but not my business.

"I'll be honest, I put my neck out for this kid. I think he's still got talent, but the owner is convinced we wasted too much money signing him." Coach looks around the room. It's not fancy, but it's not full utilitarian, either. When we bought it, the place was a shitty old warehouse, but it had excellent ceiling height for a gym. Since then, we gutted it, painted the interior in reds and blues, and put in a combination of wood and rubber floors. All the equipment is state-of-the art and well maintained. I have my own training that every employee has to go through before they work with clients, and I got a physical therapy office to move in upstairs. "Shit, Jensen. This place looks a hell of a lot better than it did a few years ago. Good job."

"Thanks, you're welcome to use anything we've got whenever you want, Coach. So what's the plan with this kid? Is there a timeframe?"

"We're going to slow-roll him out. Contractually, he's on the team and getting his paycheck, but this kid was hurt pretty bad." Coach hands me a binder full of information like it's the nineties again. "If you'll take him on, the head trainer would like to meet with you and LaVoie before the end of the week. They've sent over his files."

"Dumb question. Two actually. One, can I get these in a less archaic format?" Coach rolls his eyes, but nods. He has to know I'm not about to parse through all this shit for a paycheck unless they're sending someone over to suck my dick while I do. "Two, why me and not the team's trainers?"

"I want you to take the lead on this one. We saw what you did for Lavon Jarvis. That kid's career was over, and you brought him back to win the damn NBA MVP award the very next season." Coach shakes his head and laughs. "To be fair, seeing that opened a lot of eyes in our organization, and we're talking contracts, no matter how this goes. Our guy in recovery and our strength and conditioning trainer will take care of him during practices and any on-ice workouts once you give us the go-ahead. Right now, they've got their hands full."

"Four injuries on opening night will do that."

"You're telling me. Anyhow, you're one of the few trainers in this city that understands this shit enough for me to trust. Lots of solid people stand by what you do, and you're a straight shooter. You won't lie to me if we've made a mistake signing him. That's what I need with this kid."

"Okay, what was the injury?"

"Injuries, actually. In round one of last year's playoffs, LaVoie took a brutal hit from behind into the boards. The guy who hit him was around two fifty, he careened into the boards right along with him. Torn ACL and fractured tibia, and a broken wrist. Another player stumbled and tried to avoid him, but ended up crashing down elbow first, right into LaVoie's spine. The doctors say he's lucky to be walking. LaVoie says he's good for at least forty points if we clear him early enough in the season. The kid's young and has something to prove. I want him proving he's a damn fine defenseman, not that he should have never stepped back onto the ice."

The guy's name sounds familiar, but I'm too busy running recovery times in my head for everything Coach rattled off. The look on my face gives away what I'm about to say, but I say it anyway. "Are you fucking kidding me? That's—"

"Career ending? For most, yeah. This kid has busted his ass to get back in shape. At twenty-five, he's gone through more surgeries in the last six months than most players do their whole lives."

"Is he…walking?"

"He was out on the ice yesterday, running basic drills with Hollywood here."

I flip through the first few pages with the x-rays and general notes. For an athlete, an ACL injury can be career ending—or at least knock you out for eight months or more. Add on the other injuries, and this kid should be in a wheelchair or a recliner watching the games from home. I'm not afraid to take him on, but I need everyone to understand the limits. I have over forty professional athletes and movie stars as clients in my programs. I'm not risking my gym's reputation on someone who won't put in the work. When Devin pulls up video of yesterday's drills, there is barely a sign he went through all that, unless you know what you're looking for. I do, and the fact that he'll be coming to me means the team doctor noticed, too.

"Keep him off the ice until I have a chance to evaluate him. I'll call the team doc and trainers to set up a meeting and give you some time tables after that. If I take this, we'll start next week. Where's he living?"

"He's with Coop and I," Devin says proudly. "He doesn't have family out here, and I've known him since high school. We met at a hockey summer league thing. When he signed on, we gave him one of the spare rooms since I'm in the pool house."

"Perfect. Mini Coop is right. I can work with him and the

new kid concurrently. We can aim for a week from Wednesday. That will give us time for an eval and to send him to the specialist before I get my hands on him. Dev, tell Coop the newb is crashing the morning workout at your normal time. You and Coop will start with a run, and that will give me time to work with the kid on the basics and adjust his training schedule."

"Oh, man, come on! I can't run on Wednesdays!"

"Against your religion, Hollywood?" Coach chides with a laugh.

"It's bad luck!"

"Well, then you'll just have to play better, because you're running. So is your brother."

"Fuck!"

HOLLYWOOD
21
Ethan

CHAPTER 2
HERE IT GOES AGAIN

OK GO

THERE'S something about your own bed that's peaceful and comforting when you spend most of your life traveling and bouncing between hotel rooms. The problem? This isn't technically my bed—or my room. It's my stuff, sure, but the space isn't mine and that has me on edge. Worse than that is there's nothing to stare at. Hotel walls and ceiling have cracks or marks I can stare at until my mind has exhausted all the ways it got there or what it could be and eventually lulls me to sleep. This place is bordering on mansion, even though Chase will deny it because he doesn't want to come across as a pompous prick. It's hard to maintain a normal guy image when you're living in the Hollywood Hills and you've got a brilliant view of the Hollywood sign from your fucking pool. Hell, I'm not even in the guest room, I'm in a *spare* guest room.

When I go to get out of bed, my back tenses up and tells me it's going to be a shit day. It doesn't matter how nice the mattress is when your spine gets cracked in places that should never crack. I take my time—grinding my teeth through the pain—and ten minutes later I'm at least sitting on the edge of my bed. This can't happen on the road. Not until I have earned a solo hotel room for road games. Then I can wallow in misery without the judgmental company.

Usually, it's only rookies who double up when the team travels, but I'm only a small fraction above them in the pecking order. I'm also new to the team and late to the season. Coach said it will help me get to know my teammates better, but I think he's going to use it to spy on me. See just how fucked up I am and how much I'm hiding. I don't blame him. I'm hiding a lot.

"Yo, Lala?" The voice and knock are both timid, so I know it's Devin. The kid can be the life of the party, or he's a shy guy trying not to piss anyone off. He's not scared of me getting annoyed, he's just trying to be respectful and give me my space in his house. Well, his brother's house, anyway. Chase Cooper is Devin's older brother. He's also a bona fide movie star. I'm grateful they're letting me crash here while I find my footing, especially since that dollar amount on my contract isn't what it was a year ago. Housing out here is a fucking nightmare, too. Gotta love Los Angeles.

"Yeah?"

"Sorry, man. I'm leaving for the rink in twenty if you want to ride in together."

Twenty minutes should be more than enough time for me to get ready, but it took me ten just to fucking sit up. "Make it twenty-five and you've got a deal. I'll buy the coffee on the way."

"That works!"

I do a few stretches—ones to loosen up my back fastest—and shamble like a damn zombie into the bathroom. Fuck. I look like shit. I splash some water on my face and run a wet hand through my hair. I've let it grow into a shaggy mess since the injury, rarely bothering to get it cut. I'll need to find a barber soon, though. Or, I might keep it since it works with the whole California vibe.

By the time I leave the room and meet up with Devin by the front door, I'm moving better and the pain is manageable. Manageable pain for me just means I'm not wincing or anything else people might see. Maybe it's more hidden than managed. Coach is out on the ice when we get to the rink, along with a handful of other players in for morning drills. He hops off when he sees me and tells me to head up to the trainers. I expected that, since Devin told me about the meeting already, but I'm still nervous as fuck.

It's eerily quiet as I walk down the empty hallway. I expected to hear the standard blaring music coming from the gym, but the silence tells me no other players are up here. I guess that makes sense. No need for everyone to spread rumors about how fucked up my back is. I open the door to find one of our trainers, Tommy, and some other guy in the middle of a deadlift competition. Judging by the sweat and the gulping for air, Tommy is losing. Badly.

"Okay, last one!" Tommy huffs. His face is fire engine red, but looking at the weight, I'm not surprised. Tommy's built like a hockey player, lean and strong. The guy standing in front of him looks like a fucking mac truck. When Tommy tries to lift the weight, nothing happens. I do the math in my head and realize they've got over five hundred pounds on that bar. My back hurts just thinking about it. Mr. Muscles walks up to the bar next, and that superhero movie where nobody can lift the hammer pops into my head. Just like the movie, the guy who can lift it does so like it's made of air.

"Lala! Dude, you look like you've seen a ghost or something," Cole, our head trainer, says as he notices me by the door. "Come on in, don't worry, you're not lifting that. These two meatheads got bored after sitting in a forty-minute meeting with Doc. This is Steve Jensen. He runs a local gym, and he's currently the trainer for your two housemates."

Mr. Muscles turns around and holy fuck. He's got a bit of a messy faux hawk going and he's smirking at me, winking his ice-blue eyes I can't stop staring at. My mind goes completely blank and I've forgotten why the hell I'm even here. He holds out a hand and, thankfully, my brain kicks back into gear enough to shake it.

"Nice to meet you. Would have met you sooner, but I've been training Coop at my gym for the last few weeks. I'm sure you know about that." His grip is strong at first, but softens just a little as I smile at him. Then I remember where the fuck I am and that I can't be gawking right now.

"Yeah, Dev mentioned it. Something about a rock-climbing wall?" I take my hand away, even though I don't want to. "So, uhm, Coach said to come up and meet with you guys."

Steve picks up a binder that I know well and starts flipping through it. "I do a lot of personal trainer work with the local teams and studios, cases like yours that will be more intensive time-wise. We were just going over the plan for your workouts to make sure you're ready and able to step them up."

"Great. I have everything that I've been doing in the files. I thought it would help as a starting point."

"Uh huh, it's detailed and pretty extreme, but hell, you being on the ice right now is crazy." He flips through more pages, but he's not reading them, which means he's read the reports already. Something about this feels off.

I panic, internally freaking out that this fucking guy is coming into my fucking rink and about to tell me I can't play. Who the fuck does he think he is? He doesn't even work for the team. "I have medical clear—"

"Oh, I know. Coach wants more than just clearance, though. So, I just wanna ask you something before we do this." He slams the binder shut and lets it drop onto a nearby bench.

I'm not entirely sure what *this* is or why this guy is being such a dick, but I'm ready for whatever he feels like throwing at me. I hope.

"Why don't you retire? Why don't you hang it up instead of risking it all for a game? The wrong move, the wrong play, the wrong turn, and you could be in a wheelchair. For life. That's the best-case scenario."

My eyes flick between Tommy and Cole and I can see they're asking themselves the same thing. It pisses me off. "Because I can do this. I *can* come back from this stronger and smarter. I *can* be a better player if people just let me do this and stop questioning me. This is my fucking life, man. It's not just a damn game."

He looks me up and down and nods. He's not hot anymore. Okay, he is, but I'm too pissed off to care about that.

"We start Wednesday. Already cleared it with Coach and Devin. On Monday, you get checked out by the specialist—Doc already has the appointment scheduled. You'll be with me on Mondays, Wednesday, and Fridays. The rest of the week, you're on ice with these two shitheads. If it's an off day here, you're still training with me at the gym or the house, don't care which. We start at eight in the morning because Chase can't get his ass out of bed any earlier than that."

"Wait, what?"

"I'm your personal trainer now. At least until I think you're ready to come back."

"I didn't agree to—"

"Listen, when I'm done with you, Coach, the GM, and the owner are all going to feel a whole lot better about the price they paid to let you play." He turns to Cole and says, "Gimme a minute with him."

They walk away and heat rises from my collar. I signed a contract that said I wouldn't start the season until Coach felt like I was ready, but I thought that meant a game or two after everyone else, not this. My jaw ticks and my fingers are twitching, so I cross my arms and stare up into this Steve prick's eyes, challenging him in some weird, macho, not at all *me* way.

"Kid, I know what you're thinking. I do. The thing is, I asked them what to expect. I met with Doc, and I read through your files. You're doing one hell of a job hiding your pain. Chase could learn a thing or two from your acting skills, but you shouldn't be playing in pain like that."

"I'm not in pain. I feel fucking fine. You just want the pretty paycheck they're sliding your way to get me out of their hair."

"The paycheck is cute, but next time you want to lie to me, learn how to stand still and hide the pain. You can hide it when you're in motion, and you almost had me and Doc Smith fooled. It was when you stood still, then tried to move on ice in the drills. Dead giveaway, baby." He picks up the giant binder and hands it to me, pats me on the back, and heads for the door. "See you next week, Lala."

HOLLYWOOD
Steve

CHAPTER 3
FUCK YOU

LILY ALLEN

COOP IS OUT OF TOWN, so instead of watching the game with him and our buddy Jamie, I'm stuck at home, trying to watch what I can through a thick head of blond hair while Kennedy bounces on my dick. From the outside, she's my type: petite, big tits, and loves to fuck, but there are two problems: I stopped believing in love, and she loses points for having very little between her ears.

When we first met, it took all of five minutes before we ended up in the bathroom with her sucking my dick like a Hoover. Now, she might not get herself off, let alone me. If I have to jerk off in the shower later, why the fuck do I need her around? Dani can yell at me later. Besides, Jamie's going to win the breakup pool that Cooper setup, and he'll split it with me.

Like a lot of rich Los Angeles brats, she wasted too much of Mommy and Daddy's money. Three years ago, they cut her off and told her she needed to learn how life works. That tactic rarely works. My parents threatened the same for me, but I stopped taking handouts the second I could get a job. Dad would have held it over my head.

Kennedy dreams of being the next big influencer—in her

mind, all it takes is connections and a phenomenal body. She's got the body, and I've got the connections. It's the only reason she's bouncing on my lap right now. Meanwhile, she's damn close to getting fired from her actual job because she's late, hung over, and lets guys like me fuck her in the bathroom behind her boss's back. Guys like me, but not me, because I know Sam, so I take her out back and fuck her in my car.

I'm already planning to dump her next weekend after the party. Coop says I should dump her now, but when I asked him who'd give me a birthday blowjob if I did that, he sure as hell didn't jump up and volunteer. I'll get what I want, then I'll slide her a few low-level connections. She's as bored in this half-assed relationship as I am, and neither one of us is doing much to cover that boredom up, either.

I don't picture her when I jack off anymore. Hell, her tits are in my face right now and I'm wishing she'd move so I could see the damn game. The only way I'm getting off right now is by thinking about my newest client. The TV goes to commercial and I rock my head back against the wall, closing my eyes. It's not her anymore, it's him bouncing on my lap. I grab her hips and slow her down, lifting and lowering her at the speed I'd want to fuck him the first time. Picturing that back of his arching as he whines for my cock.

"Stevie!"

"What?!"

"Come on, I was close."

"No, you weren't, but I was." I circle her clit with my thumb. I don't care if she gets off or not, but I'm rock hard thinking about Ethan LaVoie, and I wanna finish my fantasy. I wanna run my hands through that shaggy blond hair and fuck his face while he looks up with those big, green—

"Oh fuck! Oh, fuck!" I hold her hips and imagine slamming

into his ass as I feel my stomach muscles clench, hearing him cry out for me, cry out for more. The problem is, it's still her voice.

"Yes! Oh Yes, baby! Just like that, baby!" She ruins the entire fantasy with that fake vocal fry and low-budget porno screaming. It's not what she's saying, it's how she says it that just takes me out of the moment.

As I finish, Rage Against the Machine blasts from my phone, so I move her off my lap, grab the phone, and head to the kitchen. I've never been so happy to be interrupted by my sister during sex.

"Yeah?" I answer, shoving my dick back into my shorts.

"*Yeah*? That's how you answer the phone for your perfect and most loved sibling? We shared a womb, and you answer me with *yeah*?"

"You're my only sibling. By birth, anyhow." This is normal banter between my sister and I. "What the fuck do you want, psycho?"

"I'll let you think about that for a second."

I roll my eyes and grab a beer out of the fridge. When I shut the door, the note I left myself so I wouldn't forget about tonight stares me in the face. Family birthday party. "FUCK! Gimme five, I'll be right out. You're still here, right?"

"Yep. Wear the suit. Associates from the firm are coming to the house after."

"Double fuck! Be right out!" I hurry through the house, downing the beer as I dig through my closet. There should be a suit in here somewhere. Or at least an emergency dress shirt with sleeves. Shit, it's not here. I spin around and the sigh of relief that comes out of me makes the bag on the back of the door flutter. The suit is hanging there, dry cleaned, with a tie, socks, and shoes ready to go. My sister is the fucking best.

I get dressed, check my hair, and head for the door. As my

hand hits the knob, I stop and realize Kennedy is still here. We fucked, we got off—what more does she want from me? When I turn around, she's in a short, smoking hot fuck-me dress that sparkles from the light of the TV. This moment represents the glowing neon sign telling me I'm over her and this relationship. A month ago, I would have bent her over the sofa and had her screaming my name while Laurie waited. Now? Not even the four-inch stilettos are doing it for me.

"Where the fuck are you going?" She rolls her head and I'm praying it just falls off.

"Family dinner. I gotta go. *Now.*"

She scoops up her purse and walks out of my apartment in a huff. I was probably supposed to go with her. I've known for a while Dani set the two of us up because Kennedy is the chick version of me. We just fucked, and I guarantee that tonight, she's bringing at least one guy home with her. Whatever. I'd do the same thing if I wasn't going to Beverly Hills. Hell, I still might. Woof, fucking, woof.

"Yo," I say as I toss the jacket and tie into the back of Laurie's sports car.

"What's her name?"

"Does it matter?"

"Someday I'll ask you that and you'll give me an answer. That's when it will matter. Get in, we're going to be late."

"Not the way you drive. Hit it, Lando Norris."

Family dinners with the all too honorable Judge Michael P. Jensen are so much fun. Appetizers laced with bickering, main course reminders of my failures as a son, and a dessert of acerbic insults slung in all directions. After dinner, we'll head to their house where Dad will hold court and his minions will kiss his ring.

"You're late and smell like booze."

"Must have borrowed your cologne. Hey Ma," I lean forward, kissing my mother on her cheek and ignoring the insult my father is preparing. "How's the shoulder?"

"Oh, it's much better now. Those stretches were—"

"For Christ's sake, Elaine, he's nothing but a gym rat. Let's go."

My uncle, Bob, is at the table, seated so that we're separated from our parents. Bob stands, giving my mother and Laurie each a kiss on their cheeks, and a firm handshake for me. Dad just sits down and picks up the menu. Bob is Mom's brother and the only other family we have out here in Los Angeles, but he's also the only family we like. The rest are all arrogant pricks, so at least I come by it honestly. Bob understands our father's toxic outlook on life, and he grew up with the flighty, out of touch way Mom handles everything, but he's always been there for us.

"Doesn't your sister look lovely tonight, Steven?" My mother asks in her posh New England way after several awkward, silent moments. This is her attempt at small talk. Unlike the rest of us, my mother sounds like she came from New England's finest—because she did.

"She does," my uncle replies before I can slide in with something snarky. "Radiant, my dear, as always."

It's a pleasant moment until my father scoffs and says something under his breath. Luckily, Bob puts a hand on my arm, so I keep my head down and my mouth shut. That's how we make it through dinner. That's how we always make it through dinner. Mom and Bob keeping things as pleasant as possible, Laurie trying hard as hell to impress Dad, and Dad and I trying to goad each other into fights.

Happy fucking birthday to us. I hate these damn things.

Somehow, the main course gets to the table before Dad orders a drink. That fucking hypocrite wants to talk about my drinking when he's the one who can't get through a meal without lifting a bottle. We all know what will come next, so Laurie and I shovel our food into our mouths as fast as we can, like we're in a food eating competition or something. It's why Laurie and I only order a salad when we have to make these appearances. We finish before Dad is done with his first glass. In customary fashion, we excuse ourselves and walk the two blocks to the Cheese Store. Laurie loves this place, and now and then, we spot a celebrity. Honestly, we'd go to McDonald's if it meant avoiding the show our father makes of paying the bill.

"Next year, we get a ride share." Laurie jokes as she nibbles on the cheese board she pre-ordered. "I need to be drunk or high to deal with them."

"I brought the weed, but I have a better idea. Let's skip out next year and see if it gives him an aneurysm."

Her phone buzzes and we know it's Bob telling us they're leaving the restaurant. Laurie buys two bottles of wine and we head back to her car. Twenty minutes later, Laurie parks up the street from the ostentatious house our parents live in. We're walking up the front steps, sharing a joint, when Bob stops us and ushers us over to the side of the porch and lights a cigarette before leaning against the porch railing with a sigh. "Your mother means well. You know that, right?"

"What do you mean?"

"She put out pictures because she's proud of you two. She wants to celebrate you both on your birthday. Not because she wants to hurt either of you."

"What are you talking about?"

"You got here before I could take them down. I didn't want you to walk in blind." He turns to Laurie, putting his hands on her shoulder. "Your brother can help me, but I need you to not make a scene about it. I'll talk to her later. I promise."

"Pictures?" Laurie laughs, then her face slowly drops as she realizes he means pictures of our whole life, not just the last ten years. "No. No, there are people coming to this, people I respect, and they—"

"I know, sweetheart," he pulls her to him, comforting her. I can see her eyes welling up with tears and it makes me fume with rage. This has my father's stink all over it. Bastard.

"Fuck this—"

"Steven!" he barks at me, then lowers his voice. "We have to do this with more tact and finesse than your parents have, for Laurie. If we make a scene, people will look at the pictures. *Closely.*" He kisses Laurie on the head and brings us both inside to where our mother sits, greeting guests like the queen. Clueless.

We wait a few minutes, then Bob and I discreetly duck out to the front room. Just like he said, there's a table with over fifty frames on it. A few photos from when we're so young you can't tell, but it's painfully obvious in the other half that the pictures are of me and Spencer—not Laurie. Me standing beside a shy, tall, skinny kid who isn't comfortable in their own body because it's not the right body. Not yet. My fists ball up, and I'm ready to swing on the first motherfucker that opens their mouth, and in a lot of ways, I'm hoping that's Dad. He's never accepted Laurie. Hell, he's never accepted either of us.

I shove the frames into a closet and slam the door shut, hoping they all crack and break while they're in there, then I go back and stand by Laurie so she knows it's done.

Laurie's confidence comes back with each person to congratulate her on her law degree and taking the bar. I'm proud of her for doing what I couldn't. After they talk to her, they step over to me and offer disappointing glares as I grin and shake their hands. They're associates at Dad's firm, but he's not in the room right now. Likely fucked off to the bar again. He's old and drunk and these people have made him into the damn king of Los Angeles. Although, some are here because Laurie is supposed to be taking over the company in the next few years and they know how to get in the proper position to kiss her ass. I'm laughing to myself, picturing her firing half of these fuckers on her first day.

I hear our uncle doing damage control and laughing off the pictures, saying someone grabbed the wrong frames and clearly they were pictures of me with our cousins. Of course they'd buy that. Half of these people couldn't even pick their own children out of a lineup, let alone Laurie in her pre-op days. A commotion coming from the hallway grabs our attention in time to see Dad stumbling into the main room. He trips over a chair that hasn't moved in years, and my mother takes his arm to help him along. He mumbles about the chair, giving it a dirty look and then laughing it off like nothing happened.

"Ladies, gentlemen, and those of you who are neither," he starts.

I grab my sister's hand, whispering, "Let's go."

"No, he might announce me as a partner, you know, for a birthday present." The champagne speaks for her, disguised as hope. Deep down, she knows that. She's about to come crashing back to reality, and it's going to hurt like a son of a bitch.

"Some of you are here tonight because I made you come here or lose your job. Some of you came here to show my family your respect and support."

"Jesus, he sounds like the fucking godfather," I joke, still trying to get Laurie to leave.

"But we know most of you came here tonight to drink my booze and *lie* to my face." I watch Bob head over and try to stop our father before he can say any more, whispering something to my mother as he does. Her face pales and her eyes meet ours. The lightbulb has clicked, but it's too little, too late.

"Mike," our uncle tries again to interrupt. No one saw the punch coming until too late. Mom and I rush to Bob's side as the crimson pours from his nose. Dad scoffs and continues.

"But the biggest lie of all is the one in the pretty red dress and million-dollar smile. Well, over a million really, once you tack on the price of the new body, identity, and a move clear across the country for his ungrateful ass."

"Dad!" I try to jump up, but Mom holds me back. I should never have left Laurie alone.

"Get her out of here. Now," Bob whispers as my mother holds a napkin to his face to catch the blood. I wonder, in that moment, if it's her taking care of her brother, or the carpet. "Hurry."

"The biggest lie is you fuckers calling him *Laurie* and telling me I have a *beautiful daughter*." He scratches at his neck as he snarls. He's never done this before, never stepped this far out of line.

"Daddy, no. Please," Laurie begs, tears in her eyes and hands shaking as I reach for them. I need to get her out of here, but there's a wall of people hanging on every word my father says while they stare at us.

"If you want the law firm, my legacy, everything I worked for so you spoiled fucking shits could steal it from me, then you have to fucking earn it. Not as Laurie, the lie, as Spencer. My goddamned son." He takes a swig right from the bottle. "I'll have my accountant send you a bill for the party in the morning. Happy fucking birthday. You're cut off. Both of you."

HOLLYWOOD
21
Ethan

CHAPTER 4
EVERYBODY HATES ME

GAYLE

"HEY, MOM."

"Oh Ethan, it's good to hear your voice," she says, as if we didn't talk two days ago. *"I just got back from visiting your sister for her birthday. You should see her view since they took down that awful building across the street. And the flowers? Gosh, so many!"*

"That's great, mom. Did she get my flowers? And the bear?"

"Charlie knew those were from you!" She's been with Charlie for almost ten years now. He's so much better for her than Dad was. *"They look beautiful, baby. I think they're the prettiest ones you've ever gotten her."*

"Was Dad there?"

She's quiet for a minute, but that could mean anything. *"We think we saw his car across the street. He might have gone to see her after we left."*

He didn't. It probably wasn't even his car they saw, just Mom trying to make me feel like Dad is trying. Trying would mean he picks up the phone and calls, but I haven't talked to him in four years and I'd like to keep it that way. Mom and I talk about my sister's birthday and the weather in Boston, simple things to keep us from circling back to the topic of Dad. She asks me how

I'm liking the team and how Devin is doing—she remembers him from hockey camp.

"What about the trainer? Have you started with him yet?"

"No. He's, uhm, I dunno. I guess he can't be that bad, since he's over at the house all the time and friends with Chase. He's just...intense?"

"Intense? As intense as his pretty blue eyes and those dimples?"

"Mom!"

"What? You think I wouldn't look up the man who's going to get my baby back out on the ice where he belongs?" It's one thing she and Dad agreed on. We were all meant to be hockey players. *"He's cute, Lala."*

"Don't start, mom."

"What, you can't be single forever! You're too handsome for that!"

"Mom, seriously? Do you want me to get cut from the team?"

"No, I want the team to accept you for who you are. I want you to accept who you are and stop being so afraid."

"Yeah, okay. I gotta get going. I have to meet with some specialist about my back."

"How is your back?"

"Better, I think. Guess I'll know more in a couple of hours, though. I'll call you tomorrow before the game."

"I love you, Ethan. Single or not, you'll always have me."

With the number of times my family has been in and out of doctor's offices and hospitals, I should have built up some kind of immunity to visiting them by now, but I haven't. In fact, since the injury and the accident, it's been worse. I get nervous and my mind races, anticipating the worst. My knee isn't healing. My back needs another surgery. They've found something new. I can't play anymore. Everything runs through my mind at once while I sit there waiting. Some things are outlandish, like the fear that they're going to amputate my leg. Some things are laughable. But together, they're all the terrifying messes of my brain overloading.

"Mr. LaVooeeeyah?"

"LaVoie," I reply under my breath as I stand and give a half-hearted smile to the nurse.

"Oh, that's like all the vowels smashed together. Never seen that before." She doesn't look back at me, as she makes small talk while we traverse the hallways to a room in the very back. It makes me more nervous when I see the x-ray room is right across the hall. I'm pretty sure I'm only a few scans away from being whatever the x-ray version of Hulk is. Or at least I should glow in the dark. "The doctor will be right in to see you."

At the rink, I see the team doctor, but he's not a specialist, so he refers us out when it's a case like mine. The longer I'm part of this hockey club, the more I feel like I'm only here to cause the team trouble and wrack up medical and PT bills. It's frustrating and I want to get out on the ice even though the season is only three weeks in. Missing games means I don't get to work through the early season jitters or bond with the team the way I could if I started on time, and that worries me.

"Ethan!" The doc greets me, hand outstretched, even though his eyes never leave the chart he's holding. I shake his hand, and he walks over and tosses the folder onto a small table before leaning against the wall. He fumbles with a piece of fabric in his pocket before finally pulling it out and wiping his lenses. I'm not sure if this is how he calms his patients down normally, but it's not helping me one bit.

"Did the team send you everything?"

"Yes, it looks like I have all of their reports, as well as the files from Boston. That's an excellent doctor you had out there. She's one of the best."

"Yeah, that's what they told me."

"Tell me, are you related to Aaron LaVoie?"

"Yes, sir. He's my brother."

He purses his lips and shakes his head as he stuffs the cloth back into his pocket. "Damn shame about him. He had talent. Too good to be stuck coaching kids leagues."

Here we go. This is how any hockey fan starts a conversation with me. First, he'll talk about my brother's career. If he's a big fan, we'll start with college days, otherwise he'll jump right to the pros. Once he's exhausted his opinions on my brother's single professional hockey game, he'll switch over to one of my other brothers, or my dad. This is how it will go for at least thirty minutes. Not once will he mention me, my career, how I beat the odds, how I lead the league in defensive goals my rookie year. If he talks about me at all, it's only going to be discussing the hit and the treatment after. I'm the only one who made it to the big leagues and stayed, but I'm an afterthought. The one who never should have been in the pros in the first place.

"So, how's your dad doing? He still coaching over there on the east coast?"

I lean back in the chair and get comfortable, letting my mind go into autopilot and rattle off the answers my father programmed us to say. I never say what I want to because that would blow their mind. To tell them Aaron, my oldest brother, fucked up and my dad paid to have it covered up. Or that my brother Briar should be in jail right now, but the universe took care of him for what he did. Cole had his own demons before he put his car through a tree. Oh, and dear old Dad? More wins than any other coach in New England? I bet none of them know the real reason he turned down the chance to coach in the pros.

"Let's take a gander at how you're healing and get some new x-rays on the knee for our own records."

When I leave the office, I don't want to go back home yet because I know Steve is still there. It's getting harder and harder to avoid staring at him for too long, and it's going to get me into trouble—eventually. I'm worried he knows about me. I'm more worried that I don't think he minds one bit. Steve's not straight, but he doesn't like being called Bi either. The more I listen to him talk about past conquests, the more I think the guy might be omni sexual and never heard the term before. Whatever he is, it's none of my business, and I need to keep it that way. Although, him being at the house almost every damn day since we met isn't making any of this easier. Devin says it's because Chase is back in town and not filming. I can't help but think that's only part of the reason, and those are the kinds of thoughts I need to get the hell out of my head.

I waste some time at a comic book shop before swinging over to a regular bookstore. I grab lunch at a sandwich place called Fat Sals. It's my last cheat day before I start workouts with Steve, and I'm gonna cheat hard, ordering a sub that comes with pastrami, mozzarella sticks, and onion rings piled high with other shit that's just as bad. I top it off by adding a milkshake that has a piece of cheesecake on top of it to the order. Steve would kick my ass if he saw this, but he's not my trainer yet.

I put gas in Devin's car and pick up beer and a few bags of Reece's Pieces for later. Like I said, I go hard on cheat days. I'll pay for it tomorrow, I'm sure.

When I've killed an extra three hours after my appointment, I head back home, ready to hide in my room, read my new comics, and watch a movie. Preferably one where the hot lead is shirtless for at least half the movie so I can end the night jerking off in the shower before passing out in bed. Big plans. I love when I can make plans like this because I'm an introvert and my spoon drawer has been empty since I got here. I need a recharge. Tonight is going to be perfect because Hollywood has a game, and Chase is taking Steve out for his birthday or some shit. No one but me and Lulu—Chase's boxer. She's loaded up with energy, but once she settles down, she's a cuddler. The other dog, Pongo, goes with Chase almost everywhere.

I'm running through a list of movies in my mind as I pull into the driveway, and my stomach drops. Parked crooked like always is a '68 Dodge Charger. The hood is up, but no one is around it, so I grab my stuff and pray as I make a dash for the door. I sneak in, moving like a ninja down the hall, but I'm spotted just before my hand hits my door.

Damn.

"Lala! Dude, where have you been, man?" Devin asks, arms thrown out to his side and a big smile on his face.

"Out at the doctor. I ran some errands, too. Why? I'm not going on our away trip, man."

"No, I know! Steve's car is being a dickhead just like him—"

"I can hear you, asshole!"

"Whatever, you're just mad I beat your ass gaming. So, anyway, it's being a dickhead," he repeats, giggling like he's five. "But you know cars, right? I mean, you fixed your sister's car, right?"

My sister's car—I wish we'd never fixed the damn thing for her. "I had help."

"Well, can you take a look? We were gonna call a mechanic, but those two decided to get higher than the space station when they got back from the beach, so I figured we'd be better off waiting on you."

"Uhm, yeah. Gimme ten?" I shut the bedroom door behind me to give myself time to breathe. I need a routine right now, so I add the books to my stack on the nightstand, organize the comics, and put the candy away in the drawer with my other personal items. I'll pull them all back out later, but keeping things neat and organized helps me center myself.

"Hollywood?" I yell out as I head back out to the front. "Grab me some tools, would ya? And I don't mean your brother and Steve."

"FUCK YOU, LALA!" Chase yells out as the two of them laugh so hard they snort.

I'm surprised at how clean the engine is on a car this old. Steve must take excellent care of it. It's not surprising since he has that work hard and play harder mentality. I find the keys sitting in the front seat and wonder how high they were when they started this endeavor. I turn the key, and I get a whole lot of nothing. I hop out and start poking around, making sure the obvious things are all where they should be and nothing has come loose. It's not long before the sun reminds me that a black shirt wasn't the best idea, even in October. I strip it off and tuck it into my back pocket before getting back to work.

This might be better than my original plans for the afternoon, since no one else has bothered to venture out here yet. There's not much noise at this part of the street, which helps me get into the zone faster. It also helps that I'm focused on something outside of my problems. I'm working around the battery and a loud bang scares the shit out of me. The subsequent clatter doesn't help either, as it damn near gives me a heart attack. When I turn, I find the box of tools dumped all over the driveway, and Steve standing there staring down at them.

"Shit, uhm, butterfingers." He stoops to pick the tools up again, so I do the same to help him, shoving the ones I need into my back pocket as we go. I go to reach for a hammer and our hands brush together before our eyes snap to each other's. We're about six inches apart, so close I can see how long his eyelashes are, and he can count my freckles. I want nothing more than to fall forward and let him catch me as our mouths meet. I bet he tastes like cinnamon.

No! No! Bad idea, Lala. Very bad!

"I, uhm, you can take it," I murmur as I pull my hand back and stand, spinning on the ball of my foot so I'm facing the engine again instead of Steve's piercing blue eyes. "I have everything I need."

"Do you?" He asks in a way that makes me think it's a loaded question. "Because I can get you anything you need if you don't already have it."

My face scrunches together, and I glare at him over my shoulder.

"Christ, that was cheesy as fuck and sounded totally wrong. I mean tools. I can run in and get you whatever Dev forgot."

"Thanks."

"Yeah, sure."

I don't hear him leaving, so I assume he's still standing behind me, a bucket of tools in his hand like it's an Easter basket, and someone told him I'm the bunny with the eggs.

"Something else you want, Steve?"

"Can…I help? Or watch? Shit, that sounded bad, too."

"Come on. Stand over there and you can hand me shit like you're five."

"Yeah, never did that when I was five. Or fifteen." He scoffs and leans against the car. "That how you learned to work on cars? Working on them with your dad?"

"Stepdad, actually. My sister found a clunker and fell in love with it, so we fixed it up for her." His eyes burn a hole through me and I'm at a loss, so I keep working. "I'm not a mechanic or anything, but I know enough to be dangerous."

"Oh." He fusses with the wrench in his hand. "The scar on your back, they did a pretty amazing job on it. You can barely see it."

I don't bother looking up when I shrug. "Not really something I can see anyhow."

"Yeah, uhm…yeah. Can I ask you something really dumb?"

"So long as I can give you a dumb answer back, sure."

"I'm from Boston, so I gotta know. Are you one of *those* LaVoies?"

Fuck. Here we go again. "Yeah," I lash out before busying myself by cleaning my hands off.

"I didn't mean to—"

"I'm one of those fucking LaVoies. One of the legendary sons of the all mighty Rene LaVoie. Let me guess, he was your coach? Or you played against him? Looked up to him? Thought he was a fucking hockey god like they all do."

"No, I—"

"Oh, wait. Don't tell me. You wished you were his son, huh? Well, he was a fucking dickhead and a shitty father." I can't stop myself from answering him with all the snark and annoyance I've felt since the doctor's office. Hell, since my childhood. Gotta love unresolved family issues. "Now stop talking and let me fix your stupid car."

I finish up after an hour of silence from Steve, but he doesn't leave. I'm sore from leaning over and I'm pretty sure I've got a sunburn now, but I still feel bad for snapping at him. I toss him the keys and tell him to start it up for me. He almost drops them before he scurries around the car, scuffing his flip-flops the whole way.

She starts up, purring like the beauty she is, and all I can do is grin. I slam the hood shut and finish cleaning my hands. As clean as the engine looked at first, I found nothing but grime and dirt when I got in there. Maybe the car is a metaphor for Steve—a shiny, nice exterior, but something else hides in the parts you can't see.

"Thanks."

"Sure. I'm sorry I—"

"Don't bother." He turns to head back into the house, leaving the tools and the bucket on the edge of the car for me to deal with. As he gets to the door, he yells back, "You know, you're not the only one here with a shitty family."

"What an asshole," I mumble as I clean the tools off and put them away. I'm not sure if I'm calling him the asshole or myself. Or both.

HOLLYWOOD
Steve

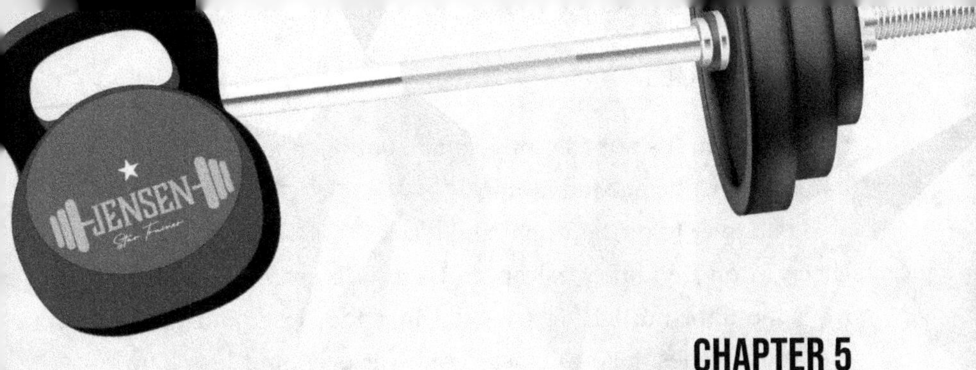

CHAPTER 5
SABOTAGE
BEASTIE BOYS

HE'S RIGHT THERE, right in front of me—licking his lips. All I have to do is lean forward and I'll taste the—bee?

Buzz. Buzz. Buzz.

Buzz. Buzz. Buzz.

I slam my hand down on the phone, shutting the alarm off and trying hard to drift back into that dream. I was back at Coop's house and Ethan was working on the car. Except he wasn't. He and I were working on each other. The damn alarm went off just as I pinned him to the hood of my car, our mouths so damn close. I've known him for all of a week and I'm already having hot and heavy dreams about him.

"Fuuuuuck!" I moan as I roll over, pulling the blanket over my head. This is how it felt when Zeus birthed Athena. This is what I get for letting Coop drag me around all day before he conned Laurie into going out to some club with us. I'm dehydrated, sore, and so fucking hungover.

I take a deep breath in. My apartment smells like three-day-old In N' Out thanks to Laurie insisting on bringing her leftovers here in case she got hungry. I sit up, waiting for my body to scream in pain after a night of dancing, followed by passing out on the couch. It's not a crappy couch, but it's not my bed, where Laurie slept. She needed it more.

I pad over to the bedroom and crack the door open enough to check in on her. She's asleep, but she rolls over, turning away from the light I'm letting in. I slip into the closet and grab my workout clothes, take the fastest shower ever, and kiss Laurie's head before I head out to my car.

There's nothing on Earth that relaxes me faster than sliding behind the wheel of my '68 Dodge Charger. Especially since Ethan fixed her up yesterday. Now, she's back to being my pride and joy instead of my worthless piece of shit that I threaten to junk once in a while. She's painted to match my gym—red and blue with silver accents—and still smells like brand new leather. I'm in love with the way she purrs.

Maybe I shouldn't have been so hard on the kid, but it's his own fault. I need to think of some way to repay him for helping me out. We got off on the wrong foot and it continued getting worse. Kennedy blowing my phone up all day, wanting to hang out, didn't help the situation any, either. I could have answered her, but when it came down to it, I had more fun standing out in the heat and watching Ethan work than I would have with her in my bed.

"Hey, you're here early! The car sounds phenomenal, man!" Devin greets me from the front steps, newspaper in hand and Lulu dancing at his feet. We train at their house because his brother, Coop, is my best friend, and he's also a movie star. I helped him set up a beautiful workout area with the best equipment, and he isn't bringing swarms of paparazzi to my gym.

"Oh, don't use the pool for Lala this morning. They put chemicals in it like twenty minutes ago."

Fuck. I never picked up the records from the specialist, didn't review the rest of his records, and never wrote up a new workout plan. I should have called this off and stayed home today. Eh, I'm a professional, and I can wing it. "Fine, get your ass ready. Five minutes."

"My ass will never be ready for you, Stevie."

"Okay, shithead, where's your brother?"

"Seriously, it's before eight. Where do you think he is?"

I storm up the stairs, kicking the door in before I stride across the room and rip the curtains open. I turn around to find Coop buried under the covers and a suspicious lump next to him. If he wasn't my best friend, I'd think I walked in on something I shouldn't have. That's not his style though, it's mine. The lump moves and I hear the thump-thump I was expecting.

"Good boy, Pongo. Wake your lazy ass, dickhead of a daddy up for me, buddy." The sheets jump up and down as his tail wags. There's groaning and what sounds like sloppy, wet, dog kisses.

"Fuck you!" it's muffled, but I was expecting it. "Don't call me daddy!"

"You get your ass downstairs in three minutes or I'm gonna scream that you're my daddy in front of the paps!"

"You wish," he grumbles.

"You couldn't handle being my daddy. Now, move it, Coop!"

"Fine! I hate you!"

I grab his head as he appears from under the covers and lay an obnoxious, over the top kiss on his forehead. "Morning, asshole."

"Gross."

"Two minutes." I jog back downstairs, ready to tackle the next one as I yell out, "LaVoie, you better be—" I skid to a stop in the hallway because he and Devin are there, wearing sunglasses and leaning against the wall with their arms crossed like a couple of idiots.

"Standing here waiting on your slow ass?" Ethan glances at his watch and shrugs.

"How late do you have to be before we're allowed to walk out?" Devin asks.

"Oh, you wanna play at that game, do you?"

"I mean, you were a whole minute late," Ethan points out. I can't put my finger on what about this entire situation that's pissing me off, but I'm done playing around.

"Keep it up, wise ass. You'll run with Devin and Coop." I slap Devin's hat off his head and he straightens up and takes the sunglasses off. "You can't run on Wednesdays? Guess who's running two laps. Get the fuck out there."

"But what about—"

"CHASE!"

"WHAT?!" Coop yells back as he fumbles down the stairs, failing at an attempt to pull his hair up.

"Get the fuck outta my sight. It's your fault I'm hungover!"

I flick on the lights to the garage and glance around, not sure where I want to start LaVoie off. I need something easy so I can run through his new medical updates and check a few exercises I have in mind for him.

"Should I be thanking you for not making me run? Or is this going to be worse?"

I turn to snap at him, but I'm thrown off by the genuine worry in his pretty eyes. What the hell does this little shit have to worry about? "Bike for thirty minutes. Break it down by ten-minute intervals. Warm up, hard push, and cool down."

"I thought we were—"

"Don't think, bike." I bark at him. "Don't slack off, either. The room has cameras. I'll be outside, working on your nutrition plan."

He's reluctant, and I am not in the mood for the back and forth that's becoming too typical between us. In fact, I need to put an end to that game entirely. I can dick around with Coop and Devin, but Ethan is a paying contract. I unpack the tablet from my bag and pull up the form I use for new clients. The blank spaces are accusing me of being a fuck up. They sound a lot like my dad. When I look up at LaVoie, I notice the son of a bitch can't even ride a fucking bike properly.

"Angle your back and tighten your abs. This isn't a fucking Sunday ride through the park." He shakes his head but does what I ask. I head to the back and turn on some music so I can focus better. Devin's pop playlist comes on and I leave it— listening to rock would have made me more of a dick.

"Taylor Swift? Are you serious right now?"

"Don't fucking knock her. She's a genius and clearly you know who she is."

"Everyone knows who she is, dude."

"Just shut up and peddle the damn bike!"

"Don't be such a prick," he grumbles, and I've had enough.

"If you moved your feet more than you moved your mouth, you might be getting somewhere."

"Not on a stationary bike, bro."

I growl, grab my tablet, and head to the living room where I can get some fucking work done. Usually, I keep it professional with a touch of snark. Except with Lala, all I want to do is stand behind him and stare at that ass of his. Okay, maybe that's not all I want to do. I'm a dog. It's well established that I have no shame. This is going to be the longest, hardest contract to work through, and I mean every innuendo possible by that.

"Lala, you can fix a car, but you don't know how to ride a

damn bike?" I yell over the music when I come back into the room twenty minutes later.

"I do!" He yells back, defensively. "I can't keep my back like that, though."

"Bullshit. You can skate like a normal person, so you can bike like a normal person."

"What the fuck? That doesn't even make sense. I'm in cool down. Who cares?"

"I fucking care!" I storm over and start manipulating his posture. It's fine right up until I press on his lower back. He tenses up immediately and draws in a sharp breath, trying to hide the pain from me still. I barely touched him—he's hiding more than I thought. "Get off the bike. Go stretch that out."

"What the fuck is your problem?" He snaps as he climbs off slower than I'd hoped. "Just because I live here with Chase doesn't mean you get to treat me like this. If you don't want the fucking gig, tell me. I'll go back to what I was doing and the team can take back that fucking paycheck they gave you."

"What you were doing clearly wasn't working. How much are you hiding from Doc and I? How am I supposed to fix you if you're so fucking broken you can't even ride a bike?"

"Fuck you!"

I try to stare him down, but...I can't. I'm too busy watching him lick his lips and remembering how he looked the other day, hunched over my car, shirtless and covered in grease. Remembering the dream and how close we came. I have this strange sensation in the pit of my stomach. Probably something I ate or my hangover from last night. I know it's none of those things, though. I don't want to admit what it really is.

"Go stretch," I repeat myself.

"Whatever. I'm done with this shit. I don't need you."

He storms out of the room, and I can't blame him. I would

have, too. I'm supposed to be here to help him get stronger, to help him improve his game and build up his strength in ways to keep him safe and healthy on the ice. Instead, I'm too busy sticking my head firmly up my ass, moping around about my own issues, and being a self-righteous prick. Brilliant business strategy.

His words hurt, too. For whatever reason, I want him to need me. As more than just a trainer, though. I head out to the back yard, spotting him dangling off a pull-up bar, trying to stretch his back. Even though he's turned away from me, I can already guess his face is contorted in pain and he's trying to hide it. I pushed him too hard. I did the exact opposite of my damn job.

"Lala?" I keep my voice calm and quiet. I want him to know right away that I'm not out here to continue being a fuckup. He drops from the bar and rolls his shoulders before turning to glare at me. It might be the sun, but I'm sure I see a glisten in his eyes, but my attention doesn't stay there long.

With a shirt on, you can't tell how ripped this kid is, but right now, he's standing in front of me shirtless, with his shorts low on his hips. The view is even better than when he was fixing my car. He's got a six-pack and the deepest cut to an Adonis Belt that I've ever seen. I pick my jaw up off the floor and rub the back of my neck as I stare at anything else I can find because I'm going to need a very cold shower in a minute.

"I'm sorry, that was unprofessional of me in there and, look, I had a rough night and that's no excuse. That's on me." I hold my arms out at my side. "Let me help you stretch your back out and we'll see if we can try again, okay?"

He crosses his arms over his chest and I'm sweating bullets. His arms are just as defined as his abs when he holds them like that. What the fuck is wrong with me? It's got to be the hangover. I'm still drunk. It could be the stress I've been under lately with my dad. Or, I find this guy attractive as hell and I want nothing more than to run my tongue over every damn muscle he has. Fuck, the things I would do to this kid.

Kid. Shit. I've got ten years on him, probably more. He doesn't need my dumb ass fucking things up for him.

"Yeah," he finally says, taking his hat off long enough to run a hand through his shaggy, sandy blonde hair. He puts the hat on backwards and my knees get weak. I'm in so much fucking trouble.

"Okay," I squeak out and he gives me a raised eyebrow. I clear my throat and try again, not about to elaborate on what he said. "I need you to do something for me, though?"

I need him to do a lot of things for me. And to me.

"What? Your car messed up again?"

"No, I need you to tell me the truth from now on. If it hurts, you say so. If it stings, tingles, does anything at all when you move, you tell me. Tell me everything, so I can do this right by you."

He nods and we go back inside, working on some basic stretches, and finding his comfort zone. I work up a plan on the fly and take him through the motions, getting a better handle on how much he can move and how we can structure the workouts and tailor them to what his body needs. I get my mind out of the gutter and into the workouts. I'm not here to break him, I'm here to help him become a better player. I needed to remember that.

"Hey," Coop yells from the front door. "Why the hell did I just do three fucking laps around the neighborhood?" He stumbles to the door, ripping his shirt off before he drops dramatically onto the cold tile floor with a deep groan, rolling onto his back and gulping air.

"Lap one was for still being asleep when I got here. Lap two was the lap you were going to take anyhow. Lap three? Yeah, that one is on Devin, so I got nothing." I'm secretly surprised he made it that far. Running in the Hollywood Hills is no fucking joke and the route we run means he ran four and a half miles of steep inclines.

"I had to!" Dev pants, leaning against the wall. "I can't do two laps. I did two laps last week, and we lost the next game. Three laps. Or one. Not two."

"I fucking hate you both!" Coop groans, throwing a towel at his brother.

"What did he do?" Devin nods to Ethan before he joins Coop on the floor. "He doesn't look tired!"

"I was riding a bike in the beautiful air conditioning," Ethan flashes him a cocky grin.

"Don't get cocky on me, Lala. Next session is probably going to kick you ass." There's the slightest tick at the edge of his mouth when I say that, and I think he might be looking forward to it.

HOLLYWOOD
21
Ethan

I'M SUCH A FUCKING LOSER.

The team is on the ice, losing, and meanwhile, I'm up in the stands. What makes it even more awkward is I'm in the luxury suite that Chase and some guy named Sam own. They invited me up since I'd be here anyway and Coach said it would be fine so long as I didn't make an ass of myself. I wouldn't do that anyhow, but I'm also not exactly having a good time either. I want to be on the ice. I want to be down there proving myself. Instead, I'm up here being the odd man out at a party.

"Hey, what's with the frowny face?" Steve asks as he plops down in the seat next to me. I thought sitting alone in a corner would be enough of a hint to leave me alone, but he's not taking hints tonight thanks to the beers. "Look, I get it, I really do. You want us to leave you to your pity party since you can't play yet, but man, lighten up a bit, yeah?"

"It's just frustrating sitting here and watching them lose. Girard has missed four goals tonight, Hollywood can't catch a cold with that glove, and the D isn't clearing a damn thing." It feels good to vent, but I doubt he gives a shit about any of that. We've been getting along better since we blew up at each other the other day, but it's not like we hang out and shoot the shit very often.

"Yeah, I know all of that because I've been watching."

That's a bit of a surprise to me. Every time I look up there, he's got his tongue lodged so far down his girlfriend's throat that I'm convinced she must have gills or something in order to breathe. I don't care. That has nothing at all to do with me, but there's this weird feeling I get when I see them making out.

"You'll be out there soon. I know we just started, but trust me, I'm gonna get you out there. How was the workout this morning? Cole and Tommy treat you, okay?"

"Yeah, they were—OH COME ON!" I throw my hands up, almost spilling my Reece's Pieces all over the place, as I watch another goal go in. "Fuck."

"Yikes. Uhm, you may wanna ride home with Coop tonight after the game. Dev's gonna be super pissed off." Steve pats me on the leg, realizes what he's doing, and pulls his hand away like it's on fire. I pretend I was too in the moment to notice. "Let me go grab you a couple of napkins in case they score again."

He leaves and I pull out my phone, checking the scores and highlights of other games. He comes back a few minutes later, but he smells different. He's also sitting a whole lot closer than before and popping bubble gum. I glance up and I'm looking right into the eyes of his girlfriend—they're like two flashing danger signs. I swallow hard and look back down at my phone.

"I'm Kennedy."

"Uh, hi."

"You're cute."

"And you're dating Steve."

"Eh, we're really just screwing, not so much dating. You wanna slip out to the bathroom? I brought some ecstasy. I stole it from my dad since his weirdo shrink prescribed it for like PTSD or something. Steve won't do it with me, though. I mean, he'll fuck me, but he won't do anything but weed." She leans toward me. If I were straight, I don't think it would be possible to look away from her chest right now. Hell, I'm not straight and I'm having trouble keeping myself from looking.

"N-no. No thanks. I can't do that kind of stuff."

"Oh, right—You play, don't you?" She smiles and licks her lips. "We can skip the E if you want. I've never fucked a pro hockey player before. I bet you fuck real hard, don't you?" She reaches over, squeezing my biceps. When she feels the muscle, she sucks in a quick breath and grins. I don't understand why, since she's dating—or not dating—the Hulk himself. Her hand slides down my arm until she gets to the bag of candy and helps herself. "Yum."

"Yeah, I get a sweet tooth when I'm nervous."

"I promise, I can help you relax, cutie."

"Uhm, I'm kinda, you know, busy."

"I can keep you so much busier." She drops some of the candy down her shirt. "Oh, so clumsy. Why don't you help me get them out? With your tongue?"

"Christ, Kennedy. Can you not offer to suck someone else's dick for one game? I swear to god!" Steve sits next to her and slides a hand around her shoulders. I wouldn't think much of it except his knuckles brush against my arm and I freeze.

"I didn't offer to suck his dick, Steven." She snipes back, and the arena gets colder. "I asked him to fuck me since you're too much of a whiney bitch to do it here!"

"I'm not a whiney bitch! Are you on something again?" He stares at her while I try to act as if I'm not hearing any of this. She gets up and storms off. "Sorry about her, Eth. We're, uhm, trying to get her into rehab. She's fighting us on it, though."

"I wasn't hitting on her, I swear! She came onto me and I—"

"I know. She hits on Coop all the time, too. She tried with Devin once and he wasn't polite about turning her down, so she hasn't tried with him again. I guess that's the trick."

"Wait, then why are you with her?" I don't mean it to come out so blunt, but I can't take it back now.

"Long story? Eh, not really. Hooked up by a friend at a party, the sex was fun, now it's not." I see him take a drink out of the corner of my eye but try to keep some focus on the game. "She's too young for me, and she's going through a lot of shit, but thinks she knows everything. I kind of feel bad for her in a way, but she was broken when I got her. Hell, so am I."

"So you bring her to a hockey game where she hits on other people?"

"Bro, at least she was just hitting on you and not riding your cock. I've already paid for the damn group Halloween costumes, and my sister is excited to go—I don't want to break her heart. My sister, that is, not Kennedy."

I chuckle, "So, you'd rather be miserable for another week or so than just find someone else to wear her costume? Dude, that's pretty fucked up." I glance over at him, staring at his jersey. For a split second, my mind imagines it's my name and my number on it, not Hollywood's. Then it dawns on me there are no sleeves. He's wearing a fucking sleeveless hockey jersey. "Nice sweater vest."

"Thanks. Coop made sure we all had them before Hollywood got here, and of course I had to make it my own and ditch the sleeves. Can't hide these guns, baby." He laughs and takes a long pull off his beer, then moves to the seat Kennedy was in. Our legs touch and I'm too terrified to move. It's possible there's a full moon tonight or I'm in some weird alternate dimension, but whatever it is, I'm not used to all this… attention.

"It's a style choice," I stare forward, looking at the ice with no clue what's going on in the game right now. I've never wanted to talk to someone this badly before, but I know it's not a good idea. Talking at the gym and during workouts is one thing—we're both sober and focused on work then. Now, though? I keep reminding myself that I can't ask him out for a drink sometime like normal people do. If I'm not careful, our little talk right now could end up on ESPN or the Jumbotron and I'd be running damage control for weeks. I don't pay my agent enough to deal with that kind of shit.

"I fought wearing the jersey at first." He takes out his jersey and shows me some pictures of the group all wearing jerseys with Devin's number. "I didn't need it looking like I'm dating the little prick or something. You ever have that?"

"What, people thinking I'm dating someone because they're wearing my jersey?"

"No, I mean, have you ever had someone you're with wear your jersey?" I'm starting to think Steve might be hitting on me, or someone's spiked my drink.

I take a minute, acting like I'm thinking it over, but I don't think he's buying my bullshit anyhow. He's poking around, trying to see if I'll bite, and god I wish I could. Even just for one night, to get it out of my system, to pretend for just a little while that I could be with someone.

"Nah. Closest I had was someone in my family wearing it. I, uhm, I don't date much. Takes away from the game."

There's that lie I know so well.

"Oh man, I would absolutely wear a hockey player's jersey if I were dating one." He leans slightly, flashing a lopsided grin.

"You, uh, you would? That could get a guy in trouble if he was, you know, in the show."

"Maybe, but they'd have to catch us first." He winks. The butterflies in my stomach jump start to life and lodge in my chest while my mouth turns into a desert. The game is gone, so are the fans. Just like the other day in the driveway, we're close enough that it wouldn't take much for us to kiss. He smirks, and in a voice thick with desire, he continues. "Take you, for instance. Once you hit the ice, hundreds of people would be in your jersey. No one would get the idea that you're dating one of them, you know what I mean?"

"Yeah, I guess."

"In fact, if I was dating a hockey player, I'd wear his jersey to every single game. Right after he fu—"

"Steve?" Chase's voice pulls us out of the fantasy and back to a very loud, crowded reality. Chase crouches down in the row behind us. "You're, uhm, you need to come take your girl home. Or somewhere else she can explore her daddy issues with a professional, not us. If she keeps this shit up, Sam's gonna fire her. If she hits on Jaim again, our sweet, kind, wonderful Lexi is gonna throw her over the fucking railing."

He sits back in the chair, looks forward, and sighs, clearly annoyed. "Couples Halloween costumes aren't worth all this bullshit."

Meanwhile, I'm wondering how many people saw that and if the entire arena can hear my heart racing or just this section. There's arguing up in the box, but I tune it out, focusing even harder on the game now. I wonder if anyone would notice if I snuck downstairs and took a cold shower. I glance up at the scoreboard and see we're still down by three and there's only two minutes left. They pull Devin for the extra skater, so I stand up and get ready to head downstairs and listen to Coach bitch us all out for the sloppy game play.

"Hey," Chase's friend Jamie stops me as I head for the door. "You okay? You're in a daze."

"Huh? Oh, yeah, man. I'm good. Just, uhm, bummed about the game is all."

"Okay. Don't let Steve get to you. Or Kennedy, for that matter. They're both walking time bombs, ready to go off without warning, and neither one of them will go to fucking therapy like they need."

"Yeah," I laugh nervously as he stares at me. I glance toward the back of the box and Steve is looking at me while Kennedy gives him an earful. The cocky son of a bitch winks at me and I wait for the wrath of his girlfriend to be unleashed, but thankfully, she didn't notice. "Thanks for the heads up."

The air changes in a hockey rink depending on the mood of the team. Electric if we're hyped or winning a big game, and colder than an iceberg if we've lost. Tonight, I'm pretty sure I can see my breath as I head to the locker room to meet up with the team. I'm almost to the door when it flies open, slamming into the wall as Devin shoves Lewis out of the room. Lewis is a rookie, and he's only on the ice because I'm not. Poor kid was thrown into the fire and tonight, he couldn't take the heat.

"I told you not to fucking stand in front of me. I told you. Your fucking job is to clear the rebound! You have one fucking job and you can't do that right, so why the fuck are you trying to do my fucking job?!"

There are a lot of unspoken rules in hockey, and close to ninety percent of them have to do with the goalie. It takes a special level of skill and insanity to be one, and they are more superstitious than most people can keep up with. They can be your best friend, or your nightmare, which says a lot when the game sits squarely on their shoulders night after night.

"I'm—I'm sorry, Hollywood!" The kid blathers on with excuses, and that's just pissing Devin off more. So I step in.

"Lew, get back in the locker room," I say, pulling him out of Devin's grasp. It's a dangerous move and it could get me clocked, but I'm banking on our friendship to save my face right now. I'm beyond grateful when Dev chooses to lean back against the wall and let the kid pass by us. There's some kind of irony in calling him a kid since I'm only twenty-five, Devin is twenty-two, and Mike Lewis is nineteen. He's promising, but they put too much pressure on him too early and he isn't handling it well. A year or two in the minors and he'll be fine.

"He was in my crease!" Devin's anger hasn't lessened any since Lew went back into the room. I lean against the wall next to him and nod in agreement. This is what Dev needs right now, and as a defenseman, it's always my job to know what the goalie needs, even if he doesn't say it. My dad always wanted me to be a forward, just like my brothers, because that's where he found fortune and glory. I never agreed with that, and while I won't be scoring eighty goals in a season, I could keep far more than that from hitting the back of our net.

"Oh, hey. I saw you and Steve talking at the end of the third." He wiggles his eyebrows and elbows me in the ribs.

"What the hell is that supposed to mean?"

"Nothin', man. Just, you know, saying." He leans in close so no one else will hear, even though no one else is out here with us. "You should slide him one of your jerseys during the next session."

My head rocks back, hitting the concrete wall a little too hard. "You can't fucking say that, Dev! Someone's gonna hear you."

"Lala, I'm the goalie. I'll threaten to cup check every one of these fuckers if they say anything. You're also in Los Angeles. You're in fucking Hollywood, California! Out is cool here."

"Uh huh, name one. One pro out athlete in Los Angeles." I wait while he thinks, watching his face morph from cocky to unsure, then confused. "Yeah, exactly. None."

"It's... getting better, though. I think."

"Dev, this is only your second season in the show. You're not exactly an authority on how it works, and you're not in my shoes. I'm begging you, as a friend and teammate, please. Please don't say anything. Ever."

"Okay, man. I've got your back, though." He flashes his big, dumb smile and slaps me on the shoulder. "Now, let's get in there and beat the ever loving shit out of that motherfucker who stepped into my goddamn crease!"

"Not gonna let him off the hook, huh?"

"Fuck no. That little shit tried to hand me my stick earlier. MY STICK, LALA! You don't fucking touch my stick! Hey, you wanna get In-N-Out on the way home?"

"Gross, no. Wait, is this a goalie thing or a Devin thing?"

"It's an LA thing, you heathen. Now we're beating up Lew and then we're making him pay for In-N-Out!"

"God, you're so weird."

"Yep. And you're so giving him a jersey. I don't mean Lew, either."

HOLLYWOOD
21
Ethan

DEV and I spend every spare minute we have running around town to the different Halloween stores. We're buying anything and everything we can like we're twelve and stole our parent's credit card. We've got fog machines, animatronics, pumpkins, and even sound effects. If it was even remotely spooky, we put it in the cart. We might have also grabbed a few things that were a little on the goofy side and way too much candy. Not the cheap, fun size shit either. I'm making up for all the Halloweens I didn't get to be a kid and have fun.

Living with the Cooper brothers has been a little on the weird side. Not because they're assholes or anything. I'd be used to that—I'm the youngest of the four boys in my family. Chase and Dev are the total opposite. They've not only opened their home to me, but their circle of friends as well. For being as rich or famous as each of them is in their own right, it's nearly impossible to tell that from just talking to them.

At the house, Chase's artist buddy, Jamie, adds more details to the animatronics and other decorations, taking them from plastic and lame, to realistic and creepy. They're so good, I get the heebie-jeebies from walking by them. Steve said it was fucking stupid and wouldn't scare anyone, so Jamie turned on one of the big animatronics when he wasn't looking. Steve screamed like his life depended on it and ran away when the thing moved unexpectedly. Devin now threatens to post the video of that on social media every time Steve makes him run.

The party I expected involved a few of Chase's friends, watching horror movies, and drinking, because that's their style. What I've stumbled into is the exact opposite. Around seventy people I don't recognize fill the house in the coolest costumes I've ever seen. The doorbell rings non-stop with kids looking for candy. Inside and out back, there are bars set up, a karaoke machine, and two different DJs keeping the party going. It's fucking amazing, like an amusement park right outside my bedroom door.

"So, like, what are you supposed to be?" Kennedy asks shortly after their group walks in. Steve's distracted by someone, so she's walked over to me and is running her hand down the zipper of my flight suit. "Because I do love a man in uniform, but I'd much rather see you out of it."

"Oh, come on, Kennedy! We're Maverick and Goose! Seriously? Top Gun? Nothing?" Devin is somewhere between annoyed and put out. He worked hard on these costumes. Scouring the internet for at least ten minutes. "Besides, since when is Daphne blonde? She's a smoking hot redhead."

"Fuck off, Devin." She snipes back and I have to hold in a laugh. Devin's plan of acting like a dick to her is still working.

"Seriously, are you two even old enough to know Top Gun?" Steve jokes as pulls Kennedy's hand from my chest. She giggles like she's stoned. There's a very likely chance that she is. He moves to kiss her and, for whatever reason, I'm elated when she ducks away from him. I also feel a little bad for Steve. "Baby, go get me a beer, would ya?"

"Get your own beer. I'm gonna go find Coop." She flips Steve off as she leaves.

"She's allowed to call him Coop?" I question. Most people that are friends of his call him that. I just can't get used to it.

"No, she just assumes she is," Steve mumbles, annoyance on his face.

"I guess that's a no on *her* being old enough for Top Gun." This is our routine over the last week or so—banter. I fuck with him. He fucks with me. It's bordering on flirtation, but so long as it stays on this side of the border, we'll be alright. Although, I'm not sure that's going to happen since we're both dancing a little too close to the edge lately.

"Hell, I don't even think you are, Stevie." Devin smacks him across the back—brotherly love. "What are you supposed to be? A weird nineteen seventies asshole? Disco Doofus. Oh wait, someone from Austin Powers?"

"Fuck off, Mini Cooper. I'm…reasonably certain I am older than Top Gun. Also, this is Fred! From Scoobie fucking Doo."

"Sure, pal."

"I dig the ascot," I snicker.

"Yeah?" He smirks and I have to look away as the red creeps up my neck.

"Kennedy sure isn't old enough," Devin adds in.

"Kennedy is old enough to—well, to *know* of Top Gun." He watches her work her way through the crowd and frowns. "I mean, everyone knows Top Gun, don't they?"

"Top Gun was eighty-six." Devin adds as he flips Steve off with both hands, nearly spilling his beer. "Dad watched the shit out of that movie, but that also means you weren't born yet either, dickwad."

"Whatever. Is Xander here?" Steve scans the crowd.

"Yeah. I saw him gothing around with Dani earlier. I think it was goth, I dunno."

"You are such a loser. Where's your brother?" Devin points his beer toward the patio and Steve nods. "Alright, don't drink yourselves stupid, but no workout tomorrow. I am going to drink myself stupid, and I don't wanna puke from looking at the two of you that early in the morning."

"There's three of us. You forgot Chase."

"No, I didn't. Chase is the hot one," Steve chuckles as he walks away, grabbing his girlfriend's ass on the way to the patio. She smacks him in the arm, and he holds his hands up. They're not going to last much longer at this rate, but that's none of my business. I look over and have to hold back a laugh. Devin looks truly offended by Steve's comment. I don't know why, considering everyone knows he's got the slightest edge on Chase in the looks department—solely because he's younger. They could almost pass for twins.

"Don't let him get to you, Hollywood. He's just a jealous prick."

"Yeah, he is. Like, even before he became the total dickhead he is now, he was still a prick. Come on, let's go get another beer and see who's out back. There might be someone hot, single, and ready to hook up with a pro goalie that is one hundred percent the cute one." We turn a corner and nearly run into a rock band straight out of the eighties. Devin stops and stares at them with his head cocked to the side. From his description earlier and their clothes, I see he was way off target with the goth comment.

"Revolver?" I ask after a quick glance at the rest of the band members behind them. I point each one out and name which member of the band they are. "Bell, Ophelia, Johnny, and Shaun?"

"Yes! Oh my god, finally!" the Ophelia cosplayer shouts,

ecstatic that I recognized who she was dressed as. "We had a Troy, too. But his idiot self came as Fred with a dumb ass blonde Daphne. I should have never hooked those two up, but in my defense, I really didn't believe they'd last the weekend, let alone a few months."

"Dani, no one remembers Revolver," Devin quips, just trying to get under Dani's skin. She's one of the circle of friends they share, and she's an absolute live wire from what I've heard. She hasn't been to the house much, though.

"They do too! They're fucking epic! They're so epic, I'll be playing them full blast while I fuck Xander later tonight and you're busy jerking off in the shower and crying over your stupid costumes." She hits back and there's a moment of seriousness that breaks apart quickly as they both start laughing. "Jesus, I can't get over the blonde Daphne situation."

"Right?! Everyone knows she's a redhead! I mean, even Laurie is wearing a wig for Velma. Oh dude, Steve should have dressed as Scooby Dumb."

"Or they should have come as dumb and *oh my god I am a vortex of stupid here to devour the entire universe.*"

Dani snorts out a laugh as Devin cracks up, "Shit! But which one is which? Oh fuck!" He takes a long drink of his beer, finishing it off, before wiping the tears from his eyes. "Oh man. I gotta remember that. Who are you guys again? Oh wait, don't tell me, Korn?"

"Funny. So funny. Stick to playing sports. At least we're not eighties rejects like you two fuckers!" She throws her hands up, nearly knocking her tall, broody boyfriend's drink out of his hands. "I can't understand how more people don't recognize us! I mean, fuck, Xander is the spitting fucking image Damien Bell! Like seriously, he could be his love child. But they know exactly who you two and your stupid brown onesies are?"

"Flight suits! We're fucking classics!"

I laugh at Devin, then give Xander a quick glance that last longer than it should. He winks. Cute. I assumed Dani was dating him from her comment about fucking him, but maybe not. "I've seen Bell and his wife doing smaller festivals and shit in the last few years. I guarantee that man has never once stepped out on her. But you're right about the resemblance." Revolver's lead singer, Damien Bell, was one of my first crushes when I was a kid. I found my mom's collection of memorabilia and it was love at first sight. That could explain why I can't take my eyes off Xander right now.

"You've seen Revolver?!" she practically screams at me.

"Christ, Dani, calm the fuck down," Xander says, rolling his eyes.

"Uhm, yeah. Portland I think? It's been a few years. They're my mom's favorite band, so I flew her out to see them even though it wasn't the whole band." I smile at the memory. It was a fun trip. "He still sounded amazing, and I swear neither of them has aged. Vampires, or something."

"OHMYGOD, that's fucking epic! Do you like live music?" She digs something out of her pocket and shoves it into my hand. "We're in a band, well, I am anyhow. We usually cover a couple of their songs just to get the audience really into it. I'm Dani! I've seen you around, but we haven't been formally introduced."

"Ethan," I say, taking her flier. She bites her lip and giggles, so I just offer her a smile back before I glance over at the tall drink of brooding next to her. The booze is going to my head tonight. I just hope it's the right one in charge at the end of the night.

"Are you fucking kidding me?" Xander growls in a low voice. "I'm right here and you're gonna hit on him."

"What? You weren't eye fucking him? That would be a fucking first. Go find Steve!"

"You hitting on him isn't part of the deal!"

I glance around while they bicker and realize I've lost Devin. I give the group a nod and scoot by them to go find him before I cause any more trouble. A few months in LA and I've been hit on more than I have my entire life. I check the kitchen and the living room, but I don't see him, so I head to the back of the house where Chase has set up the karaoke machine. Devin is a moth and karaoke is his big blue flame, so I'm sure he's hanging around there somewhere. He absolutely cannot resist them. I spot Steve's girlfriend cutting through the crowd, looking pissed off and Chase across the way, shaking his head. Guess that didn't go well. Nights like this make me glad I'm terminally single.

When I come around the corner, Devin's standing there, arms wide open, with a mic in his hand. I feel myself go paler than pale because I've just walked into a Hollywood Cooper trap. I'm surprised he can still get me like this since I've known him for so damn long and he hasn't changed. He does this to all of us at some point, dragging us up on stage to join him in idiocy.

"She's lost it! Come on, man!" I hear Chase yell from the back before Devin even starts the bit. I know it's coming.

"He's right," Devin chides. "I think she's lost it."

"No! No, she has NOT lost it, so I'm not doing this with you!"

"Say it!" Devin goads me on as Steve hands me another beer with a wink before disappearing into the crowd.

"Fuck it. I hate it when she does that," I quote the movie into the mic and chug half the beer as Devin starts the song. The part of me that's embarrassed doesn't stick around long because we're dressed like Maverick and Goose. We have to do this. I do remind him that he's getting the best scene in the movie wrong, though. "Should have been wearing the white uniforms for this scene, dickhead."

"Yeah, but these are cooler!"

"Not if you're looking to get laid."

"Oh, I am," he smirks, then winks at a group of women by the bar.

Just like in the movie, the whole damn crown joins in. This is what Devin does best, he entertains. Between the pipes or on a stage belting out lyrics, there's a magnetism to him I could never handle. He also rarely gives a fuck what anyone feels about him being a little nuts. It's a goalie thing. When I scan the crowd, I spot Xander and Steve talking by the pool. They're sitting a little too close, acting a little too comfortable with each other, and I feel jealousy in the pit of my stomach. I'm not sure which one I'm jealous of, though, or why. Then something unexpected happens. They both stare right at me and smirk. Not a friendly, 'hey you're fun' smirk, but an 'I want to rip your clothes off and toss them out a window' smirk. Both of them.

For a split second I forget the words, the movie, everything. Devin punches my shoulder, and I shake myself out of whatever just happened and finish the song, but I can't shake the butterflies in my gut. There's clapping and a call for an encore, but the expression I give Devin tells him that isn't going to happen.

"I can't believe you did that with me, man!" Devin laughs and hugs me as we walk back over to the bar by the pool. "Dude, that was fucking epic! I expected you to punch me in the damn face, not actually sing with me! We need to do that again!"

"Once is enough, but seriously, how could I not? There's probably jail time if you dress like this and don't sing it, even if you are Canadian." The bartender hands us both shots while he compliments the song and the costumes. "Dude, careful or he'll have me up there doing shit from Cocktail next and I can't juggle a bottle to save my soul."

The bartender gives me a wink and I flash him a smile. Finally, someone who isn't tied down is hitting on me. I won't act on it, but it's nice to have a little eye candy and someone to picture later tonight. Although, tonight, I have more than enough to work with. This is nothing like the parties for Halloween in Salem, but it might be better.

Devin's had a gorgeous brunette all over him since we got to the bar, and I'm happy for him. However, now that my wingman duties are over, I'm wondering if I should call it a night before I make decisions I'll regret. I take another shot as someone brushes their fingers along my back. When I turn, Xander nods as he walks by, blowing me a kiss.

My brain screams to go hide in my room, while my gut and my dick say I should follow him and find out where this leads. Before I can, shouting and cursing ring through the crowd. Everyone in the backyard turns in time to see Steve getting screamed at by his girlfriend and smacked hard enough that I felt it from back here. She's so drunk that I can't make out most of what she's slurring, but she keeps gesturing toward us. Possibly toward Xander, who shrugs and walks back into the house. I catch a few words at the end before she storms off.

Well, then why don't you go suck his dick then?

"Who is she talking about?" Devin's new best friend asks, looking between the two of us.

"What? Oh, it's Steve. Could be anyone. Absolutely anyone." He answers before he tucks a piece of hair behind her ear and she giggles. He's smooth, but right now, he's just proving to Steve that he's the cute one.

As much as I want to believe Kennedy was yelling about Xander, I'm pretty sure it was actually directed at me.

HOLLYWOOD
Steve

CHAPTER 8
BONES

IMAGINE DRAGONS

GETTING SCREAMED at is the last thing I needed tonight, but getting screamed at because my now ex-girlfriend thinks I want to blow my damn client has me above and well beyond pissed off. She's not wrong, but she doesn't need to announce it to the world. My sister stepping in front of me before I can run after Kennedy is probably the best thing that's happened to me tonight. So far.

"Hey, don't let her get to you like that. She's kind of a bitch, and she's a gold digger, but in reality she's just screaming for help and doesn't know it yet," Laurie says before handing me a beer. "You wanna talk about what she said?"

"Why would I need to talk about it, Laurie?"

She leans in closer to me so no one around us can hear her. "Well, Steve, how about we start with the fact that she's not wrong?"

"What the fuck is that supposed to mean?"

"You're my brother, and while I love you dearly, you're also a fucking asshole. You had one foot out the door since you two started dating, and you know it."

"Yeah, but so did she!" She gives me a glare. It's one I know well. It's the 'what happened to you,' glare. The one that reminds me how much I've changed over the years. I get it from her, Chase, and Jamie pretty regularly. "It was never going to work out, okay? She and I are a fun fuck, but beyond that? Nothing. Dani will tell you that, and she's the one that set us up."

"And what about him?" She nods to something behind me and when I turn to see what she's looking at, I'm locking eyes with Ethan. My heart thumps in an unfamiliar rhythm. Xander I can handle, but Ethan? Totally different story. "Why don't you try talking to him?"

"Lala? I know him already because he's my client, which also means he's off limits."

"Uh huh, which means you've talked to him about manly man stuff like weights, sports, and all kinds of boring shit. Go lay some of that smooth Jensen charm on him, little brother." I shake my head, but before I can argue with her, she's laughing. Not just laughing, she's doing that loud cackle. She knows something I don't, as usual. "Oh Jesus, that never gets old. You know, for a player, you have absolutely no idea who's on your team and where the scouts are sitting, do you?"

"Would you please translate that into something resembling English?"

"He's been eye fucking you and Xander all night! Possibly the bartender, too. The kid is taking appointments, Steve. Go book one."

"No! Ethan? The guy dressed like Goose from Top Gun?" She stares at me in a way that screams duh. "Ethan's is—" I stop and peer over my shoulder at him again.

"The word you're looking for is blushing. Every time you stare at him, he turns away and gets all flustered. It's actually pretty adorable if you think about it." She pats my arm. "I'm going to the back. I saw Chase and Jamie duck out while you were fighting. Why don't you invite him?"

"To the back?"

"Yes, you idiot. To the back!"

The back is what we call the garage during parties. It makes it sound like a secret hide out or a speakeasy—something old Hollywood instead of just a garage gym. It's our hide out when we're done partying, but don't want to look like losers and shut the place down early. I don't always make it back there, too busy taking someone out to the car to get my dick sucked. Or headed home to fuck all night. When I do hang out, I never take my hookups to the back. I never even took Kennedy back there. I don't want them in my inner sanctum. Ethan's different from anyone else I've hooked up with at one of these parties, though. Something tells me he wouldn't be another hookup, and not just because he lives here.

What the fuck am I thinking? He's a client, and a big one at that, so that means this is a terrible idea. And yet, here I go, walking right toward him with that fucking swagger, my body not listening to my mind.

"Hey, can I get two of whatever he just ordered? Oh, Hollywood, we're going in the back." I flash a smile to the bartender and wrap an arm over Ethan's shoulders, never looking at Devin. It feels a little like I'm staking my claim right now, and I can feel the bartender back off. I could be wrong, but I swear Ethan leans into me a bit. He's probably just drunk. "Lala, you wanna come with me?"

He stares at me and I can't hold back the laughter as I down the first shot. I hold up the second shot, offering it to him. "The garage, Lala. We're going to the garage. Would you like to join us there?"

"Yeah, I mean no. I mean, I knew that's what you meant." I

hand him the shot and give him a wink before I head into the house, not waiting to see if he follows. He will.

As we walk in, Coop flicks his lighter and holds it up to a joint. He looks up and smiles drunkenly as Ethan walks in behind me. "Hey, you made it Lola… err… Louie… Lala! Whatever." I roll my eyes at him and head toward the fridge in the corner, grabbing a pint of ice cream.

Jamie starts shuffling a deck of cards. "So, Ethan, it's a house rule. When Steve gets publicly dumped at a party, we all call it a night and hide in here while he eats ice cream and sulks about it."

"Oh, fuck you. Both of you."

"Nope. You're not my type, dick." Coop ducks the plastic cup I toss at him and then gives me a stare.

"Calm down, it was empty."

Not much has changed since high school when it comes to my best friends and I. Chase and Jamie are my brothers, Devin, too, even though he's so much younger than us. Hell, the three of us practically raised him, so I'm surprised he's even still alive. Once in a while, we'll get a new addition to the group, so long as they work with the dynamic. Jamie brought in both his wife, Lexi, and Dani. I can't even remember where we found Dani, because that's what she is—found. She's our feisty stray kitten that we all adopted and take care of. I brought in Laurie, but she walks the fine line between outsider and part of the group.

The way the night plays out once we're all in here rarely changes. Chase is always drunk, too high, and trying to play poker. Jamie is high as fuck and actually playing poker or making out with his wife. I'm either hitting on someone, or avoiding the poker game in other ways—like my little game with Xander.

I flop down onto the couch next to Pongo, who wags his tail

when I pet him. We watch Chase as he shows everyone how not to deal a hand of poker. Jamie, as always, cleans up the deal behind him, inviting Craig and Ethan into the game. Ethan takes up their offer. Craig passes, so Dani takes his spot. Meanwhile, I sense someone behind me, and I don't need to turn around to know who's there.

"Hey, Xander. Thanks for starting shit with the girl I was gonna tag later tonight."

"No problem. She looked boring as fuck." He takes a drag off the joint that's being passed around and hands it to me next. "Dani's gonna lose."

"She always does." I look over at Jamie and nod, reminding him to turn on the fans and air filters so we don't get any smoke near Devin or Ethan. "Pretty sure I should be thanking you, though. Kennedy grabbed some dude to take home as her prize, and now I'm looking to do the same. Who to choose?"

"Yeah, but Kennedy's a wreck and she's going to get her revenge one way or another." He leans in closer and I can smell his cologne. I'd be lying if I said it wasn't turning me on. It's a game we play and Dani knows that while he would absolutely jump my bones in a heartbeat, I'm not interested. I'll let him shoot his shot though, because I like to see just how close I can make him think he's getting. "I think you and I have the same little stuffed teddy bear we wanna win from the fair tonight. We could bring him home to play or stick to our usual shit."

"Kennedy's mess is partially your fault. Also, hands off. I'm winning that prize."

"I stopped giving Kennedy any of my stash months ago. She gets it from one of her daddy's now." He nudges the side of my head with his nose, "How about a bet? If he's not on one of our dicks by sunrise, I'm on yours."

"Oh, you are so on."

"Five hundred dollar cash prize if we take him to Paris together." I have competition over the guy I'm not even allowed to want. And the competition has just asked me to join forces. Tonight just got fun because, win or lose, I'm getting something out of this stupid breakup. Maybe I should be thanking Kennedy for the opportunity. "I'll even let you have first crack at that pretty mouth of his."

Forty minutes and three more beers later, Coop is cussing up a storm, Jamie has his wife on his lap, and I'm pretty sure Ethan just won Coop's Jag. It's all for fun, thankfully. Coop loves that Jag. Meanwhile, I'm sitting on the back of the couch while Xander sits between my legs. I rub his shoulders and continue to make eyes at Ethan, but there's a chance I've underestimated my ability to fight Xander off when I'm this drunk. Xander might get his wish for the two for one special after all.

"This game is rigged!"

"You're the dealer, asshat," Jamie yells back to Coop, knocking his hat off his head as he laughs.

"We should play spin the bottle," Xander suggests as he stares at Ethan. Laurie shoots me a glare and I know she's telling me not to be an idiot or do anything stupid. Too late for that. I glance over to Ethan, who has his head down and he's peeling the label off his beer. It's the same beer he came in with and I think he's trying to sober up.

"You know," I say as I climb off the couch and walk over behind Ethan. "Peeling the bottle's label is a sign of sexual frustration."

"Oh, shut the fuck up, Stevie!" Jamie's wife cries out, holding up two bottles without labels. "I guarantee you I am not."

"She is not!" Jamie echoes and flips me off. He's right, those two fuck like rabbits.

"Come on," Xander goads, winking at Ethan. "We've got four

stunning ladies in here, and six pretty damn decent guys. Odds are in our favor that we'll all get whatever we're looking for. Odds are better we end the night in a wild, drunken Dionysian orgy."

"We're not all eligible," Jamie points out. "No one here but me is kissing my wife. Unless she says otherwise."

"Yeah, and I could get stuck kissing Chase," Devin laughs, then goes back to making out with the girl he found.

"I'm not kissing any of you fuckers," Laurie chimes in, draping herself over Craig.

"Well, actually, if we narrow it down to no siblings or couples, that only leaves—hell—Dani, Steve, Ethan, and me."

"Aren't you and Dani dating?" Jamie asks.

"Meh," Dani answers. "Open relationship slash looking for the final piece of the triad. I'm in."

"What in the fuck does that mean?" Coop asks, eyes definitely not open.

"I'm in," I say, letting my fingers graze against Ethan's back as I walk by him.

"I suggested it. Of course I'm in. How about you, pretty boy? Are those odds in your favor or against?"

"Okay, whatever, go play over there in the corner or something." Chase vaguely gestures across the room, a weak attempt to try to save Ethan. "I'm still playing poker!"

"No, you're taking a nap, big fella." Jamie and Alexis help Coop up and over to the sofa, where Pongo curls up with him instantly.

"I gotta take a piss," Ethan mumbles as he uses the distraction as an escape and leaves the room.

I check in with Laurie again and she's practically pushing me out of the room with her eyes. "I need something to eat. Anyone else want anything?"

"Dude, pizza! We should order a pizza," Coop shouts, half asleep.

I feel Xander's eyes on me as I get to the door, but I'm not letting him get to Ethan first. I get to the door and glance back, seeing my beautiful, amazing sister run blocker for me as she grabs Xander's arm and starts asking him about Revolver. I know Ethan said bathroom, but the look said anywhere but this room, so I need all the head start I can get. I check the patio first since he was hitting on that bartender earlier. I don't see him, so I head to the other side of the house where the bathroom and the two guest bedrooms are. He's got to be staying in one of those, but if he's in his room, I'm not crossing that line.

Xander might.

The bathroom door opens and I turn in time to see Ethan practically walk right into me. It's like a tractor beam and I am caught in his pull.

"Ste—" I don't even let him get my name out. Grabbing his face, I kiss him, backing him into the bathroom and kicking the door shut behind me. He's not stopping me, not fighting back. Laurie was right again. I still shouldn't be doing this. Fuck, he feels so damn good, though. Like victory and rock hard abs that I wanna lick. He tastes like beer and cupcakes.

"Shit," I grunt out as I pull back. "Man, I'm so—"

Now it's his turn to cut me off, slamming me against the bathroom door and kissing me back. His hands go to my ass, my hand goes right for his dick. He moans into my mouth and it's the sexiest noise I've ever heard. I take over again, pushing him against the sink. A soap dispenser and some other things fly off the counter and we clumsily explore each other, but I don't give a shit, grinding hard against him. I bet Kennedy would love to see this. I guess she was right, too.

"Are you too drunk to want this?" I ask, feeling him growing hard against my hand, listening to him whimper.

"No. Fuck, I mean… shit, don't stop!" He whines, pulling my head to his neck as he thrusts against my hand. He's blubbering and swearing under his breath, pulling me closer. I let go of his dick and we grind on each other like there's no tomorrow. He throws his head back and I go right for his neck. "Oh, fuck! Harder!"

"Atta boy, tell me what you like. Tell me what you want me to do to you, Lala. Tell me exactly how to take you apart." We crash together again, tongues lashing and teeth in the way. We're like teenagers who've snuck off to the bathroom for the first time. If he wasn't in this stupid costume, I'd be on my knees for him right now.

He chirps like a bird as we get closer and closer to making a mess of ourselves, so I cover his mouth with my hand and thrust harder, damn near ready to explode.

"Good boy. Keep quiet and I'll suck your cock so hard it will blow your damn mind, then I'll bend you over this sink and show you—"

"I—I—damnit," he stutters and pushes me away, a breathless mess. "I can't do this!"

He rips the door open and takes three steps into the hallway before he stops dead in his tracks. I expect to see someone there, to see that we've been caught, but there's no one. Maybe he's thinking about coming back. I'd like another shot at that mouth of his, if not more.

"Can we talk about this?"

"There's nothing to say. I can't do this, I'm…sorry."

"Why? Because if you don't want to, that's one thing and I can live with that. But you kissed me back, and I think you do fucking want this." I walk up behind him, my hand on his hip as

I press against his back and whisper, "If it's because you're worried someone's going to find out or out you, then you just have to be quiet for me, baby. Come on, one night. One drunken, stupid night."

"Steve, I don't know what I was thinking. You're my trainer. You're Coop's best friend. I can't risk my job and my house for a quick fuck." His head tilts back onto my shoulder as I slide my tongue up his neck. I breathe his scent in. He smells like whiskey shots and citrus. I'm not holding him back. He has every opportunity to walk out of my arms and into Xanders. But god, I hope he stays.

"I can assure you, Ethan, I am a lot of things. Arrogant, a bit narcissistic, and a total pain in the neck. But I can promise you one thing." I turn him around and look into his green eyes. They're like jewels the way they sparkle, calling to my greedy soul. I press him against the wall and trace my nose up his chin. A whimper of desire escapes his throat as I growl in his ear possessively. "I am not a *quick* fuck."

HOLLYWOOD
21
Ethan

CHAPTER 9

I LIKE THE WAY YOU KISS ME

ARTEMAS

STANDING THERE in the hallway with nothing between us but sparking electricity, all I can think is how badly I want to kiss him again. How right it felt having his body pressed hard against mine. Did he feel it, too?

"I…should…I mean, we should—"

His hand is on the wall next to my head in an instant as he takes a step closer to me and the air around us thickens. He's taller than me, so I have to look up to meet his eyes. His knuckles drag over my cheek and I'm reduced to a babbling idiot on fire. The word *no* quickly vacates my vocabulary. He moves closer, arm still against the wall, preventing me from running away—caging me in.

"Which room is yours, Sweets?" His voice is low and authoritative, and I have to swallow hard before I can even move my eyes toward my door. It's just across the hall, but he would have known that. Both guest rooms are back here. He smirks at me. "Good. Farthest one from the party. Guess you don't have to be *that* quiet for me."

His mouth slots over mine and he swallows the questions, along with my loud gasp. His lips are softer than I expected them to be, but his mouth is demanding. His hand slips behind my head, holding my face to his, and it's like I can't catch my breath—and I don't want to. I'm convinced I'll melt into the floor any second now, but when his knee slides between my legs and bumps against my raging hard on, I throw my arms around his neck and kiss him back. Hard. I'm fucking grinding against his leg like a dog, a moaning, whimpering, begging dog.

"This…" I squeak out like I'm eleven years old again. I clear my throat to finish my thought, but it doesn't help much. "Might be a bad idea."

"Does it feel good?" His velvety voice against my ear makes my eyes roll back. I need to stop this needy whimper sound I keep making, but I can't. I have no control anymore.

"Yeah." My fingers play at the back of his neck, making him groan and push me harder against the wall.

"Then fuck it. Let's feel good together."

"One…one night?"

"That's all. One night of me rocking your world, then you go back in the closet. Safe and sound."

He kisses me again, then picks me up. He fucking *picks me up!* And I'm so turned on, my legs wrap around him before I have a chance to even think about this. We could get caught. We could get outed. I could lose my fucking spot on the team that I worked so hard for. All of that slides to the back of my mind when he opens the door to my room, kicks it shut, and carries me to the bed.

He doesn't throw me down, even though I wish he would. Instead, he holds me, moving us both to the middle of the mattress before he lets me down gently. We're both still in all of our clothes and when I glance down, I can't stop the laugh.

He looks pissed at first, then he looks at himself and joins me in laughing.

"Shit, we're an eighties gay kid's wet dream right now, huh? Freddy and Goose."

"I always knew Fred was a sucker for a man in uniform." He licks his lips as he unzips my flight suit. He's taking his time when all I want him to do is get my dick in his hand. I purr like a cat when he pushes my t-shirt up and flicks my nipples with his tongue. My head rocks back and I stare at the ceiling as he bites down while grinding against me. When he lets go, his tongue travels south, licking at the muscles of my stomach and I never want him to stop. I've never done anything like this before, not even in college. It's always anonymous quick hookups or pretending I'm attracted to women. Hidden away in bathroom stalls and broom closets.

It's been a long time since I had the luxury of foreplay or dry humping. When I did, it was as an inexperienced, dumb teenager. Even then, no one ever explored me the way Steve has, or left any marks like I'm sure Steve is doing to my hip right now. I'm floating outside of my body, giving control over to him and letting him do whatever he wants to me.

Steve's on a mission to shatter me, and I want him to. I need him to.

"You're so fucking pretty, Lala."

He works his way up my chest, rutting against me while he bites at my neck. Meanwhile, I'm a useless blob of jelly. I think he likes that, though, because the few times I've tried to take off his shirt or feel him up, he swats my hands away. He moves back down my body and when I think he's about to make another trip up, he reaches his hand into my boxers and pulls out my cock. It's already fucking dripping for him, and he's salivating like a hungry bear. I don't know if I should be embarrassed by it, but I'm not. I want this so fucking bad.

"So, so pretty."

I should tell him to stop. I almost push him away. Instead, I lay there whimpering and yelping while I watch him lick and tease. My hips buck and my head falls back again when his tongue lazily slides over the tip, licking up the pre-cum. I couldn't stop him now if I wanted to. I've only ever dreamed of someone touching me like this, and the last time I was with a guy was seven years ago when I was starting college. We hooked up in the library and he sucked me off—nothing special. I liked him, though, and when he wanted to see me again, I was so fucking excited. Dad couldn't stop me from getting what I really wanted. When I got to the guys dorm room, the bastard threatened to out me, showing me the pictures he'd taken. I had to give him five grand to keep his mouth shut. I used to worry he'd come back for more money later, and because of that, I've hardly touched a man since.

This is like losing my v-card all over again, and for whatever reason, I'm not afraid.

"Ahh, Stevie! Oh fuck, Jesus Christ! Just like that, please!" I beg and whine as I squirm underneath his rock hard body. He's holding me down, taking me apart piece by fucking piece. "Yes! Oh fuck, yes!"

He looks up at me, mouth full of my cock, and winks. I'm in some kind of shock when he takes my hand and presses it to the back of his head, because I don't even know what to do. His hair is softer than I expected it to be as I slide my fingers through it and hold him there, gently thrusting into his mouth, chasing a release that's built up for too long. I know I shouldn't be doing this with Steve. He's my personal trainer, and he works for the team. This could all backfire tremendously, but I can't worry about that right now. Not with his pretty lips wrapped around me. He hums and everything inside of me clenches.

"Fuck, I'm close. I'm so damn close. Please!"

He cups my balls, and that's the end of me. I'm grabbing his head and letting my body do whatever the fuck it wants while his fingers dig into my hips, holding me against the bed. The things he does with his tongue. Shit, I didn't even know half of that was possible. It's fucking hot. Soon enough, I'm emptying all I've got down his throat. My vision blurs, there's a ringing in my ears, and I'm not sure if I'm high or in heaven. I get the vague sense that he's moving up my body again and when I open my eyes, he's staring back at me.

"You alright?"

"Fuck," I croak out. "That was the best damn blowjob I've ever had, Stevie."

His nose rubs against mine. "I like it when you call me that, but I like it more when you whimper it. I bet you make all kinds of pretty noises when I'm buried in your tight ass." His lips are on mine, slow and lazy. I taste myself on his tongue and it's another first for me. Even the few women who gave me head usually ran to the bathroom to rinse their mouth out or brush their teeth before kissing me—I always thought that was weird. I wonder how they would have reacted if they knew I was picturing a man's mouth instead of theirs.

"God, you're fucking perfect, Lala." He murmurs against my neck, his cock pressing against my belly. "Roll over and tell me where the lube is before I come on your damn chest."

"I...I don't have any. Just, you know, lotion."

He stops what he's doing and leans back to stare at me with a face full of questions.

"I just, I haven't, uhm, It wasn't—"

"Are you a virgin?"

"No! I mean, I just don't...date."

"Ethan, have you been with a guy before? Beyond a BJ?"

"Yes!" I'm not sure why I'm being so defensive all of a sudden. "Look, I don't...I'm not really—"

"Gay? You're bi then, right? I mean, you're not straight, are you? Not that it matters."

I stare at those blue eyes, sparkling like stars and making my stomach flutter. "Straight for the cameras, if that makes sense. I've dated a few women, even tried having sex with them, but it's for show."

"So, when was the last time you had sex?"

"Uhm, a few years ago. She was—"

"With a guy."

"With a guy? Oh. I... high school? I was, uhm, I was the top, though." I close my eyes and cover my face, letting the embarrassment wash over me. I've fucked this whole thing up. "Fuck, I'm sorry. I'm sorry, I should have said—" What the fuck was I thinking? I wasn't. I was letting the booze do the talking. I'm expecting to hear the door slam shut any minute now, but he's still lying on top of me. He pulls my arms away from my face and starts biting at my neck again and moaning into my ear. His cock presses against my stomach as he grabs my ass, squeezing as he moans.

"Fuck, how do I get this damn suit off you? How do people fuck in these this?"

"They fly planes in them, not fuck. Switch places, dumbass." I roll us so I'm on top now, grinning at him as I unbutton his pants. We both freeze at the knock on the door, then slowly turn our heads to watch the handle, but it doesn't move. Steve starts laughing, but I'm still freaking out since it's my dick that's out right now, and my hand down his pants.

"Shower. Now. We'll see what you've got in there that we can use."

"What?!"

"I'll be gentle. I'm not gonna hurt you, Sweets. Not unless you want me to."

"No, I mean, what if they come back?"

"They won't. It was my sister telling me she's leaving. Two knocks, pause, two knocks. We had to come up with a system. She'll text me the excuse she gave everyone. Now, get in the damn shower so I can claim that pretty little ass of yours, Lala."

"Do me a favor?"

"Yeah?"

"Keep the ascot on?" I finger the bright orange piece of fabric as he watches me. I like this shifting power, this play for control. I know what he wants. Hell, I want it, too. "Let me have that fantasy when it's my turn to fuck you?"

"Switch hitter, eh? We are gonna have so much fucking fun tonight."

In the bathroom, while Steve's checking the water temperature, I grab a box of condoms and check the dates, relieved that they're still good. I'm not even sure where they came from. I hold up the box and a bottle of aloe vera that I found, and he nods before he pulls his shirt off, then drops his pants. Jesus, there's not even a trace of fat on him. It's muscles on muscles on muscles. I swallow hard and glance down at myself, wondering how weird it would be to turn the lights off.

"You coming in, or chickening out?" He steps into the shower. "Or were you hoping for Xander?"

"Xan—No, no it—" I have to think for a minute because I'm not sure I know the answer to that. Would I have stopped either of them?

He nuzzles against my ear and whispers, "Take off this stupid fucking suit and get in the shower. It's okay to be nervous. Be glad I got to you before he did, though. He's a kinky little fucker."

"Did you two—?"

"Nope. He wishes."

"I've, uhm, I've got scars. They're pretty gross. I'm, you know, I'm not built like you, either."

"Baby, not an inch of you is gross. I told you, you're fucking pretty, Lala."

"Are you always like this?"

"Nice?" He laughs as he slips the suit down my arms. He stops for a second when the suit falls to the ground and he sees my back. Again, I expect him to leave. Again, he stays and wraps his arms around me. "I've seen you without a shirt on, Ethan. Trust me, I stared, and it wasn't because of the scars. What do you tell people?"

"Car accident. Or that I fell off my bike."

He runs his fingers over some of the worst of them. "Did you notice that Jamie won't take his shirt off around anyone unless he knows them really well? He's got a few a lot like yours. You're not alone, Ethan, and they don't make you any less pretty. You don't have to hide them from me, Sweets."

In the shower, he doesn't move fast like I thought he would. He takes his time with me. Slow kisses under the water lull me into that safe headspace I haven't had in a long time. He runs his fingers along my scars and kisses the ones on my shoulders. His hand slips behind me and he teases me, praising me every time I make a little noise or scratch my fingers down his chest. I'm getting hard all over again, and he hasn't even gotten off yet, but he's not stopping. I turn around and he holds my hips as he rubs his cock against my ass. Every time I start to panic, he slows down, taking his time with me just like he said he would.

"Bend over a bit, Lala." He repositions the shower head, so it's not hitting my face as I lean forward. "Good boy. Now, you need to breathe. If you focus on that, you'll be fine. If it's too much, I'll stop. But you *will* take every fucking inch of this cock tonight. Do you understand?"

"Yes. Yes, sir."

"Sir works, but don't call me Daddy."

I laugh and he uses the distraction to push the tip inside me. I damn near crawl up the wall as I yell out. At first I think it's pain, but it's pressure. True to his word, he stops. It takes a few tries, but eventually he pushes a little deeper and I lose my god damned mind.

"Jesus, Lala. Take that cock, baby. Take it so fucking good for me." He reaches around me, stroking me in a rhythm matching the roll of his hips.

"Oh god! OH FUCKING GOD!"

"That's right, Sweets. That's exactly what I am. I'm your god, now."

He speeds up, pulling me up so he can nibble on my ear while he fucks me. His hand wraps around my neck and he gives the gentlest squeeze.

"More," I hiss, so he squeezes harder.

"You feel so good. Come with me? Fucking paint your chest while I fill you so fucking full you'll damn near burst. That what you want, Lala? My fucking come dripping down your thighs all night?" He lets go so I can breathe, then squeezes again. "I'm gonna bend you over Devin's net, and I'm gonna listen to you scream my name into the stands while I show you how much of a god I am, Ethan. You'll be my little fucking play thing."

I can't form sentences anymore. Everything is a blur of pleasure and Steve's voice. He pulls my hair back and bites down on my ear just before he loses control of his thrusts, fucking me harder and faster. There's a strange warmth inside me when we come, and I'm surprised I don't black out.

"Fuck, Lala." He praises me, and I want more of it. I want

more of him. His arm is around my chest as he reaches over and grabs the soap, washing us both as he kisses me so softly it makes my heart flutter. There's an emptiness when he pulls out of me, and I want to spin around and kiss him long and hard. I want him inside me again already. But my legs are done and my body is telling me I need a break.

"You okay?"

"Uhm, yeah. Yeah, I will be. I just, I think I need a minute." He turns me slowly, his body pressing me against the cold shower tiles. He can't keep his hands and mouth off me, and I'm sure as hell not complaining.

"You should get some sleep."

"Don't go," the words run out of my mouth in a panic before I can think about the repercussions. "Please?"

"It's your room, Lala. I can stay as long as you want." He hums against my ear before he runs his tongue up the shell. "Don't worry, I'm not done with you. You just need some rest and water before round two."

HOLLYWOOD
Steve

CHAPTER 10
THE DIRTY GLASS

DROPKICK MURPHYS

THERE'S a knock on the door and I crack open an eye, seeing sunlight hitting the floor. "Fuck," I moan as I read the clock. I'm about to cuss out Devin when a hand slaps over my mouth and a pair of absolutely breathtaking, but panicked, green eyes lock on mine.

"Yeah?" Ethan yells out as he stares at me, willing me to keep quiet. I lick his hand so he'll let go.

"Uhm, Coach texted, and we don't have to be in till like two, so Chase and I are going to grab breakfast if you want to join."

I glance around the room for the first time, surprised at how sparsely decorated it is. No posters, no pictures of family, nothing personal on the wall that says this room is lived in. There's a painting, but it's a generic one Chase's old girlfriend put in here to be forgotten. There's a stack of books on the nightstand, a few more across the room, and what appears to be a box of comic books tucked away in the corner. Seems I bagged myself a nerd last night.

"Thanks, man, but I think I'm good. I'll be ready to head out to the rink when you come back if you still want to run drills."

Christ, he's so fucking cute when he's nervous. I slip my hand under the blankets as I kiss his neck. He jumps when I brush against his cock playfully. I could easily go another few rounds with him, even after last night.

We wait to make sure he's gone, which he isn't. "Hey, man, uhm, sorry about the way Steve and Xander were last night. They're, you know, kind of assholes sometimes, but they're mostly harmless, if you know what I mean. Chase said he'll talk to Steve about it, if you want."

"Uhm," I roll my eyes at Ethan while he thinks about how to answer that. I kiss him to shut him up, but then we both start laughing. "Yeah, good idea. Let me know how that goes."

"You're such an asshole!" I whisper, pulling his face to mine for one more kiss. Then another. Then another.

My alarm goes off and I reluctantly climb out of bed and head to the bathroom. A few minutes later, with my clothes in my hand, I'm staring at Ethan, wishing this could go another way. He's still in bed, propped up on his elbows with the navy blue sheet barely covering him. Fuck, he's gorgeous, and the drive to crawl back into his bed is strong. Which makes this next part hard as hell.

"That," I gesture around the room, "never happened. When I walk out the door, we're back to being like we were before. The successful, rich, hot guy and the sexual frustrated pro-hockey player, got it?" I pull my pants on and tuck the rest of my clothes under my arm.

"Yeah." I turn away because there's disappointment in his voice and I can't look at him right now. If I do, I'll give in. "Yeah, I get it."

I swing by the kitchen on my way out, grabbing a bottle of water and a slice of pizza. Checking my phone, I see I was too drunk to drive and Laurie gave me a lift back to my place. It's more an excuse for Lala than for me. My friends already know I'm a fuckup. They don't need to think he is, too. I forward him the message so he knows as I get into my car. But when I turn around to back out, I stop and sigh. I'm not sure what the fuck is wrong with me, but I don't want to leave. I'm about to go against my better judgment and storm right back inside and figure out what the fuck is wrong with me when my phone mercifully rings.

"Hey Laurie, what's—"

"Are you home yet?"

"No, just got in my car to head down to the gym."

"Come pick me up, but don't dick around or go see your girlfriend; come to my place and pick me up."

"What's going on, Laur? Are you okay? Did something happen?"

"I can't talk about it right now, but I'm okay. I'll see you in thirty."

This can't be good, and I immediately check my messages and emails. So far there's nothing raising any red flags, but I could be looking in the wrong place. I pull into her apartments twenty minutes later and the security guy waves me in. I'm here enough that he knows me. They aren't the swankiest apartments in town, but they're new and have that whole modern box style. I sling my workout bag over my shoulder so I can get changed before I leave. As I take the elevator up, my stomach growls and I realize that my head is throbbing. I'm too old for this shit. I grab a granola bar from my workout bag and call the gym as I step into the hallway.

"Hey, Kylie. How was open?" I always call, but not in that annoying boss way, more out of legitimately caring about my employees. They're all well aware I'd drop everything and come in, even just to cuss some dude out for treating my staff wrong.

I'm an asshole, and I have that reputation to uphold, but I'm the only asshole allowed in my gym.

"Uhm, it was, uhm—have you talked to Laurie?"

"I'm walking in her front door right now. What the hell happened, Kylie? Why do you and Laurie know something I don't?"

"Because, fuck face," Laurie yells and she comes out of the kitchen carrying two travel mugs of coffee. "You broke up with the wrong damn girl last night."

"Uh, no, she definitely broke up with me and she was the right girl to be doing that."

"Uh huh, except when you pissed her off, she paid you back by driving a fucking car through your front window."

"What!?! Why am I only just now hearing about this? Wait, I live on the second floor. How'd she do that?"

"Hang up, Kylie." She calls out to the phone that's still in my hand. "I've got it from here."

I stare down at the phone and remember that I haven't hung up yet and the reality of what she's telling me clicks. "My gym? She fucked with my gym?"

"I intercepted your calls so you wouldn't know." She walks over, handing me the mug and then rubbing my arm gently. "I thought you deserved a nice morning next to a cute guy before I swoop in and fuck it all up. How did that go, by the way?"

"It…went. Don't change the subject."

"It went? What does that mean? Seriously with all those sparks flying, no second date?" Her face turns to worry and then pity. "He wasn't into Xander, was he?"

"No, he's just—he's not out, Laur. It was fun. Now he's my client again, so it's super awkward. It can't happen again, though."

"Steve, it's called discretion. I get it, it's not easy. I understand more than most people how hard it is. But—"

"I can't do that to him. Pro sports isn't where you come out, and especially not to introduce the world to a fuckup like me as the boyfriend."

"But you like him?"

"No." I answer too quickly. "I dunno. It doesn't matter."

"So, you were leaving and if I hadn't called you, you weren't thinking about going back in again? Is that the lie you want to go with?"

"Drop it, Laurie. Just tell me what the hell Kennedy did."

The glass crunches under my boots as I survey the damage. Thankfully, no one was here last night. Any other day and her driving skills would turn midnight CrossFit into a drive-thru class. I'm sure Laurie is still waiting for me to ask if Kennedy is alright, but to be honest, I don't care if she cracked her damn head open. She fucked with my gym.

"You want to talk about it?" Laurie asks.

"I was gonna break up with her anyhow. She was fucking some other guy, which means this was purely out of spite, which means I'm also not going to give her those damn contacts she wanted. Once we're done here, I'm going to call Sam and Jamie and tell them what happened, and Sam's going to fucking fire her ass."

"Now, who's doing things out of spite?"

"Not the time, Laur. Not the fucking time."

I walk across the gym and grab a broom from the supply

closet. If I'm standing around, I'm losing my mind. I need to be doing something. Laurie likes to tell me that's what's wrong with my relationships, and I like reminding her she's a lawyer, not a psychiatrist. I am well aware of what's wrong with me. From the outside, people think if I stay in a relationship too long, I get annoyed and have to move on. It has nothing to do with annoyance or boredom. It has everything to do with getting too close again. Yet another reason I need to stay the fuck away from Lala. I'll just end up hurting him when I get the need to run away.

"So what happened last night to make her want to drive her car through the gym? Was this all because of Ethan?"

"She said I was cheating on her. I wasn't. I swear, this time, I wasn't. She said she saw Ethan looking at me and heard Xander and I talking about him. So that's why she was yelling at me. Meanwhile, she's been fucking some guy named Brad who has a wife and two kids."

"I'm sorry, what?"

"It doesn't matter, she's got…seriously unresolved daddy issues. She hit's on Chase and Jamie right in front of me. She even did it at the hockey game, and hit on Ethan, too."

"And you dated her because?"

"She was a loose cannon when we hooked up. I just expected a volatile relationship and incredible makeup sex. I didn't expect the front end of a Beemer in my fucking gym."

Craig ducks under the police tape. "Hey, babe. Sorry, got here as fast as I could. Steve, we can't open like this. You need to get on the phone while I get some people to clean up." He kisses my sister before holding his hand out to take the broom from me.

"Insurance has to clear first," Laurie reminds me. We used to have a nice little savings between the two of us. Then Laurie needed money for the transition and insurance didn't cover shit. I was more than happy to help. The gym was how we were going to make the money back, and we are. It's just taking longer than we thought. We also thought Laurie would be in at Dad's law firm by now. I'm doing my best, and so is she, but it's a struggle neither of us wants to admit to facing.

"Look, I've got a call about franchising. I was gonna tell the guy to fuck all the way off, but I dunno. Maybe I should check it out. Give it a chance. We could use the extra cash flow." I stare at the glass and bent window frame, the rubber flooring I'll need to replace. More and more money that I just don't have. "Not sure he'll want to franchise with a gym that can't even open."

"Franchise? Really?" Craig asks as he and Laurie sweep.

"Steve, you hated that idea. You wanted to be the one and only full-time location."

"Yeah, well, that was before I fucked up by getting laid, okay? Besides, I already have Chase and Devin with their own gym at home, so how would this be any different? I've got to do one fucking thing right in my life at some point."

"I'll get one of my friends that studied business and franchise law to come meet with us later and talk it over, so you appreciate what you're getting into. You can't just blindly stumble into something worse just because of me."

"It's not your fault, Laur." I step over to her and pull her in for a hug. None of this has been easy on her and she always blames herself instead of blaming our fucking father. The sky could fall and she'd insist it was her fault. Hell, she blamed herself for my fiancé leaving me, which she had nothing to do with.

"It is. It's my fault. If I hadn't... If I had just stayed—"

"Miserable? Depressed all the time? No, fuck that. I would have sold everything I own to make sure you got to be who you are. Besides, I can't wait till the old man retires, and it's your damn name on the law firm, not his. Fucker."

"It's the same name, bro," Craig butts in again.

"Fuck you, it's not the same name because it's her name, not his. Whatever, you get what I mean. I'm going to my fucking office to call the insurance company."

Laurie can handle the press that's still lingering around, she's always been better at that anyhow. Livid doesn't even begin to explain how I feel. I want to call Kennedy and cuss her out. I want to scream at her the way she screamed at me last night.

There's a knock on the door and Laurie pokes her head in. "You have a call on line four."

"I'm a little busy to take a call right now. Or at least a little too annoyed to deal with anyone who wants to talk to me."

"Okay, but it's Chase. He's called three times, checking on you and you're not answering your cell. But, uhm, you might want to come back out here for a minute before you answer."

"Fuck, now what?" I storm past her after I transfer the call to my cell phone. "Dude, I'm a little—"

"Busy?" Coop replies. "Yeah, we heard. Jamie and Lex are on the way. If you have any clients this morning, you and your employees can use the house gym. I'll head back there in a bit so I can let them in."

"I uhm—No, I canceled all my—fuck. Did you bring everyone?" I ask as Devin, Ethan, and two of their teammates I used to train step into the wreckage. I can feel the wave of emotion coming and I'm fighting back tears at this point. The one thing that would make me feel better is the one thing I can't have, but I can sure as fuck see him standing right there. Right out of reach.

"Yeah, of course I did. Now, get back to work, slacker." I reach for a broom and he sighs, rolling his eyes. "Now, get your ass in the office. You need to call about a new window and get some security footage looked at once Dani gets here with that PI guy."

I'm barely back there ten minutes before Coop walks in and tosses a credit card on the desk.

"What's this?"

"Put all the damage repairs on there and let me know if there's any trouble."

"What are you talking about?"

"Well, I figure you've been training me for—shit—ten, twelve years now? And you charge me by hanging out at my place, drinking my beer, and having me do two commercials for you. Based on your monthly gym rates, I'm looking at around twenty-five grand. Double that for sessions with Jamie and with Dev. Dog sitting. Charge me for that, too. Lulu isn't cheap to board and you do that and house sit. Designing the whole garage gym. Yeah, that was all you, too. Fuck, I owe you, man."

"I can't take this from you, Coop. You're my best friend." I don't need to tell him that he's been there for me as much as I've been there for him. He doesn't owe me a dime, but he's not going to let me refuse his help.

"You're not taking anything and you're not my friend, Steve —you're my fucking brother. Do you think I'd let Devin or Jamie struggle like this?"

"I'll pay you back."

"The fuck you will." He plops down into a chair and scoots it close to the desk. He takes a deep breath, giving himself a second before he blurts out, "Hey, uhm, E's been acting weird today. Did something else happen at the party last night? Like, other than the argument, the poker game, and me blacking out?"

I stare at him, unsure how to answer. I could lie, and he might let me get away with it like he always does, but he'll see right through it. It's why I refuse to play poker with Coop or

Jamie anymore, they know my tells. They don't know each other's tells, but they know mine—assholes. I blow out a heavy breath and drop my head into my hands.

"I think I fucked up, Chase."

"No shit, Stevie. Your front window already told me that, but that's not what you're talking about, is it? How bad, Stevie?"

"I don't know. I... wait, what do you think happened?"

"I'm not falling for that trap, but I will say this. He's a good kid, Stevie. Don't hurt him, and for the love of the fitness gods, do not fuck this up."

"What do you mean, don't fuck this up?"

"You know, be cool about it."

"Do you think I'm going to take out and ad and out him or—"

"Woah, I'm only saying he's not Skylar. He's also sure as hell not Kennedy. Give him a chance?"

"Coop, buddy, you are barking up the wrong dick. We had our fun, but it's over. One and done, baby. It's over."

"Yeah, sure. Dude, you don't even sound convinced of that." He runs a hand through his hair and checks the door before he continues. "Steve, a few months ago, we watched our best friend find the love of his life—his fucking soulmate. Do you expect me to believe it hasn't opened your eyes a little to the prospect of finding someone? Possibly even settling down? Not even a tiny bit?"

"No fucking thank you, pal. Bachelorhood is my calling. I'm too damn good at it."

"Mmmhm. So good you turned your gym into a used car dealership. Alright, well, I'll see you at the house tomorrow, right? To watch the game?"

"Yeah. I'll be there. I can pick up bee—"

"You will pick up nothing. You worry about this place. I'll

take care of the drinks and weed. Jamie gets the food. Exactly like when we were younger, and you'd forget your wallet every time we were out."

"You're such a dick."

"Coming from you, I'll take that as a compliment. I gotta get back to sweeping up your mess."

HOLLYWOOD
21
Ethan

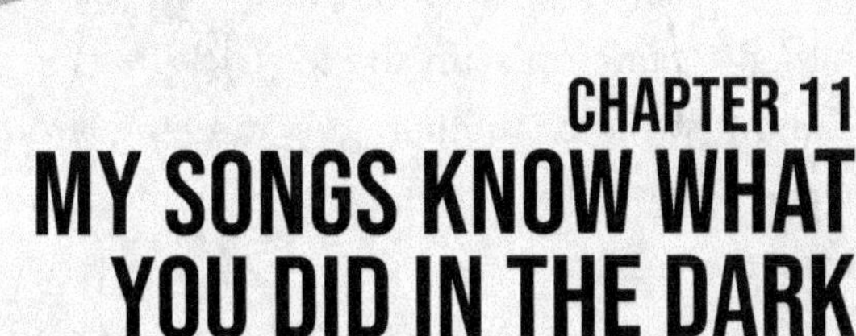

CHAPTER 11

MY SONGS KNOW WHAT YOU DID IN THE DARK

FALLOUT BOY

MAGIC HAPPENS when I step out onto the ice. A transformation from the awkward, shy kid who'd rather be at home in his room to a confident hockey player and teammate. The locker room, the outside world, the past—it all melts away the second my blade cuts into that smooth, hard surface. If I stare hard enough, I can see my reflection in the freshly flooded rink, and that's what I do. Every game, every practice, I search for myself under the ice. It's how I separate from that weaker version of me, trapping him there, locked away where he belongs. If I come out to cut up ice, I'll grab a water bottle and pour some out. It looks like I'm clearing something off the ice— spit, blood, whatever—but I'm clearing the voices out of my head.

"Hey, Lala, are you okay or are you ready to hurl?" one of the guys asks as he skates by, tapping my skate with the blade of his stick.

"I'm okay, man, thanks." I push off and wait for the cold air against my face to complete the transformation. I open my eyes and stare down—it hasn't worked. Shit.

You shouldn't even be allowed in the damn locker room. It's disgusting. I don't even want to call you my son.

I take a deep breath and concentrate on my footwork as I glide around the rink, trying to out-skate the memories of my father. I came up with the ice trick in high school after my dad caught me and another guy messing around. I thought we'd locked the door. I thought we were careful, but we were just idiot teenagers.

It was almost two weeks before I came back to the team. I blamed the bruises that remained on a fall from my bike that never happened, and no one questioned it. Why would they? My dad was the most sought after coach in college hockey at the time. At home, it was never brought up again, not directly. I learned how to hide who I was—who I am—so deep down, he gets frozen in the ice.

Bro, we're going to a strip club. You should come out with us!

Why don't you ever go out, like with girls and shit, man?

I found excuses in an unlikely place—my father. I used practicing and training to escape the questions and the answers. I would tell them hockey is more important than girls and good times, echoing what my father preached to his teams regularly. In reality, I was hiding in my room, staring blankly at Playboy magazine and trying to force myself to become the one thing I'm not. That didn't go well, either, because it just proved to me what I was and made me try to hide it even more.

Either pay up, or I'll out you, and I've got pictures. It's like that game, Clue. It was your cock in my mouth in the library.

Ever since the Halloween party, I can't stop thinking about Steve and what we did. I haven't seen him since we helped clean up the gym after Kennedy drove through the front window. Later that day, after practice, I had a text with all the workouts for the week and an excuse—schedule conflicts brought on by the damage to the gym.

I'm not sure if he's serious about that or just avoiding me, but either way, he's gotten in my head and I need him out. Now. I didn't ask for this to become weird between us. I didn't want a one-night stand either. I mean, I did, and it's what I needed to happen, but it wasn't what I *wanted* to happen.

I lean over, letting the ice and momentum carry me around while I hold my stick across my knees. Luckily, today is just open drills and not a full practice where everyone can see how messed up I am. I glance down again and the reflection is showing me years of crying myself to sleep, knowing I was a fucking mistake. Years of solitude, pretending and hiding just so I could be accepted by people who barely knew me. I'm nothing but a fraud in every possible way.

I was never supposed to be like this. I was supposed to blend into the background while my brothers soaked up the limelight. They were supposed to be stars while I got to remind the press that I was their younger, less talented, and certainly not gay brother.

"Lala!" I pick my head up and stare down the ice at Devin. "Come down here and take shots on me while everyone else is dicking around in the locker room!"

I knock a stack of pucks off the dashers and push a dozen or so between the circles. My first few shots are wide and Devin cocks his head, holding his arms out. I don't wait for him to get back into position, blasting one down low and into the back of the net. It's good to be distracted. When I glance down to pull the next puck over, I check the ice again. It's still the wrong me stuck under there with my confidence, my skills, and my façade. I don't think I can do this. I don't think I can hide who I am much longer if I can't fix my head.

Maybe I don't want to hide anymore.

"Hey, you gonna shoot or what? That last one doesn't count just because it went in!"

I take the shot and it goes wide. Shaking my head, I pull another puck over. "Sorry."

You sure as hell are sorry. A sorry excuse for a hockey player, you can't even hit the broad side of a fucking barn. We should sign you up for cheerleading with your sister. That's what you want? Pigtails and a pretty little skirt?

The next shot dings right off Devin's helmet, and that's a big no-no in hockey. You never aim at your own goalie's head. Especially not as a defenseman. I search around to see if anyone saw that as he skates toward me.

"First off, what the actual fuck was that? Second, what the actual fuck was that?"

"Devin, I'm just having an off day."

"I hear ya on the off day. It's like I can't get my head in the game because of fucking Steve."

I stare at him, hoping that was just a poor way of saying that and not something I should read into.

"Wait, no, I mean, not actually fucking Steve. You know, like, I'm so used to him bitching me out and being a hard-ass during workouts, but with him ditching us is fucking with me. Like the season isn't real anymore. I need to call him later. He can't do this kind of shit to me."

"Dev, it's not really his—"

"I mean, you don't fuck with the goalie's superstitions. We're supposed to work out, get a lot of shit out of my system, and run me stupid so I can focus. That's not happening with him not being there. I mean, it's probably better for you that he's not, or it isn't, I dunno, man."

"What the fuck is that supposed to mean?"

"Oh, shit. Right. I mean, uhm. I'm not gonna say a damn thing to anyone, okay? You're my D, I told you before. You got my back and I've got yours. Right?" He pats my shoulders with that big dumb grin of his. "Now, get your dad and Steve the fuck out of your head, and let's play some damn hockey, okay?"

He goes to skate away, but I reach out, grabbing his arm. "Who else knows?"

"Nobody. I mean, Chase knows. Probably Jamie, too, which also means Lexi. But seriously, it's no big deal, Lala. I don't care either. Not in a mean don't care way, just in a none of our business kind of way. You know? Like, how Steve and you work out is your own business." He gives me that goofy as hell grin before he squirts water in my face. "Lighten the fuck up, bro. There's, like, what, three guys on the team that might give a rat's ass about your ass and what it does on weekends."

"Jesus, Hollywood!" I swat the water bottle away from him. "Look, there's nothing, okay? He's just my trainer, nothing else, understood?"

"Fuck, sorry!" He looks around and drops his voice down. People don't realize how much echo there is from the ice with the boards and the glass the way they are. "So, you guys aren't, like, a thing now or?"

"No. No, it was a—it was…it doesn't matter. It was never anything." I didn't realize how much it would hurt to say that. It hurt when Steve left. It hurt when I saw him again later at the gym and he could barely look at me. It hurts just standing here thinking about it. It's my own fault, though. These are my rules, and Steve and I both agreed to follow them. One fucking night. Nothing more.

"Bummer."

"Why do you care?"

"I dunno. I mean, you two seem happy around each other. It's like a cute college crush or something. Escándalo!"

"Bro, stop watching telenovelas on our days off."

"Fuck no. Those things are amazing! I wouldn't sweat it too much, man. Steve's totally gonna come back for more of that cute little ass of yours." He winks before letting out a hard laugh as he skates backward toward the net. "Either way, you're my D, Lala."

"That sounds so wrong, Hollywood."

"But it feels sooooo right, baby!"

"I hate you."

"Love you too, Lala. You're muy caliente!"

I head straight for the hydro when I'm off the ice, only stopping long enough to ditch my gear and change. The hot water and jets are exactly what I need after spending far too long fighting my demons in the cold rink. Doc wants me to come check in with him after on ice workouts, but I always swing in here to relax and loosen up again before I see him. No one else is in the recovery and training area yet, so I've turned the music off, and it's just me and the sounds of the water. I'm almost where I need to be when the door flies open with a crash and our team captain comes stumbling in like he's drunk.

The guy is an absolute prick and the only reason he's the captain is because he's got the fan base and that's what the owners wanted. None of the team likes him, but it's a team sport, so liking someone doesn't matter when it's game time. He turns the music on and cranks it up louder than normal.

Thankfully, one of the other guys comes in right after him and turns it back down.

"It's a fucking training room, man, not a Metallica concert. Save that shit for the gym," Mickey Fowler says as he heads toward the trainer's offices. He's an alternate captain, and even he has very little respect for Josh Girard.

"Metallica? How old are you, dude?" Girard hits back weakly. He doesn't climb into the tub like everyone else. He jumps in, sloshing water over the sides, being a dick about it. "Metallica. Jesus, my dad listened to that shit."

Five more minutes. Just leave me alone for five more minutes, man.

"So, Lala, what's up?" Normally, I like my nickname. It's fun, and my sister gave it to me after my brothers got all the good ones. My dad hated it, but like she said, it's just our name. When Girard says it, though, it sounds like a schoolyard bully trying to poke fun at me, because that's exactly what it is. I can feel the disdain oozing off of him and into the tubs. I really fucking hate this guy. "You looked a little sloppy today."

"Leave it, Josh."

"I just wanna know if you're still planning on slowing us all down." He splashes water toward me, but I'm in a state of Zen he's not gonna break. "I can't wait to see you out there in a full practice when we run scrimmages. I'm sure you're gonna be fine against the boards."

It's easy to ignore his bitchy attitude because I've known the asshole for most of my life. Further back than Devin and I. There's nothing more fucking annoying than being rivals in the peewee league, high school, and college, only to become teammates in the pros. Bullies who call you every homophobic slur in the book, even though he has no proof I'm gay, make such amazing teammates.

Sometimes guys grow up and out of that stage of life, other times, they're Girard. I'm not even sure why he signed with Pasadena since teams were clamoring over him, offering him more money than he's worth. He's flashy, but if you break him down, he's nothing special. He pulls the same moves every game, and the only thing he's really good at is disappointing his female fans. He's a mid-level player with stats not far off from mine—which isn't great since he's a forward and I'm on defense.

"Yep. Fucking hilarious, aren't you, Josh?"

I can feel him staring at me, but I don't bother to open my eyes. There's no need. I know the look he's giving me because he's been giving it to me since we were eight. He knows I'm better than him, and that bothers him to no end. That's why he picked the gay card to go after me for. That and, to be fair, I don't have a wife or girlfriend and don't bother to try. He doesn't need to know he's right, though. He doesn't need that kind of ego boost. Besides, every time we've gone head to head, I win. Every time he gets a breakaway—in scrimmages or games—if I'm on the ice, I stop him. Always have, and I always will. I also don't get intimidated like some of the rookies do around him.

"Josh, you know the last time you tried to take me into the boards, it was you on your back, not me."

"Psshh. Oh hey, speaking of being on your back, I hear you've got a new girl. Blonde, tall, muscly. Just your type, huh?" I ignore him, or at least try to. He's grasping at straws, anyhow. Steve is out, and he's my trainer. That's all Girard has and all he'll ever have. "What was her name? Oh yeah, Steve! Is getting your ass pounded by a gorilla like him good for your back?"

"Why don't you try it and let me know?" I'm done. No sense in hanging around any longer since this fucker won't shut up. I climb out of the tub.

"Hey, no need to be hostile! I can't fault you for hooking up with him, man. I heard he's hung like a horse." I wonder what he'd say if I turned around and told him he's absolutely right, and that he fucks like a god. I'm glad I have my back to him. He doesn't need to see the way I'm smiling as I remember the other night. "And you got the team to pay for it and call it training? Your agent is incredible."

"Yep, she is."

"Wait, before you go, this is important. How'd you learn to take all that man meat?"

"Watching you, obviously." I snatch a towel from the shelf and slip my flip-flops back on. I give him a one finger salute on the way out of the room.

Did he just seriously say man meat? Fucking tool.

Doc's ready and waiting for me in the exam room, so I hop up on the table and lie on my stomach. Doc's never one for small talk, which I appreciate, but his hands are always freezing cold. So, when he touches my scars, I flinch every time. I squeeze my eyes shut and wait for it, but it doesn't come.

"You get sucker punched out there? That's a hell of a bruise," He asks, his fingers poking at my thigh. "Otherwise, whoever she is, it looks like she tried to suck your soul out of your leg, kid."

"What? Uhm, no." A flash of Steve waking me up with his head between my legs has me wishing I'd worn pants. "Must have gotten it wrestling with the dogs."

My entire body blushes and I bury my head in my folded arms. I need to tell Steve to take it—Shit. There's that guy who should be stuck in the ice right now, rearing his head up again, reaching in and squeezing my heart for no good reason. There's nothing I need to tell Steve. We're never going to be in that position again, according to him. According to me.

It was fun. It was more than fun, actually. But that doesn't matter—it was a one-time thing. He's out, he has nothing to hide. I like my job, my team, and my paycheck. Or that's what I'm trying to convince myself of. What if I just need to see him again one more time? He said I was the sexually frustrated one, and that's exactly what I am. Frustrated. What if that's my problem, why I can't get out of my head? It could have absolutely nothing to do with Steve, and everything to do with my sex life being dormant and then springing to life.

I don't even believe myself. I felt real that night. Like I could be who I am, let go and be…me. I want that again because that was more than just sex. It was acceptance. It wasn't because I'm a pro athlete or for bragging rights like some people; he wanted me for me. It has nothing to do with primal urges or other bullshit. Or it does. What if he was so pissed off that his girlfriend broke up with him, and he was horny, and I was… willing?

"I'll, uhm, be more careful next time."

We go through the rest of the exam with nothing but the standard questions about how I'm doing physically and checking my range of motion. As I'm leaving, Doc stops me and checks for anyone nosing around.

"Kid, don't let Girard get to you. He's a prick and you two have a history, I get that, but you're on the same team now."

"Yeah, I know, but I don't think he knows," I say, pulling my t-shirt back over my head and heading for the locker room. I'm not worried about Josh Girard right now, anyhow. Right now? I think I need to talk to Steve.

HOLLYWOOD
Steve

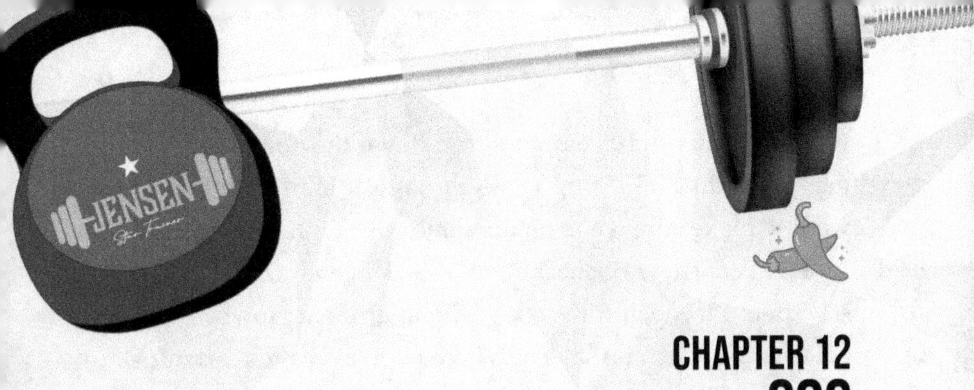

CHAPTER 12
SOS

RIHANNA

"YOU PLANNING on staring out the window all day or are you going to work?" Craig asks, sneaking up behind me and punching me in the side. He's right, I've been standing here daydreaming, but it's not all about the fancy new windows Laurie talked me into. Well, it is, but it's more about who I want to put against the windows to test out just how tinted they are.

"Fuck off. I don't have any clients for a few hours." I nod to the windows. "Did you hear they self-tint? Like those glasses that turn into sunglasses and shit?"

"Yeah, Laurie told me about that." He glances back over his shoulder. "I thought the hockey team was all yours?"

"It is, why?" He turns and nods toward the front desk where Kylie, our receptionist, is talking to sandy-hair and a nice ass leaning against the counter. I'd recognize that body almost anywhere since it's the one I've been daydreaming about all week. I haven't seen him since the window fiasco. Too much going on here and more on-ice practices this week have kept us apart. It was for the best. Or I thought it was. "Lala?"

He turns and gives me a tight-lipped smile before thanking Kylie and heading over toward Craig and I. "Hey, Steve. I was wondering if you have time to run down the new workout with me? Shouldn't take long to go through it all. I just, you know, want to make sure we're on the same page with everything."

I make a show of checking the clock even though I know my schedule. I'm open for most of the afternoon. However, I don't believe him when he says he's here to go over the workout since I've texted him all the changes and Chase has said he's doing fine. I flash him a smile, letting him know that I see through his little game. It's possible that when we said only once, neither of us meant it.

"Yeah, I've got time, and it looks like the machines we need are mostly empty."

"Uhm," he stammers, as the soft pink spread across his freckles. This kid takes guys twice his size into a corner and fucks them up. But right now, he's melting faster than butter in the summer sun. It's a cute crush, and I'll admit, I wouldn't say no to another shot at him. "Can we talk about it in private? I'm, uh, not sure I understand some of the stretches you sent, and I'd rather not have people watching me stretching out here like a dumbass out in the open."

"Craig, tell Kylie we're taking room three and it's for a VIP client." Ethan rubs the back of his neck when I say that, trying to avoid eye contact with Craig and I. "That means no interruptions while we're in there, yeah?"

"No problem. See you around, Mr. LaVoie. I can't wait till they start playing you. You're a damn good D."

He has no idea how good a D Lala really is. It takes every ounce of control to keep myself from laughing at Craig's innocent comment like a twelve-year-old. I shake my head as we make our way to the back room closest to my office. It's where I take all the VIPs for one-on-one sessions, although that usually still means as a personal trainer and professional. It's no big secret among the staff that I've screwed people in my gym. Why not when I own the damn place? But a high-profile client like Lala? No, those I take home or meet at a hotel for that kind of fun. I call it professional courtesy. When I hold the door open and he walks past me, I can feel the professional courtesy van leaving the station, not to be seen again for a while.

He's on me like a dog in heat, pushing me against the wall and groping for my cock before the door clicks shut.

"Mm, somebody's a bit greedy today, huh?" I grab his hand and put it right where I want it as I lick my lips. "Such a pretty little mess you are, Sweets."

"No, I know. We said not again, but…I—I can't stop thinking about you. About the other night. I need you out of my fucking head. I need to get this out of my damn system, or I'm fucked."

"Oh yeah, you're definitely gonna be fucked. What if this doesn't work? What if we do this, and you want more?"

"I—I don't know. Please?"

I slam him hard against the wall before I swallow his words and his moans, grinding against him. He's putty in my hands, exactly how I expected. I pull his shirt over his head, taking his nipple between my teeth and biting down. Fuck, the sound he makes for me is needy and goes right to my dick. Something between a whine and a whimper. I wanna hear it again. And again.

"You think this will get me out of your head, Lala? You think it will be easy to forget what I do to you?"

"No, it… it, Stevie, we…we shouldn't…I need—I need you! Please!" He stammers, not even capable of stringing a full sentence together as he gropes for me, trying to get my shirt off.

"I told you, it can't happen again. Remember?"

"I tried! I tried to forget about you. I can't even jerk off to anyone else but you! I couldn't fucking do it! I wanna feel that again, Stevie. That rush, that high. I need to get back on my damn game, but you're all I can think about."

"Shh, Lala. Unless you're telling me to stop, shut the fuck up. I'll take care of you, baby. I'll fuck you so damn good, but it isn't gonna get me out of your head. You'll be begging me." I grab a fistful of his hair and yank his head back, exposing his neck to me. "Now, you greedy little bitch, get on your damn knees and get ready to take my cock down your pretty little throat."

I push him down by the shoulders, and he yanks down my workout pants and my boxers. His green eyes stare up at me and it's like I'm staring into the face of a lost puppy dog. "Please, tell me you've sucked cock before."

"Y-yeah. It's—"

"Been a while? It's like riding a bike, Lala. Now, open wide."

He chokes on me at first, and I'd be lying if I said it wasn't hot as fuck to watch him struggle to take me in. His tongue slides along the underside of my shaft and my head rocks back. Fingers in his shaggy hair, I tighten my grip and push him down lower, forcing his nose to brush against me as a throaty moan pushes out of me. This is definitely not his first time. Either that or he's a goddamned natural.

"Atta boy. Oh shit, just like that, Lala. Taking me so good with that whore fucking mouth of yours." I give him time to breathe before I shove his face back into my pelvic bone. "You suck cock like a pro, baby. That why you came here? To suck my dick? You missed me that much, huh? I'll take care of you, baby. I'll give you what you need."

I watch the tears streaming out of his eyes and the spit sliding into his stubbled chin. Fucking beautiful. The way he gulps air when I finally pull him off me is equally hot. I could easily become addicted to this guy. I stand him up against the wall, kissing him hard and shoving my hand into his pants. Exploring him with my tongue and my hands, still pulling whimpers from deep inside of him. I unzip his shorts and take his cock and mine together in one hand, jerking both of us off slowly.

"Stevie!" he moans like an angel getting fucked by the devil himself. His arms wrap around my neck and he's holding on for dear life as I continue to pump my fist. His whole body tenses for me, so I spin him around, drop his pants and stroke him harder while my cock presses between his cheeks.

"Open your eyes, Lala. Open your eyes and watch what I do to you." He gasps when he comes face to face with himself. Apparently, he hadn't expected a full length wall mirror to be right in front of him. "I'm gonna fuck your tight ass while you watch."

He mewls, but it's cut off by the grunts and whimpers he makes as ropes of come land on the mirror and his chest. "Atta boy. Fuck my hand, baby. Fuck it so good." His knees try to give out, and I have to hold him up, kissing his neck and whispering how good he's doing. I walk him to the stretching table in the middle of the room and have him lean against it. As I search around, I'm inundated with ideas. Things I want to try with him, angles I'm more than ready to explore. Guys like him, athletic and young, they can go for hours if you treat them right. That's exactly what I want to do, too.

Shit, I think I like this guy, but it could be because he's off limits.

Before I go grab the bottle I keep stashed in here, I check the door and make sure it's locked. When I glance back at him over my shoulder, he has this pitiful puppy dog face and my stomach knots up in anticipation. I want him, and I'm about to have him, but this is a bad idea. This goes against our agreement, but just like that morning, I don't want to stop. It's weirdly not even the sex, I just need to be near him.

I turn the sound system on to give us some cover, but don't turn it up too high since I want him to beg for me. I toss a towel in front of him as I move in behind him and pop the top on the lube. "Bite the towel if you're going to scream, okay?"

"Do I want to know why you have lube in here, Stevie?"

"Massages? Spread your legs and relax, Sweets." I push his shoulders down so his ass is all mine. He flinches at the cold liquid against his flaming hot skin, then again when I push my finger in slowly. On the second finger, his head drops to the table that he's practically climbing while I massage his prostate. "You good, Lala?"

"Don't stop. Please!" He wraps around the towel like it's a security blanket, and I watch his long eyelashes flutter as the breath catches in his lungs. He's a beautiful mess. I want him to be *my* beautiful mess, and I don't mean for one night or random hookups. Shit, that's bad, but I can't worry about it now.

"Eyes up, Sweets. Let me see you in the mirror." I lean down next to his ear as I line up. "Show me what a good little whore you can be for me, Lala. Now, lift your hips for me, and don't forget to breathe."

His back bows and his tight little ass pushes against me. I guess he likes a little dirty talk. I hold up my hand and stare at his eyes in the reflection of the mirror. He nods. There's a sharp crack followed by a deep groan that's muffled by the towel. I spank him again, but this time, as my hand makes contact, I push into him. He claws at the table, but when I ask him if it's too much, he shakes his head. I give him a minute to breathe, to relax again, because he's gripping me tighter than a fucking vise. I rub gentle circles into his hips and shower him in praise, just like he needs me to.

"Atta boy, Lala. You're taking me like a fucking champ, baby. Show me your eyes. Show me those big, green emeralds." He slowly lifts his head, barely able to hold his eyes open. His eyes roll back when I rock my hips and luckily I get my hand over his mouth before he yells out. Even muffled, I can still tell it's my name he's screaming. "Shh, Sweets. You gotta keep it quiet when I'm at work."

He nods and pries his eyes open again. "I'm sorry... I'm... m'sorry."

"No, no. You feel too fucking good to be sorry. Too fucking perfect the way you take me. Such a good whore for me. Now tell me, whose whore are you?"

"I—I'm your whore, Stevie. Oh god, oh fuck."

"That's right. What do you need, Lala? What is it you want me to do to you?"

"You! Please, Stevie, I need you so bad! M-make me yours?"

I want him to mean that, but I don't want to scare him off. He came to me, though. I was doing whatever I could to stay busy, to not put us in this situation again, and yet here we are.

"You are mine, Lala. You're fucking mine, you understand that?"

"Yes!"

The sound of skin slapping against skin echoes in the room, not loud enough to hear outside, but it's still music to my ears. My hips speed up and I lean forward again, grabbing his hand and holding it tight as the knot in my stomach comes undone. Fire flows through my veins and empties into him as he whimpers my name over and over. I feel him go stiff and then thrust his own hips. I'm gonna have one hell of a mess to clean up in here when we're done.

"You okay?" I ask as he lies under me, both of us sweating and gasping for air. He nods and I brush the hair back away from his face and kiss his cheek. I used to do that with partners, soft gestures and kindness. I wrap my arm around him, hugging him to me as I nuzzle his neck. I don't want to let go. Not yet. "Lala, I uhm—"

"Don't," he cuts me off, but he doesn't try to break free of my hold. "I came here knowing exactly what would happen."

"I'm well aware of why you came here, sweetheart. We should talk, though. Unless you need more…stretching."

"No. Hell, I need an oxygen mask and a shower is what I need!" he laughs. I realize I like the sound of his laughter as much as I like the sounds he makes when we're fucking. I kiss him again and he smiles against my lips. "Can we get dressed before we talk, though?"

I pull out and he gasps and moans softly. It makes me want to hold him close and take care of him. It's been a long time since I've wanted to do that for someone else. I get another towel and pour some water on it, gently cleaning him and leaving a trail of kisses along his back and then his chest. When I stand back up and look at him, tears swirl in his eyes, but I wipe them away with my thumb before they can fall.

"Steve—I…I don't know what I was thinking."

"You know what?" I laugh. "That makes two of us, Sweets."

"What? Oh no, well, that's just great. What the fuck do we do?"

"For starters, you take a breath." I rub his arm, trying to keep him from freaking out. I decide to take my shot. I cup his face, kiss his forehead softly, and then press my head to his. "Lala, I don't know how, but, as crazy as this sounds, I'd like to give this a try. If you're interested. I know I'm a bit—okay, a lot fucked up, but I want to try to do better, to be better for you."

"Yeah, sure. You mean like just randomly fucking me until you find someone else, right?"

"Ouch, but I deserved that." I tilt his chin and run my thumb over his bottom lip. "I don't want to do that to you, Lala. I can't explain why, but I want more with you. I want dates and late night cuddles while we make out and watch movies. I want to wake up with you next to me and not have to hide out when Devin knocks. I want you to visit me here in the gym, so I can bend you over the desk and listen to all those fucking noises you make."

"Romantic, Steve, but we're already aware that isn't going to happen. It can't happen. *We* can't happen."

"We can. We can just keep quiet about it. Okay, maybe showing up at the gym during regular hours and disappearing isn't a great idea, but we've got other options. We don't have to go out in public together or do anything risky like that." My palms are sweaty and it's not from the sex. I can't slow down the words as they pour out of my mouth. I'm begging him. I don't beg. "Hell, Coop and Dev already found out about us, so we don't have to hide from them. Your place is about as private as we can get for a date. I'm already there a ton anyhow, so none of that would seem out of place to anyone so long as we're careful. I...I want a chance. I want a chance with you, Ethan."

"Steve, you just broke up with your girlfriend very publicly. You're a serial dater who's rarely unattached or at least not crawling into or out of someone's bed. Steve, you're a fucking playboy and that's not something that's kept secret. I wish it was different, Steve. I do."

It's like a punch to the gut from reality and it's my own damn fault. "Okay, yeah, you're right. I'll go to meetings, I'll go to therapy, I'll do anything you want me to." His eye twitches as he stares at me, and it's like he's waiting for me to laugh in his face. "Sweets, neither of us has had good luck in this relationship business. Fuck, I gave up on it, swearing it all off. But there's something about you, about us, that I can't explain, and it's driving me fucking mad."

"So, what would we be? I mean, if we did this."

I think about it, then I laugh. "We're a fuckin' mess, that's what we are."

"That's not what I mean, Steve."

"Yeah, yeah, I know it isn't," I whisper, gripping his hips and pulling him toward me so I can tease his bottom lip while I think. "If I say fuck buddies, I'll mess this up faster than you just came. I already know that. It's not enough. I don't want to treat you like I've treated the last year's worth of people. I never want to just throw you away."

"So?" He holds the o sound out as his eyebrows raise, questioning me and my motives with one word.

"So, Ethan, can I take you out to dinner in your own home someday in the very near future?"

"I'm going on the road with the team this weekend, so it will have to be after that."

"You're seriously considering this right now?"

"One condition." He kisses me softly and now it's me who's melting. His fingers muss up my hair before he cups my face and looks me square in the eyes. "You wear my jersey next time we fuck. With the sleeves on!"

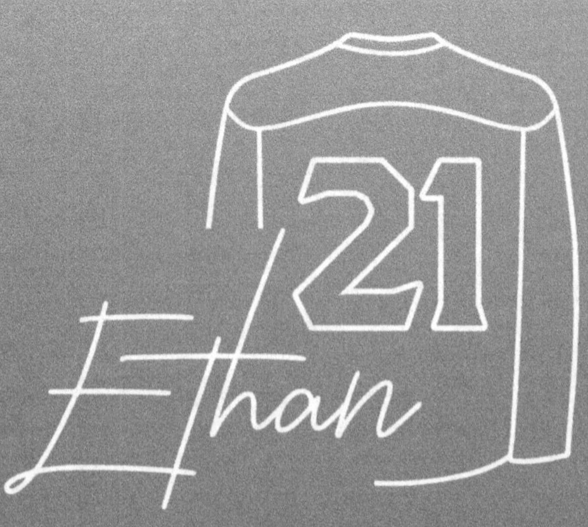

HOLLYWOOD
21
Ethan

CHAPTER 13
ELECTRIC TOUCH

TAYLOR SWIFT, FALL OUT BOY

I CHECK the oven for the tenth time, the candles for the fifth time, and switch out the bottle of wine I picked for what I believe is the third time. To say I'm nervous would be the understatement of the year. I check the mirror and think about changing again. I wonder if the tie is too much, or if I should grab the jacket that goes with the suit. The rules for dates at the house you're crashing in are a little wild west, which is making it worse. It also doesn't help that I've been overthinking this whole situation since we decided to give this a try almost a week ago.

I take a breath and glance around while I hold it in, hoping the exercise will calm my nerves. Around the house, there are still Halloween decorations up that might stay up through Christmas at this rate. Chase took Pongo to a movie set in Vegas, and Devin has Lulu with him on his own date. It's eerie how quiet it is in the house when it's only me and my rapid fire, freaking out thoughts. Quiet isn't good—I need something to make this less quiet.

"Shit!" I run around the corner and try to figure out the sound system. I must hit the TV button first, because an ESPN announcer's voice fills the room. Next, I find the radio in the middle of a car commercial with someone screaming at me; definitely don't need that. Who the fuck listens to that anymore? Finally, I find the streaming, drop the volume down, and set it to shuffle one of Dev's classic rock playlists, since that's what Steve listens to in the car. For a guy in his mid 30s, he really tries hard to be older. The first song is Fat Bottom Girls by Queen and I shake my head and laugh. If this is a sign about how tonight will go, I'm doomed.

The doorbell rings and I freeze. Who the fuck is here? Why now? I need an excuse in case it ends up being someone who knows me. I run around in a panic before finally heading for the door. I stare at the knob, praying it's a delivery because Steve wouldn't ring the damn bell. The out-of-body experience I have while I watch my hand pull the door open slowly is a little trippy. I peek out, not sure what to expect, and I'm met with an entire field of daisies with the slightest hint of Steve's head somewhere behind them. When he lowers them, my jaw drops. He's in a dark polo that looks like it will rip if he moves the right way, and tight black slacks. I swear he buys his clothes a size smaller to make the rest of the men around him feel inadequate. He leans in, giving me a quick peck on the cheek, and I'm hit with the scent of whiskey and cinnamon. Okay, maybe he's kind of perfect.

"Seriously? Ringing the damn bell like you don't practically live here? Get inside before someone sees you standing there with flowers!" I pull him in and shut the door, but when I turn back around to look at him, he looks…scared?

"I'm sorry! I haven't done this in a while!" He blurts out, shoving the flowers forward again, hope playing in his eyes as he tries to force a smile. It looks absolutely ridiculous, and I love it. "They, uhm, they're for you. You look great, by the way. I'm sorry, I should have come in, but I wanted to do this right for once."

I stare at the daisies for a minute and chuckle. "I've never gotten flowers before."

"It's stupid, isn't it? Fuck, I always fuck this part up. I really gotta stop listening to Chase on this shit."

I take the flowers from him and put them on a table near the door before I cup his face and guide his lips down to mine. Slow, soft kisses, no one in control, no one fighting for power, nothing but us being equal for once.

"Lala?" He moves away from me, but thankfully not far. "What smells so damn good?"

"Oh, uhm, I made dinner. You said we could order out or whatever, but I wanted to—"

"You cook?"

"Yeah. My mom taught me. I can also do my laundry like a grown up. Oh, and I tied the tie all by myself." I quip, wrapping my arms around his waist while he rolls his eyes and continues to sniff at the air. "Look at that, the gruff old hockey player can be domesticated."

"Gruff, a bit, but old? If you're old, then what the fuck am I? Don't answer that!" He jokes, kissing me and backing me against a table. He stops abruptly and sniffs once more. "Baby, did you cook Yankee fucking pot roast?"

"Is that bad? I just thought since we were both from—"

"Will you marry me?" I stare at him, unimpressed by his sudden proposal. "I'm kidding. Sort of. It's my favorite! We had this lady who would come cook meals for us when I was a kid and, hell, I haven't had Yankee pot roast since I was about twelve."

There's something different about Steve tonight, but not in a bad way. It could be that I'm seeing the real him for the first time, relaxed and playful instead of a cold, snarky asshole. He's like a damn kid headed to his first school dance. I catch his fingers twitching nervously as he takes in the house, as if he doesn't recognize a place he's been in a hundred times or more.

"I kind of hoped a little something from back home would be good." I pull away, rushing into the kitchen like it's on fire and check the oven. I guess we're both nervous wrecks right now.

Dinner is cooked perfectly, much to my surprise. I grab a couple of oven mitts and carry it into the dining room, careful not to let my tie drop into it. I don't think this room is used much as a dining room since it's not like a house of single guys are hosting dinner parties anytime soon. I put the dish at the end of the table where I've set two places. No need to set the whole table with just the two of us. I also didn't want to recreate the Batman scene where he has to walk the salt down to her.

I turn and Steve is right there behind me, cupping the back of my head and pulling me to him. We kiss each other without ego or agenda, just the two of us being honest and ourselves. It sends sparks up my spine and makes my toes curl in my uncomfortable shoes.

"When are they back?" He whispers against my lips.

"Tomorrow night."

"Did you make dessert?"

"Uhm, no?" A pang of worry hits me. Why didn't I think about dessert?

"Good, cause you're all I'm going to want after this. Hell, you might be the appetizer if you keep looking at me the way you are right now."

I'm jealous that his nerves seem to have dissipated, while mine has doubled since he walked in the door. I keep checking the windows to make sure the blinds are closed and my tie to make sure it's straight. I pull away, biting at my nails as I head back to the kitchen, but he catches my arm and pulls my chair out for me.

"Sit. Stop freaking out on me. We're safe. Tell me what else we need and I'll get it, Sweets." He pulls a lighter out of a drawer behind him and lights the candles before he turns the lights down low through the house. He pops the cork on the wine, pours us each a glass, and holds my glass out for me to smell like he's some kind of sommelier.

We're both unsure what to do at first, talking over each other to ask questions or staying quiet too long to give the other person a chance to talk. You'd think we'd be better at this since we've already seen each other naked and even had a few verbal spars. He reaches out, taking my hand and finally we relax enough to talk. He tells me about his sister and growing up in Boston. About the move to Los Angeles and quitting law to go into personal training and physical therapy. I keep my family stories vague and talk about what it was like growing up in a family like that. We tiptoe around the family drama and only talk a little about work. There are brief moments of tension when it's obvious there's more to the story, but there will be another time for that. Or at least, that's what we're both hoping.

"Lala, that was delicious. I thought for sure you were gonna tell me Chase made it or you had someone come in and cook."

"Nah, this one is easy. Came out exactly like my mom used to make."

"You don't talk about her much."

"Yeah, she left when I was still pretty young. I don't blame her, in fact, the opposite. I was so glad when she got out of there. I only wished she'd have taken my sister."

"Not you?"

"Dad would have never let that happen. It was hard enough getting him to let us go see her from time to time. Being the youngest of the four boys, I had a little more freedom until he, uhm, found out about certain things. Before that, I'd spend weekends with Mom and her new husband, Charlie, down in Boston. He's a nice guy, British, and so different from my dad. He brings her to the games when I'm in town and treats her well."

"That's great, that you still get to see her and all." His smile is warm, but his eyes are sad. I wish I knew why, because I know he still has both of his parents and they're still married, but neither of us really talked much about parents.

"Yeah, we talk on the phone every few days. She, uhh, likes you. Thinks you're cute."

"Oh yeah? Well, you'll have to break it to her that I'm kind of seeing somebody, so she'll have to wait till I screw it up," he laughs. He's got a great laugh, unapologetic and real.

We rinse the dishes and get everything put away, kissing and teasing each other every opportunity we get. At one point, he has me pinned against the fridge, and he's loosening my tie while he nibbles under my jaw.

"I like it better when you have stubble, but this is still nice," he whispers. I swear my eyes roll back in my head. Next thing I know, he's pulling me through the house by my tie, leading us into the living room. "Come on, let's catch a movie."

I couldn't tell anyone what he turned on. Before it even has a chance to start, he's pulling me into his lap and we have our tongues down each other's throats. It's as if Steve has my checklist and knows exactly what I want, what I've never experienced before. He pulls my tie off ever so slowly before he shifts and lays me down across the couch. He's got the tie in his hand still as he crawls up my body, dropping his hips at just the right moment and making us both groan with pleasure.

"You should wear ties more often. You're fucking hot." He purrs. "Do you trust me, Lala?"

"Yeah."

He uses the tie as a blindfold and climbs off me, telling me to stay put. I hear him walk away and the drive to pull the tie off my eyes is intense, but I want to do this right. I want to make Steve happy. Seconds go by, but they feel more like minutes. His footsteps come closer, but I'm not relieved by that. Instead, I'm worried he's gone to get a camera or call the paparazzi over to catch us in the act. I'm worried he's coming back to humiliate me. I'm worried this was all a lie, like so many times before.

"Hey, I'm here. I'm back." He nuzzles against me reassuringly, but he feels different. It takes me a moment to realize he's taken his shirt off. He pushes my chin down so my mouth opens and I can feel his breath on me, but it's cold. "Hold this for a second, yeah?"

I nearly choke on the ice cube because I don't know that's what it is at first. I'm cursing myself in my head for thinking it could be anything else and for my throat trying to open up and take it. If I am just a whore, I'm not a successful good one, given my track record.

"I'll buy you a new shirt." Before I can ask him what he means—not that I could around the ice—he rips my shirt open. The tiny sound of buttons bouncing across the tile floor echoes around the room.

"Okay, give it back." I go to reach into my mouth and he stops me with a snicker. "Not like that, Sweets." His mouth presses against mine as he takes the cube from me. My heart is racing and my mind is all over the place right up until the cold ice touches my bare chest and I jerk upward.

"Fuck!"

"Shh, relax, baby. Trust me." He hums as the ice circles my

nipples, leaving water that he blows on gently. Every ounce of blood has rushed out of my limbs and straight to my dick. I'm so hard it hurts. He's sucking on my neck, still teasing me with the ice when he unzips my pants and pulls my cock out. "Atta boy, relax for me. I'll take care of you."

The heightened sensations of his hot mouth, the cold ice cube, and the fact that I can't see anything have me hard as a damn rock. Without warning or time to prepare, Steve takes me all the way down and I'm bumping against the back of his throat. I scream out his name, which is, of course, right when the doorbell rings.

I rip the tie off my eyes, but before I can do anything, Steve is striding to the door, not bothering to put his shirt back on. "Stay there." His voice is—protective. Like he's going to save me from a serial killer or something. Like I'm not a two hundred pound NHL defenseman who's perfectly capable of keeping myself safe. It's protective and dominant, and fuck, I kind of like it. "Stay hard, too!"

I shake my head, trying to fight back the panic of trying to figure out who is at the door.

"Hey, Christ, you are a big fella, huh?" the voice is familiar, but I can't place it until they start laughing.

"What's it to ya, shrimp dick?" Steve asks, his Bostonian accent coming on strong. I'm pretty sure that means he's pissed off.

"Oh, we're here to see Lala. We wanted to—"

"*Ethan* isn't here, so fuck all the way off."

"Oh, come on, man. He's expecting us! Just let us in, we'll do our thing, and then we'll get out of your hair."

"Bullshit. If he was expecting you, why'd he leave two hours ago?" I peer around the corner and see him cross his arms while simultaneously puffing out his chest. He's daring them to try anything. "Bro, if this is some kind of team hazing thing, fine. He's on a date at one of the AMCs in Burbank, so good luck with that."

"Why's his car still here, asswipe?"

"Because that's not his car, you fucking tool. Also, because when you want to impress a girl, you borrow the fucking jag. And then, when you're done, you pray to the baby Jesus himself that you can get the stains out of the backseat before Coop comes home."

It's hard for me not to laugh at the way he's taking Girard down a few notches, but I try to stay as quiet and still as I can. I listen to the lies roll off Steve's tongue like honey, and I wonder how he got so good at leaving the truth behind. I try to stop my brain from going there, but it's too late. My mind is bouncing around ideas that he brought them here, that he's going to out me, that this is all some fucking game for him. I've gone from euphoria, to concerned, to needing to get the fuck out of here in minutes. Anxiety is a fucking nightmare.

"I know you're in there LaVoie!" Girard yells out and I hear mumbling from whoever has tagged along with him. It must be friends, because no one on the team besides Girard would try this kind of shit.

"Girard, you can't even find your own dick without one of your friends here helping, you fucking twat waffle. If you think Coop and I won't take you down because you're on the team with his kid brother, you're in for one fucked up awakening. No team will touch you when he and I are done with you. Now, take your fucking friends and get the hell off Chase's property."

I don't hear the door shut, too deep inside my own mind.

"Alright, now, where were we?"

I'm hugging a pillow as I stare straight ahead when Steve comes back around the corner. He must know what's going through my mind because he immediately wraps me in his arms around me, kissing my head.

"You're safe, Sweets."

"Get off me."

"Lala."

"No, I can't do this. They could have seen us. They could have seen you come into the house and…and…"

"Ethan?" His voice is strange, like he's calling me out of a dream. It's gentle and warm. "Ethan, baby, they're gone."

"It's my fault they were here. Fuck, who knows how long they've been out there? Or if they're really leaving. This was a terrible idea. I'm sorry. I'm sorry, Steve."

"Is this where you tell me you've endangered the mission and you shouldn't have come? I have got to stop watching movies with Alexis and Jamie."

Steve stares at me, but I can't look at him. I wanted this. I wanted this so damn bad, I was willing to mess my whole life up for a shot. A shot with a guy whose reputation says he'll probably leave me when he gets bored or he'll bang five chicks behind my back. It's my fault. It's Steve's fault. No matter who is at fault, what we're doing is wrong. Now, all I can hear is my father screaming at me.

"Lala, please look at me." He tilts my face up, but I keep my eyes down. "Hey, we'll be careful. Those assholes have nothing on us, okay? I got rid of them. Now let's go back to you and me."

"I can't. I can't."

"Why?"

"Because it's wrong, Steve. I'm…it's not right. It's not normal. I'm… I'm fucking disgusting."

He grabs my face, kissing my temple before holding his forehead to mine. "Baby, you are fucking beautiful. There's not a damn thing wrong or disgusting about being gay. In fact, I'm pretty sure there were gay people before there was this whole idea of monogamy and marriage." He brushes my hair back, and the heat rises inside me again. I can't help it, no matter how much I think I want to stop being who I am. "There's nothing wrong with you, Lala. Not a damn thing. If anyone fits the description of disgusting, it's those idiots."

"Why do I feel like I'm fucking up here? Why is my position on the team on the line, not theirs?"

"Because society is fucked up and backward, not you. You're…hypnotic." He swallows hard and I finally lift my eyes to his. He's struggling with something, but I'm not sure what. "Ethan, I don't know if I can say this without sounding like a dick, but you're changing me in ways I wasn't sure I was ready for. You're opening boxes in my mind that were meant to stay sealed forever. You're thawing out a long frozen heart, and I'm not sure I can handle this, you, us. I don't know. But god damn, I want to try. I really want to try to let myself feel again with you."

"I—I want to try with you, too."

"Come on, let's turn on the movie and lie down so I can play with your hair again while we fall asleep together."

"You don't want to—"

"We've got all night, and all morning to fuck around, Lala. And I intend to do exactly that with you. But for now, I want to hold you until you're okay again. I want to take care of you, Ethan."

"Is this a bad idea, Steve? I mean, you and me, is it a bad idea?"

"I mean, probably, but I'm here for a bad idea or two, Sweets. Especially bad ideas as pretty as you."

HOLLYWOOD
Steve

CHAPTER 14
BAD DAYS

FLAMING LIPS

TODAY HAS RANKED UP THERE in the top ten worst days of my life. There are problems with the plumbing at the gym, and the city is paving the street that leads to our parking lot. On top of that, two of my employees got COVID while we were closed for Thanksgiving. Individually, none of that is more than I can handle. In fact, living in Los Angeles, those things are practically a walk in the park. Until you add the bastard who calls himself my father into the equation. Then, everything seems a million times worse.

Of course he picks now, when the gym is short on both staff and members. I'm trying to remember enough Spanish to direct the plumber into the parking lot around the paving as I feel my father's eyes on me. The noise alone from what they're doing was giving me a headache, but now, I'm just waiting for my head to implode from overloading.

Kylie took it upon herself to keep him company while he waited, which means he's seething by now. He's a firm believer that nothing and no one makes Judge Jensen wait. I disagree and take pride in proving him wrong. If he wants to cut us off, then who the fuck does he think he is walking in here like he owns the place?

"Be right with you, Dad," I say as I jog past him to meet with the plumber, who, to my surprise, now speaks perfectly good English. Dick move, but I'm giving him bonus points for pulling it off and making me struggle through those directions. I give him the rundown of what's going on and then brace myself for impact with Dad.

"Your Honor," I hold out my hand, and he shakes it harder than he needs to. That's our relationship, a handshake and snark, and even that's hit or miss most days. "What can I do for you?"

He looks around, surveying the place like he's never been here, because he never has. I can see the growing disappointment and even though I don't need his validation, it hurts like a kick in the guts. This gym is my pride and joy. It's my safe space and also a place I'm so damn proud of, and he's walking in and pissing on the floor.

"The location is terrible."

"There's amazing foot traffic on normal days."

"The lighting is shit."

"We just had the window replaced, and the lighting is fine. Maybe it's your eyes."

"And the place is as dead inside as your soul."

"Ouch, nice to see you, too, *sir*."

If he's going to piss on my floor, so am I. I'll have a full fledged dick swinging contest with this motherfucker. It may not be the best decision business wise, but it will make me feel a hell of a lot better about the day. He hands me an envelope with my name on it.

"Sign it."

"What is it?"

"The deed to the building and the land. Sign it."

"Oh, yeah, about that. No."

"You'll sign, or I'll press charges for theft and sue you for every fucking dime you think you have."

"Sue… Sue *me*? You'll have charges pressed against *me*? Oh, that's just stellar. Don't quit your retirement plan to take up comedy, dad. The jokes are tanking." He thrusts the envelope out again, but I still don't take it. "On what grounds are you planning to sue me, Dad? I have receipts and all the backup for this place and you have no rights to it."

"Defamation of character is where we'll start. The interview you gave a few years ago in Men's Health Magazine should prove to be enough for that. As for the theft, I also have receipts and deeper fucking pockets." He chuckles and starts roaming around the place like he's taking inventory. He probably is. "Thing is, Steven, it's not even you I have a problem with. I gave up on you years ago when you decided to lose your mind and go into this fitness guru bullshit. But when it comes down to it, you're simply the fish I can fry the easiest."

"Come at me then."

"So long as I don't go after your brother?"

"Sister. Leave her out of this."

"I will, as soon as the games stop, and he pays me back all the fucking money."

"You didn't pay for her transition! All you did was move us across the country! You only did that because I found you a place to set up shop and open a new branch for your firm. You act like you moved here for us, for her, but you've never done anything that didn't benefit yourself."

My words don't even break the skin as he continues his stroll. He pushes open the door to my office and makes himself at home as he steps inside. He even whistles like he's impressed when I know what he really thinks without him having to say anything.

"Here's the deal. You have two choices, and only two choices." He walks over to the window wall and stares out at the bustling street. "You give up all of this, on everything you've dreamed of, and Spencer can keep playing his stupid game. Or Spencer stops the bullshit and takes over the company like you were supposed to and you get to keep your silly little gym. Either you're both penniless losers, or you both get to keep the legacy intact."

"That's blackmail, so I guess I should just add that to the list of illegal activities my father is cool with? Tell me, does blackmail rank above or below general corruption, or does it just fit neatly in there with it?"

"I'm offering you a way out of all this."

"You're not offering me shit. You're trying to use me and my gym to fuck Laurie's life up because you can't stand the idea of your stupid fucking firm going to your daughter."

"Oh, he's not getting the firm. In fact, if you don't sign this paperwork before the end of the week, I'm going to make sure he can't get in at any firm. I'll make sure I golf with all the right people, telling them what a disgrace he is, how he took my money and blew it on idiotic surgeries for attention."

"That's bullshit, and stop calling her Spencer."

"They'll listen to me," he goes on, as if I'm not standing there anymore. He tosses the envelope on my desk and looks up at me, staring me in the eyes. "They'll listen because I'll tell them the sob story of how he turned you into a failure and a fairy. The abuse you suffered at the hands of your manipulative brother, and how much of a fraud he is."

"Alright, get the fuck out of my gym." My hands clench into fists and I'm certain I've got fire shooting out of my ears.

"Hey Pumpkin Spice!" Ethan shouts as he heads toward the office. I wish he'd stayed up front with Kylie. "Come on, are you hiding from me? I heard about the plumbing and how empty the place was today, so I thought I'd surprise you with a breakfast date with your favorite food and favorite client. Okay, it's my favorite food, but I think you'll—Steve?"

There's a smirk on my father's face and I flip from wanting to kick his ass to feeling like I just got a face full of ice water. My father steps around the corner and into view, and the smirk has grown into a full smile. Dad follows hockey. Dad knows exactly who Lala is and just heard him say the word date. He's latched onto that. I know it.

"Oh hey, sorry, I didn't know you had company," Ethan tries to recover. "I, uhm, figured it would be okay to show up early and get the session done since no one is here."

"LaVoie, right?" My heart sinks.

"Yeah, that's me. Donut for a hockey fan?" Ethan flips the box open and holds it out to my father. Much to my surprise, he takes one, nods, and walks away. "Good luck with the rest of the season, kid. I hope you're back on the ice soon."

"Thanks!" Ethan asks in a whisper as we both watch him walking out the front door. "Who was that?"

"My father."

"Woah," he says, surprised. Then he slowly turns toward me, "Hold on, your dad? And you didn't introduce me?"

"He knows who you are." It comes out colder than I intended, but I couldn't help it. My mind is too busy racing through possibilities.

"Stevie, do we need to lay off for a bit?"

"I don't know if he'll come after you like that, but he might. I'll figure it out, though."

"Well, glad I brought donuts, then. Trejo's donuts and a little fooling around makes everything better," he winks and nods toward the office.

"Oh, I can think of several ways these donuts are about to make my day so much better."

Ethan is an hour later for dinner, and that is where I draw the line. If he wanted to stand me up, he should have done that months ago. Back when I could handle it better by finding someone else to screw for a few nights while I got him out of my head. I get that he's a little freaked out about the interaction with my father yesterday, but that's no reason to just ghost me. He's not answering calls or texts, and I've already gone through so many stages of dating grief and confusion. I don't know what to do next.

Yes, I do. I hold the phone up to my ear and wait, talking as soon as he answers. "Coop, where is he? Is this some kind of fucked up payback for something I did? Is this because of my dad?"

"What are you talking about, man?"

"Ethan! He was supposed to be here an hour ago, and he's not here."

"I saw him working out in the garage this morning," he says. My moves through the house, the familiar taps of the dog's toes on tile following him around. "My cars are both here, and D's out with his own car."

"Fuck. Is he in his room?"

"I have no idea, and I am not checking for you. You two are grown adults. Handle your shit," he snaps back. Coop and I are like brothers, but brothers that very rarely fight, so when he snaps at me, all the warning bells go off in my head.

"Are you okay, man?" I ask, as my focus shifts from my boyfriend to my best friend.

"I dunno. Yeah. I'm fine."

"I'm coming over. Ethan is AWOL and you sound like you've walked into the deep end of a shark infested pool for fun."

When I get there, I find Coop in the kitchen. He's pulled out enough ingredients to feed a small army, and he's in the process of peeling an onion. Without shedding a tear. I'm not sure if that makes him a sociopath or not, but it does in my book. Cooking is good, though. Cooking means he's coming out of it, or at least knows how deep he is.

"Hey, how do you feel about Spanakopita with coconut Panna Cotta for dessert?" he questions without looking up.

"Spanking your pita and a pina colada?" I walk in and hop up on the counter, grabbing some kind of fruit looking thing and picking at the skin. He swipes it away from me.

He stops long enough to glare at me. "Spanakopita, you'll like it. Now, get the fuck off the counter." He gets super focused when he's like this. "I've got an order in for the stuff I'm missing. Should be here in a few minutes and then dinner will be ready in like two hours."

"Did you get ice cream, too?" I'm nothing if not predictable with how I handle breakups.

"You're not breaking up with him. I don't care how late he was or what's going on. You two actually work, which is more than I can say for any date either of us has had in over a year."

"Whatever. I'm gonna go make sure he didn't fall and break his hip or something." I grab a handful of coconut shavings before he can slap my hand away and I head toward the back hallway. It's quiet, but I can see the flicker of the TV screen under his door. I was joking about the hip, but now I'm legitimately worried that something isn't right.

"Eth?" I whisper, quietly tapping on the door. "You in there, Sweets?"

"Yeah." Something doesn't sound right, though. He sounds... timid. I turn the knob and it clicks, so at least he hasn't locked himself in to avoid me.

Inside, I find a lump of blankets on the edge of the bed with a foot sticking out. I also find his phone on the charger next to his bed, meaning he heard my earlier calls and texts.

"Are you okay?"

"No," he squeaks out in a pain filled whine and I immediately forget about our date or breaking up.

"Lala, what is it? What's wrong?" My knee no more than hits the bed next to him, causing it to dip ever so slightly, and he lets out a yelp and a scream. I freeze. "Ethan? Is it your back?"

The blankets move in a way that tells me he's nodding his head, so I slowly lift my leg off, letting the mattress level back out. Gently, I pull back part of the blanket, finding a messy tuft of blonde hair.

"Can you move?"

"No." I glance up as I take his hand. His eyes are squeezed shut. Clearly, he's still in pain.

"I'm calling the specialist."

"NO!" He yells, then hisses at the effort. "They'll kick me off the team!" I brush his hair back with a free hand, feeling the sweat. Still more worried about his career than he is about his own health. Dumbass.

"How long have you been here? No, never mind. I'm going to get Coop so he can help me move you, okay?"

"No, it's...I'm fine."

"You're not fine and it's Coop—he'll understand. Let us help you, Eth. Let *me* help you."

"Don't wanna move."

"We gotta figure out what's wrong, Sweets. It's either this, or the hospital, your call."

"Fine."

I run to the end of the hall and yell for Coop, who pokes his head out around the corner. "Coop, I need your help. Eth's hurt."

"What?! Do I need to call an ambulance or something?"

"No, just, I dunno, come help me." When we step back into the room, I can see the muscles in Ethan's back as they spasm. I spin back around to Coop. "Change in plan. I need ice packs and muscle relaxants."

"No drugs!"

"Sweets, I'm not giving you pain killers for fuck's sake." I say as I head for his bathroom and Coop runs off to get the ice. In the medicine cabinet, I find all kinds of fun stuff that I assumed would be in here. Although it looks like he hasn't touched any of it. I find the one I know he needs and fill a cup with water. "Okay, looks like you never take these or anything else you're supposed to, but don't worry. I'll keep an eye on you and you're only taking one, maybe two. If that doesn't help, we need to go see someone."

I kneel beside the bed, brushing his hair back again. The look in his eyes is pitiful, and I can tell he's embarrassed, too. It takes some coaxing, but eventually, he agrees to take the meds. Coop and I help him get in a better position and I arrange the ice packs, using compression bandages to help secure them in place. Once he's situated, I work on gently massaging the area. Between the courses I've taken so far and the full physical therapy office upstairs at the gym, I've learned a thing or two.

The spasms become less intense as the drugs and ice take effect. Lala's body finally allows him to relax, so I climb into bed with him and turn on a movie before I hold him close. It's so far away from what I'm used to in a relationship. By now, I'd be looking for a way out, or at least looking for what's next. As much as I want to blame a car accident and Jamie's sister for my breakup with Skylar, I know it was me. I know I chase them away by being a cruel dick. I want to do better for Ethan, to be a better person for him and myself.

"Sorry I was late. I couldn't reach the phone to call you."

"Well, I'm sorry my head was too far up my ass to realize you wouldn't ghost me like that."

"Am I gonna lose my spot on the team?"

"No, Sweets. It was back spasms. They're common enough. We'll talk to the team's physical therapist about treating these when they happen. Especially if they're that bad."

He looks up at me with glassy eyes and a goofy smile—the drugs have clearly kicked in. "You're pretty."

"And you're pretty wasted."

"Knock knock," Coop announces himself as he pushes the door open with his ass. He's got a tray with two big bowls and a couple of bottles of water. "Dinner is served. Brought you water since you probably shouldn't be drinking after takin' the good stuff. Text me when you're done and I'll trade it out for dessert."

Ethan moves to sit up, but I make him stay put. Carefully, I scoop a small spoonful and bring it to his mouth, then realize he's staring at me funny. "What?"

"For a guy who doesn't do relationships, you're really damn good at them."

"It helps that you're cute. Now shut up and eat before I change my mind."

HOLLYWOOD
21
Ethan

CHAPTER 15

CALL IT LOVE

FELIX JEAN, RAY DALTON

MY HEAD IS under the water as I let the heat hit my back, hoping it will loosen the muscles after the last workout. It's fine most days, but the cold weather snap that's hitting Los Angeles right now isn't doing me any favors. Over the last few weeks, I started working more with Seb, the team's rehabilitation guy. The muscle spasms haven't been a problem, and I have a plan of action for when they come back to kick my ass. He and Steve assured me it's normal, and they come from me overdoing it in the gym. I don't only overdo it at the gym, though—not when Steve and I get it on as often as we can. I think my body is still adjusting. Going from the guy who never gets laid to crazy amounts of sex has probably been a shock to my system as much as it has my brain.

After the way Steve took care of me, though, I'm thinking about our situation. It felt nice being taken care of like that, and even though I'm still nervous every time we go out, I'm also incredibly happy. When we're at the house or his apartment, everything clicks between us. I've been learning he's not the harsh dickhead everyone thinks he is. It's a front—a wall he's built to protect himself. I understand walls like that since I've been building them my whole life. I'm hoping the two of us can work on taking a few more down together, though.

My phone rings and it takes me a second to place the noise before I reach for it.

"Hello?" I answer without looking.

"Hello my sweet baby boy," my mom coos. She does that to annoy me. *"I hope I didn't interrupt anything important?"*

"Hey, Mom. No, just getting out of the shower. We had an early morning practice at the rink in Calgary, so I'm getting ready to head back to the hotel for some extra sleep. What's up?"

"Oh, I can't wait to watch you again. Soon, baby." She sighs heavily into the phone as she changes gears. *"Promise you won't be mad at me?"*

"Mad at you? Why would I be mad at you for calling?"

The silence has me worried as my mind runs through possibilities. Mom's not a coy person. She's bluntly honest to a fault sometimes, so she has my attention.

"Lala, it's about Steve. I… I had Charlie look into him and I—"

"MOM!" Charlie is a good guy, and I like him, but he works in security. Mom's done this with a few of my friends, but I didn't expect her to do a deep dive background check on Steve. "You can't do that!"

"Well, it's too late! I already did and, Lala, baby, I want you to be careful, okay?"

"Why? Are you planning on telling me he's a deranged killer on the loose? Or that he isn't even Steve—it's an alias! Does he work for a deep cover spy agency sent to infiltrate pro hockey's dark, homosexual agenda?"

"No, Ethan, sometimes you're as bad as Kota. Listen, you're my baby and I had to be sure, you know that. I was so happy for you finding someone, and I wanted some assurance he's safe." She truthfully sounds more worried than upset, so at least that's

good—I hope. Like she said, she already has the information, so I might as well listen to what Charlie found. *"He's, well, he's had a lot of…relationships."*

"Sex, mom. He's had a lot of sex. That's not a crime, Mom."

"No, but it's a pattern with him. He'll date someone for a while, and when it ends, he, well, he carries on recklessly for a while, and that's when the cycle starts again. It's happened at least three times since high school, from what Charlie found."

"Jesus, how deep did he dig?"

"The internet never forgets, Lala! Criminal Minds *taught me that!"*

"Yeah, I'm well aware." I'd suspected there was more to Steve, but we've only been together a couple months. That's hardly enough time to really get all the details on someone. There's a lot he hasn't found out about me, yet. "I told you he's a playboy like that. He grew up rich and didn't do well settling down. He's got a different girl or guy in his bed every night sometimes, but not now. He's not like that with me."

"Oh, honey. If you only knew how many people have said that before."

"What do you mean?"

"Men don't change, baby. You've seen that in your father and your brothers. They are who they are, and you could be the best thing since sliced bread, but you can't change a man."

She's right, and it's something that's been eating at me for a while now. It's especially hard because of our situation. It's not like I can ask for relationship advice from just anyone, though. No one knows about us, and if we start going to couple's therapy to keep us both in check, people are going to find out.

"You still there, Ethan?"

"Yeah," I mumble. "Mom?"

"Yeah, baby?"

"What if I don't try to change him?"

"If that's the path you choose, you need to be ready to have your heart broken from time to time. You need to make sure he knows that you're in this for the long haul, not a few months of fun, sexy times."

"Jeez, mom!"

"Oh, come on. I've probably read worse in my books." She teases. *"I'm only saying you need to learn what makes Steve tick. After that, ask yourself if he's worth fighting for. I had to do the same thing with your father, and when I asked myself that, the answer was no. Your father wasn't worth fighting for, Ethan. Is Steve?"*

Recognizing that what makes Steve tick and what makes him who he is as two different things is a crucial step I've missed in this relationship. Until this conversation, I hadn't separated the two or thought much about Steve's past. I was too busy wrapped up in this crazy honeymoon phase of us being together. Which meant I fell into the trap that launched a million movies, television shows, plays, and books. Believing that I could fix someone, change who they are in their soul.

You can't change him. Her voice echoes in my head. She's right. She's right on so many levels.

"I didn't change for him. I still don't want to go public with this or admit any of this to regular people. Why should I make him change for me if I won't change for him?"

"Well, that's one way of looking at it, sweetheart. Although, you're going to have to tackle that dilemma in the very near future. You can't change him, but Lala, you can't hide him forever, either. Well, you can, but that's called wrongful imprisonment and kidnapping."

"You gotta lay off the legal shows, Mom."

"I will do no such thing!" She laughs into the receiver and it's contagious. *"Alright, Lala, I gotta go. Charlie is tapping his toes at me because he made dinner reservations for date night."*

"Okay, mom. Oh, Mom?"

"Yeah, baby?"

"Thank you. I think I needed that talk more than I realized."

"I knew you did, Ethan. I'm always a phone call or a flight away. I can't wait to see you in a few weeks! I Love you, sweet boy."

"Love you and can't wait to see you either, Mom."

I've got three days left on this away stint, and now I've got something to keep me from getting much sleep for those three days. I guess it's good I'm not playing yet.

I'm on my last set of pushups, feeling better than I have since the injury and moving so much easier. I drop, come up, drop, and there's a bag of something tossed on the floor under me. My stomach growls at the familiar sound, knowing exactly what it is before I've even had a chance to look down.

"How many more do you have left?"

"Five."

"Okay, finish up those and we'll talk after," Steve says, sending my mind racing. What does he have to talk about? Is it the same thing I want to talk about?

On the last rep, I drop, grab the bag, and roll to my back. I rip the bag open and dump a mouthful in, savoring the sweet candy shell and that smooth peanut butter taste. "Fuck, I love these things," I moan as I close my eyes.

"Congratulations."

"Fo wha?" I ask, not giving a shit about talking with my mouth full. He tossed the bag at me, knowing full well what would happen.

"Well, for being the only man I've ever met who has that level of obsession with peanut butter candy, for one." He sits down on my stomach and I immediately guard the bag like it's made of gold. He laughs and reaches over to me, knocking the hat off my head before he cages me in and kisses me. "Oh, don't worry. I'm not getting my hands anywhere near that bag. I like my fingers attached. Thank you very much."

"So, what else?" I finally ask without candy in the way, raising an eyebrow in curiosity.

"Merry early Christmas, handsome. You're cleared for duty." He smiles down at me, kissing me again. "Which means when I'm done with you, we need to pack your bag. The team heads out tomorrow for an eight-day road trip, and you're going with them."

"Seriously?"

"About the clearance or about me wanting to fuck your brains out before the boys come back from running?" He stands up and offers me a hand, but I jump up, surprised that I'm even able to do that. It's part of why I'm cleared, though. The improved range of motion and the decrease in daily pain have been amazing. Nothing short of a miracle, and it was all Steve.

"You're serious right now? You're not fucking with me?"

"Not fucking with you, Sweets, I'm serious. You'll still train with me twice a week for now, but you've worked your ass off the last few months and I talked with Cole about a new schedule. I've also given him your workout plans so as a reference to build your recovery, strength, and conditioning plan."

"So…I can play?"

"Yes, Lala. You can play. They've even sent Lewis back down to the minors as of this morning." There's sadness in his eyes, but he's trying to hide it from me. Things will be weird while I adjust to life on the road again. We'll need to be even more careful when we go out, since I'll be more in the public eye, too. I can't begin to run down what else will change because my mind finds and focuses on one thing. Us. We're going to change.

"Steve, we're okay. Right?"

"Huh? Oh, yeah. Yeah, we're fine," he says the words flippantly, like I'm not the guy whose bed he's been sharing for the last few months. He gets up and crosses the room, pulling out the clipboard he uses for Devin's workouts, and starts jotting down notes like nothing just happened.

Part of me is overjoyed. I get to play again. I can finally get out on the ice and prove what I can do for the team and, hopefully, shut Girard the hell up for a while. But the rest of me is scared as fuck. Scared I'm risking more than my career and my health, but my relationship, too. I should have already thought about what this would look like with me out all the time and him going back to life as usual. What will this do to him?

I come up behind him, wrapping my arm around his waist and holding out the bag of candy with the other. I kiss his shoulders and across his back, wanting him to react to my touch, but he's still just writing. Pretending that everything between us is fine.

"Talk to me, Stevie." He tries to shrug me away, but I persist. "Please?"

"It's nothing, Ethan."

"Bullshit. You're upset about something that's bigger than not having me to yourself for two hours, three days a week. I want you to tell me what it is. Is it me, the medical clearance, your dad?"

He turns, still holding the clipboard like it will shield him from my advances. "It's not you, or the game. It's not my dad either. It's me, okay?"

"Alright, that's a start. What about you?"

"How can you keep doing this?"

"I'm not sure what I'm doing, so can you clue me in?" I nudge his shoulder with my nose. It's moments like these that making being short annoying as hell.

"How can you date a guy like me?"

"A guy like you? What's that mean? Smart, funny, incredibly hot, and willing to put up with all the rules I make?"

"You forgot that I'm a fuck up. You can't possibly trust me, and if you do, you shouldn't." I start to respond, but he stops me. "Lala, we—no, I—I can't make this work. I can't be trusted. Hell, I don't trust myself right now."

"I trust you. "

"Why? Because I didn't out you? You really think I'll make it the whole eight days without messing this up? You don't know me, Eth, not as well as you think you do. Right now, you're here, and if I get that urge, I come here and we fuck like rabbits. When you're gone, though, there's no one here to keep me in line but myself. How well do you really think that's going to work?"

"We don't—"

"It's not going to work, Ethan, because I'm not a guy you can trust. I'll get bored, I'll hookup like I used to, and I'll be the one who sabotages our entire relationship because that's the kind of guy I am. I can't commit, no matter how much I want to."

I don't have an immediate answer to that. I don't know what I'm supposed to say to make him feel better about our situation. "Okay, I won't trust you. I'll call you every night, twice a night. I'll put a tracker on your phone. I'll make you send me videos during the game. I'll do whatever you want, whatever will help you learn to trust yourself."

"What?"

"I trust you, Steve, but that isn't the real problem here. You don't trust yourself. You're the one worried you're going to cheat on me or fuck up, but if you think about it, you're scared—like me. I knew who you were when we got together, and you knew who I was. I didn't say no before, and I'm not going to say no now."

"Right, and when I do cheat on you? Because it's a when, not an if. When I torpedo the fuck out of the best thing that's ever happened to me?"

"Steve, all we can do is try, and if you feel like it's coming, tell me. You need a support system as much as Chase and Jamie, as much as me. We have to teach you that you're not alone in any of this." I don't feel like anything I'm saying is helping him.

I shove the bag of candy in my pocket to free up my hands, and reach up and cup his face. His jaw ticks against my palms and he tries to keep a stern face as I stare at him, but I see the glisten in his eyes. He's not scared, he's full on terrified.

"Steven Jensen, I want you to listen to me, and you hold me to this if you ever need to. You're mine. You've never hidden any part of what makes you, *you*. I'm with you, and that means all of you. The only thing I need from you is for you to be honest with me."

"I…I am honest with you, Sweets."

"And that's all you need to be. If you fall, I'm gonna be by your side, not kicking you in the side."

"You can't know that. You can't know how you're going to react when you walk in and I've got the next Kennedy on my dick." He slams the clipboard down so hard, a piece flies off the corner and hits me in the shoulder.

"You're right! You're absolutely right and I might freak out. Chances are really fucking good that I will. You have to give me a chance, like I am giving you one. Give me a chance to forgive you, because I will. I'll want to, even if I'm mad as hell about it for a few days. Don't give up on us, Steve. We're a mess, but we're one hell of a hot mess together."

"So while you're gone, I'm gonna get one of those stripper party bus things and go to town. When I'm done, I'll call and tell you about it, and, like the Catholic church, you'll forgive me for my indiscretions?" He scoffs, and he's right—it's a ridiculous idea even for the church, so why should it work for us? Relationships are based on trust, but maybe trust needs to have levels.

"No, I'll kick your ass for that. But Steve, you're trying to hold yourself to a standard some old guy made up and forced onto society. I'm not saying we need an open relationship. If I wanted that, I'd probably have chased Xander, but I wanted you. We need to keep our minds and communication open about everything. Okay?"

"You're serious right now?"

I pull the candy out of my pocket and hold it out for him again. "Stevie, I promise you on this bag of delicious goodness that I will not give up on you, and that I will be there to help you. Just don't go back to Kennedy, okay? She was..."

"A mess, yeah. She's actually in rehab right now. My treat."

"Wait, when did you send her to rehab?"

"I called Sam, her boss, when she put her car through the gym windows. At first I wanted him to fire her, but when I actually got him on the phone, I changed my mind. He called yesterday and told me she's been sober for three weeks so far, and she's trying to stay single for a while since that's part of her problem." He runs a hand through his short hair and shrugs. "I'm helping him pay for her rehab, since I'm kind of getting mine for free with a guy like you."

"A guy *like* me? I hope he's not a guy like me. I hope you really mean *me*," I tease, like the asshole I am. "How about we go make out in the hot tub When we're done, I'll take you back to my room and give you something to remember for the next eight days, huh?"

"Can I ask you something? Why are you so willing to forgive me?"

I chuckle, remembering the conversation I had with my mother. "A few days ago, a wise woman—who may or may not have run a very detailed background check on your internet history—told me that if I'm in this, I need to make sure I'm really in this. Otherwise I'm wasting your time, not mine, and it would make me no better than you, just more self righteous."

"Eth," he says with a laugh. "I think I really like your mom."

"Yeah?" I smirk, stepping over to him and lacing my fingers behind his head. He dips his head down, letting our lips tease each other. "That's good, because I really like you."

HOLLYWOOD
Steve

CHAPTER 16
FADE TO BLACK
METALLICA

I RUN the numbers for what has to be the tenth time in the last five minutes—they can't be right. The number I keep getting tells me the gym is hemorrhaging money, but it's not. We're in the middle of the highest rate of new client sign ups we've ever had and we're growing almost daily. There's no rental on the equipment, since I purchased it outright, and I can't think of a single reason we could be losing money. I grab my phone and call my lifeline—Laurie.

"What's up?"

"Laur, are you busy or do you have time to come to the gym? I really need your help here on the accounting issue. Could you bring that accountant friend of yours?"

"Yeah, sure. What's wrong, forget to pay the electric again?"

I think back and jot a note down to make sure I did, in fact, pay the electric bill. I'm pretty sure I did, but right now I'm paranoid about everything. "Yeah, yeah, I paid that. Can you hurry?"

I run the numbers again and again until Laurie is standing in front of me and setting a giant cup of coffee on the desk. "So, what's wrong? I half expected to see another car sticking out the front window. Maria will be here in a bit. She's the accountant."

"How is this right?" I direct her to the computer screen and the number in red boxes. "He said he was cutting us off, but can he take back money that's fucking ours, can he? Even my personal account looks like shit right now."

I move over and let her take over at the computer to try her luck, but she comes up with the same final amounts and they're not good. We went from half a million in the bank to I can't pay my employees in less than two days. I take a long drink of coffee and scrunch my nose. It's taking me a while to remember nowhere has pumpkin spice anymore, which is a crime against my tastebuds.

"And you think Dad is the one tanking our accounts? Who would be capable of accessing those? I mean, even if it was his money, he—"

"It's not his money, Laur. It's ours!"

"No shit, Steve. I'm only asking *how*. Wait, there's no way it's Jamie's sister again, is there?"

"No, they sent her to prison. At least, I think she's still in prison. Maybe I should call him to make sure." I pull my phone out, stare at it, and put it back. I don't believe for a minute this was Elle. "It's not her style, Laurie. She would clear every dime or do it in a way that fucks me six ways to Sunday."

"Losing this place would fuck you six ways to Sunday, Steve."

It wouldn't surprise me to learn that Jamie's sister, Elle, was behind a bank hack since she's done it—and worse—to us before. That was the first time I nearly lost the business. What I ended up losing was a part of my soul and all of my heart. I've been on something of a spiral since. I saw it happening. I couldn't stop it, though. I'm not blind to how much what Elle did to me changed me, but when you're on one knee and hearing yes one minute, and praying they survive the next? Watching them walk out the door is more than gut wrenching. Much worse.

Something about what Laurie is saying has lodged in the back of my brain, but I can't figure out what it is or why.

"What about one of your exes? Did you pay taxes? Do you have outstanding debts to a bookie?"

"What the fuck are you talking about? You're the only one who has access besides me, and no, I don't owe money to anyone."

"Are you implying that I—"

"Don't be a fucking idiot, Laur. If you wanted to take my money, you would walk in and let me hand it to you."

"Fair, I was just giving you shit anyhow."

"How are you joking around at a time like this?"

"Because plenty stressed out for both of us, Steve. Breathe. It's like a week and a half before Christmas. Everyone is stressed about money, and this likely won't get fixed until after the new year with the way the banks are. Everything in our private accounts seems to be fine, so we have a little wiggle room."

"Fuck. I had plans for that wiggle room."

"It better not be a ring, and if it's not a ring, it can wait, Steve."

There's a soft tap on the door and I glance up to see a cute woman in a tight dress and a low cut top. She's what I'd imagine the love child of Zazie Beetz and Tessa Thompson would come out like. I stand and put on the biggest, fakest smile in my arsenal. With a little luck, this will keep Laurie off the questions about Ethan and me for a few more days. Although, I really hate not telling her about how it's going with him, but I don't want to get her hopes up about it going well.

"Hi, something I can do for you? How about some private lessons?"

"Gonna guess that's why your gym is losing money."

"Steve, Maria. Maria, this is my idiot brother." Laurie looks over at me as I shrug. "He's got jokes."

"What? I didn't know the accountant was going to be cute!"

"You're twelve." Laurie replies before turning her attention back to Maria. "It's not why the gym is crashing, though. We were making huge profits a month ago, but back in October, our father said he was cutting us off. Neither of us understood what that meant, since he didn't support us. He hasn't since we were around sixteen. We can't think of anything else, though."

"It was initially a trust setup by our grandfather. We were assured that beyond us, only our grandfather's lawyer and banker had any kind of access to it. It was our paternal grandfather, but even he didn't trust dad."

"Okay, well, let me take a crack at it. Where did the money for the gym come from? Loans that might have upped their interest or?"

"The trust," I answer, leaning against the windowsill. "We invested, made some money, paid off a few things, and used the rest to open the gym."

"Okay, and you're equal partners? No one else is involved?"

"Yeah, only Laurie and I. Everything in the gym is paid off, too. Including the building. We own the land, equipment, the name, all of it. I made sure we were covered."

"Clients?"

I pull out the backup logs and set them on the desk next to her. "Highest active membership we've ever had, and growing. Plus, I'm on retainer for three studios and two pro sports teams."

I get restless watching her work, so I step out and look around the gym at my employees. I'm not sure how to tell them.

Craig nods at me and I head up toward the front, putting on my flashiest work smile until I see who's standing there waiting for me.

"Mom?"

"Oh, Steven, I'm so glad I caught you. Do you have somewhere we could talk? Somewhere with less, you know, help?" She glances at Craig and Kylie when she says it, and I roll my eyes. New England is a great place if you're looking for beautiful scenery when the leaves change color, and an unhealthy dose of racism in the elites. It's why I'm glad we moved, but it didn't change my parents.

"Yeah, Mom, come back here into the spare room so you stop disturbing my clients and co-workers."

"Oh, dear, they're not co-workers when you own the business. Have you forgotten?"

"Mom, we talked about this and the shit that comes out of your mouth."

"What, Steven? I just mean to say that they are employees and that referring to them as co-worker implies they're equals to you and Laurie. That's no way to run a business, and I'm sure your father would have taught you that."

"They are our equals, mom. Fuck, Craig has been dating Laurie for months now and you even met him at the art show for Jamie a few months ago."

"Oh," she seems stunned by the revelation. "I assumed he worked for her and was helping her take the paintings to her car."

"Jesus Christ, mom!"

"Would you stop using such awful language?"

"Okay, so you can be racists and classist and I can't say fuck or Jesus Christ?"

"Don't be like that, Steven. You're well aware that isn't

entirely what I meant. You can't expect me to keep up with every boy or girl you and your bro—sister come home with. I'm not your social events coordinator." She straightens her dress and folds her hands while she searches her purse for something and continues to ignore half of what I say.

My mom has one of those permanent far away looks in her eyes that's been there most of her life from what I can tell. She came from money, married into more money. If I asked her to make a change for a ten, she'd probably say she didn't know money went to that small a number in the first place. That's our mom. The only flaw in her facade is when I push her too far, like now. That's when she shows that she's not as clueless about us and the world as she pretends to be.

"Why are you here? You never come here. You guys didn't even show up for the grand opening, then turned around and gave a bullshit speech on television about how proud you are of what we've accomplished. You're not proud of either of us and you never have been."

"Steven, we were in Rome at the time." She pats my arm like I'm a child. "Now, Michael, your father, asked me to come see you and give you this. When I asked him why he couldn't send someone else, he said I would need to be here to sign this before I could give it to the lawyers. I don't care what it is, but he insisted, so here I am."

I open the envelope and it's a bunch of legal jargon, most of which I understand. Years of law school didn't totally go to waste. I shake my head, knowing exactly what this is. "He didn't tell you what you're signing?"

"No, he said I needed you and your sister to sign this and I'll sign it after. Once it's signed, I'm going to take it back to our lawyer after my hair is done. It's ridiculous and a waste of my time, I'm sure."

"Son of a bitch."

"Watch your mouth, Steven. You'll never find a good wife with language like that."

"Ma, this is saying he's cutting us out of the will. He's saying we owe him over five million dollars and accusing us of fraud!"

"I don't know what any of that means, dear? Can you stop complaining and sign it please? I'm going to be late for my hair appointment."

"Mom, if we sign this, he's going to take everything from us." I check it over again. I should call Laurie in here, but she's busy and I don't want to upset her. She'll blame herself for this.

I've heard of cases like this: parents suing their children for the money it took to raise them when they don't turn out the way they expected them to. Parents taking their adult children to court because they felt entitled to grandchildren they weren't getting. Most of the cases get thrown out, I'm sure, but they're sensationalized. Fighting this would mean outing Laurie. I don't care about me, everyone knows I'm out and Dad never seemed to mind since I'll stick my dick in a woman once in a while. He called my sexuality a phase.

Then I remember that Dad came to the gym not long ago, and I realize he'll out Ethan right along with Laurie because that's how he'll hurt me. That's what's been tickling my brain. Losing this place would devastate me, and that's exactly what Dad is planning to do.

"He's going to ruin us."

"Oh, I'm sure it's not that bad, dear."

"Did you talk to Uncle Bob about this?"

"No. Michael and Robert aren't speaking after the incident with Spence—uhm—Laurie. Dear, can you please just sign this for your father? Company is coming over later and I need to get my hair done before they arrive."

"I need to keep this. I need you to talk to Uncle Bob while I get a lawyer."

"Dear, your father and Bobby are lawyers. Now, your father told me to bring it back. Signed." She digs into her designer purse. "Oh, look! Here's a pen. Oh, I got this pen from Nancy Reagan weeks before you two were born. We were at her house for a—"

"Mom, focus for me, okay? Tell Dad I'm going to find Laurie and get her to sign it. Okay?"

"Oh, you will? That's so nice of you. Should I sign it?"

"No. No, not yet." I know my mother is a fucking mess, but she doesn't need to be dragged into this. She can tell you about every event she's attended and each celebrity she's met. Outside of that and picking out gaudy colored couches and expensive purses, she doesn't want to know a damn thing about life or how it works.

I walk her out to the car that's waiting for her and remind her to call her brother. He won't be able to fix this, but he's a partner at Dad's firm with enough pull that he could make this go away. Some of those partners won't want this kind of publicity, and won't jump through these hoops because my father is retiring in a few years.

I run back to the office and hand the letter to Laurie, watching her fall back into my office chair as she covers her mouth.

"I didn't want to show you, but you shouldn't be in the dark about what dear old Dad sent over. I think he's found a way to freeze everything and start locking us out as if that has already been signed, sealed, and finalized."

"He...he can't." She's ready to blame herself.

"This is my fault for dropping out of law school. It's not your fault for being who you are, Laurie. You're a beautiful, talented, funny, smart as hell woman and that's who you've always been. I won't let him take any of that away from you. Ever."

"Bingo!" Maria shouts, even with her sitting right there beside Laurie. I had forgotten she was there. "Okay, partially correct on your dad, and what he's doing isn't legal. I'm going to talk to my boss and get you two the paperwork you need. I'll represent you and the gym, obviously, but I will take a membership. No private classes."

"Yes! Absolutely. Wait, I thought you were an accountant?"

"I am, but I also graduated with a degree in financial law."

"I love you."

"I'm still not going to sleep with you, Steve."

I don't tell her, or Laurie, but I don't *want* to sleep with her. I've got someone else. Someone I care about, and I don't want to fuck that up. I chuckle at the possibility that Ethan was right about me learning to trust myself.

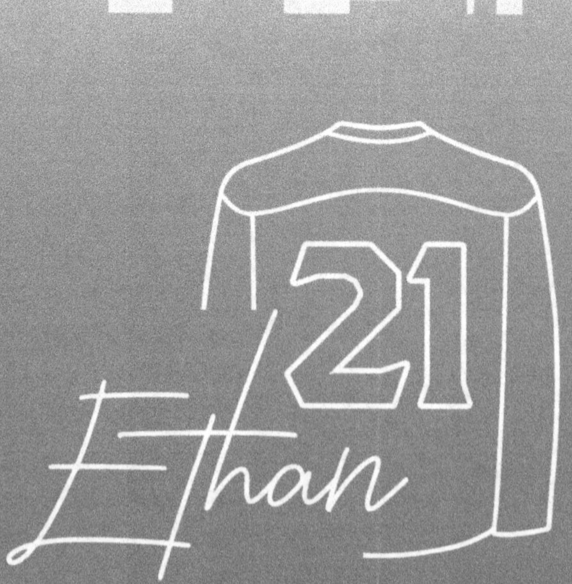
HOLLYWOOD
21
Ethan

CHAPTER 17
BAD GUY

BILLIE EILISH

"STEVE?" I yell out down the hall, but he doesn't reply. Kylie, the receptionist, said he was back here, but didn't get any more specific than that. When I don't find him in the locker room, I check his office and find him on the phone. He glances over and waves me in, so I shut the door quietly behind me. I notice when I turn back around to look at him, he's sizing me up like a piece of meat.

When he stares at me like that, I hear my father condemning me for what I am. Like he's standing right here, yelling about how I should punch Steve for looking at me that way. It should offend me and make me want to kick his ass. I do like it, though. Not sorry about that, pops. I like that being gone for an eight-day stretch means coming home to someone who wants me.

The room feels ten degrees warmer than when I first walked in as I watch him sit back and stare at me with hungry eyes. It gets even hotter when he motions me over to the other side of the desk. He pats his leg, and I can already see the outline of his dick in his workout pants. I try to look away, but I get distracted again and subconsciously lick my damn lips at the sight of his large, strong thighs. What the hell is wrong with me?

He snaps his fingers and my eyes lock on his. He can't be serious about asking me to do this right now. I glance back at the door, making sure I shut it. He leans forward and hits the mute button, then looks at me again. His eyes stop and linger on my lips, my neck, and my cock—he knows exactly what he's doing to me right now.

"Make your choice, Sweets. On your knees or on my lap, which is it gonna be?"

"I, uhm, I don't know what you mean. I was only here to ask if you wanted to go—"

"Sit down, Lala. Trust me." His cocky grin isn't helping me walk away from this. Instead, it's pulling me closer. My mouth is dry as I run my hand through my hair nervously. He takes my other hand and pulls me to him, guiding me onto his lap so my back presses against his strong chest. He's nipping at my neck as his hard cock strains against his pants and my ass. My entire body is begging for him. Fuck. This is not what I planned on doing when I came in here, yet here I am, rubbing against his cock like a needy slut.

"Just remember to stay quiet, Sweets." His arm wraps around me, slipping into my sweatpants. "The investor doesn't need to hear how much of a whore you are while we're talking."

"I—I promise!"

"Relax and lean back. I'm going to unmute the call." He hits the button with his free hand while simultaneously brushing his thumb over the tip of my cock. My hips jerk and I struggle to bite back the moan, but I manage it. His hand wraps around my throat, squeezing hard as his hand pumps. I'm so blissed out I can't concentrate. He's squeezing and stroking, and I can't hold on much longer. His big hand wraps around me and he's jerking me off slowly while he dry humps me. I can't tell him what I want or I'll get us caught. I can't tell him I want him to move faster, to fuck me right here in his office.

"No, I'm still concerned about the location." He says, and I don't think he's even out of breath. "Do you think the space is big enough for a franchise, assuming we end up going that route? I don't want to downsize."

He keeps talking, but I don't hear a word he's saying. Fuck, there's a wave of euphoria crashing against me, even though I know we shouldn't be doing this. I don't have a lick of willpower when it comes to Stevie. My feet come off the floor and onto his knees as I lean back against him, my fingers digging into his legs. He's teasing me, dancing his fingers over my shaft before he cups my balls.

"Don't you dare come, Ethan. Not until I tell you to." His breath against my ear turns to static, and when he bites down, I wonder if I'll be able to do what he's asking. I'm way too close to wait.

My back arches and I try to think of anything other than what we're doing right now. Steve's like an addiction and I'm a junkie for his touch, his voice, his cock, all of him. Especially after eight days of not even being able to have phone sex.

"Okay, but the merger? Explain that to me again like I'm five, because I think I'm missing something."

He's not missing a damn thing. Without warning, he pushes my feet off his knees and stands, taking me with him. Shoving my chest down on the desk, he whispers for me to grab the other side and hold on. He hits mute again, and then puts the call on speakerphone while he rifles through a drawer, grinding against me. My head is swimming and the guy on the phone is droning on in his underwater voice when Steve yanks my pants down and something cold drips onto my ass.

"I'll tell you when I unmute, you better stay quiet, baby. Got it."

"Steve, you can't—You shouldn't do—" I stutter as he drops his pants.

"Are you saying you don't *want* it? You don't want me to fuck your needy little ass on my desk?"

"No! No I... I do."

"Say it. Say what you want."

"Your cock, I need your cock, Stevie. Please! Please fuck me!"

"Then shut the fuck up and stick that ass in the air like a pretty whore for me."

My eyes roll back when he pushes the tip in because Steve is big. Not porn star level or anything terrifying, but thick, which means it hurts like hell going in for a few seconds. I grip the damn desk so tight it's about to break, biting down on my hoodie until he pushes far enough that the pain turns into something else. Something that sets every inch of me on fire. A shiver runs up my spine as he leans over me, filling me up until I'm not sure I can take any more of him. Thankfully, he bottoms out with a deep groan in my ear.

"You feel so fucking good, Lala. Someday, I'm gonna record this so you can see how well your hungry little ass takes my cock." A moan I can't hold back escapes me and he pulls one of my legs up onto the desk, somehow going even deeper. "I'm taking it off mute now, and I'm gonna fuck you real good while I listen to this prick try to undersell me and my brand. The more annoyed I get with him, the harder you're going to get it. Understand?"

Shit. If I'd known he was pissed off, I probably wouldn't have come in here. Who am I kidding? I want him pissed off today. I want him to fuck me so I can still feel him three days from now while I've got one of the top centers in the league facing me down. I need to learn to use this lust fueled drive during the game, and this is a hell of a way to practice. I bite down even harder, leaving bruises on my own arm as his thrusts start, slow and steady at first, like ocean waves on a perfect beach day. His hips rock gently against me and I'm struggling to stay quiet, and I think he knows it.

I'm not expecting it when he pulls almost all the way out and slams hard into me. He's testing me and I am completely failing, trying to muffle the deep moans in my sweatshirt. He does it again and again, pushing fire through my body with every thrust. True to his word, every time the guy on the phone speaks, Steve's thrusts get harder and his grip on my hair tightens. This is pure bliss.

"Must be CrossFit day. Those guys are always so fucking loud with the grunts," the voice on the phone says. Steve laughs before he slams into me again and then stops, buried to the hilt inside me. His fingers slip around my throat again. I'm so fucking full and he just stands there, his hand sliding over my skin and setting off sparks between us before he squeezes so hard I almost pass out.

"Yeah, they can get pretty into it. Always sounds like they're getting fucked in the ass to me," Steve chuckles in a low, dark tone. I'd laugh too if I wasn't trying to keep from keening and wailing Steve's name as he carries me to the edge. It's all too much, and I'm losing what little hold I have left on control.

I don't know what the guy says next, but whatever it is, Steve's not happy about it. He covers my mouth with his hand and slams so hard into me the desk moves. I need to scream. To yell. Something.

"So what do you say, Stevie?"

"Let me think about it, yeah? How about we do this again next week? I'm balls deep into something I really need to go hard on."

"You need a vacation, Jensen," the voice chuckles. *"Have a good holiday, man."*

The phone slams down and Steve grabs a handful of my hair, yanking my head back as his hips crash against me. I can't hold it in anymore, and there's no way I can scream into the hoodie now.

"Atta boy, tell me how good I feel inside that pretty, tight ass of yours. Almost got us caught there, Sweets." Cool air hits my back as he pushes the hoodie up and slides his hand up my spine, tracing the muscles as I move under him. "Someday, I'm gonna fuck you so hard, you won't walk for a goddamn week."

"Oh fuck! Oh god! Steve! Stevie—I—" I reach around, grabbing his thick thighs and trying to hold him inside me. "Please! Oh god, please!"

My head yanks back more and he's against my ear again. "Don't come yet, pretty boy. I want you to come in my mouth. You think you can hang on long enough for that, baby? Long enough for me to suck the come out of you?"

"Not if you keep fucking talking like that, you prick!"

He lets go of my hair and grabs my hips, fucking harder and harder until I hear the telltale grunt he makes just before he comes. I'm not sure how much longer I can hold on, especially after he finishes inside me. I call out his name and he flips me over like I'm a rag doll, swallowing me down. I can't stop myself from grabbing his head, holding him down when his nose hits me until he starts to choke. I let him loose, then do it again, just like he does to me. My eyes roll back again and my hips pump forward. I'm in a blizzard, unable to see a damn thing. All I hear is the howl of the blood slamming through my body and the crackle of electricity at the tip of every nerve ending.

I fall backward on top of the desk as a string of swears slides out of my mouth. My whole body feels like jelly, and he's lapping me up. His tongue sliding over my scars and muscles as he whispers about how perfect I am. He thinks I'm perfect. I'm anything but. My eyes are still closed and I'm breathing like I just did a double line shift, so the softness of his lips on mine is unexpected. Slow and lazy and somehow still full of lust. He loves kissing after oral, and I'm starting to become a fan myself.

Shit.

I'm falling too hard for this guy. This isn't right and we're going to get caught. My team will find out, my fans, my father. I'll be laughed out of the league, and he'll leave me for being a loser. I can't do this. I can't do this. What if my mom was right? What if I can't keep doing this? What if—

"I've been thinking about bending you over this fucking desk every single day since you left, baby," he coos as he licks at my neck. "I was good. I didn't—"

"I can't...I can't breathe!" I don't know what's wrong with me. The world is spinning and getting smaller by the second. All I want to do is breathe, but my air supply has been cut off. My stomach does a somersault and I need out of here, now! "Get the fuck off me! I can't do this!"

I regret the words the second they come out. He lifts his head from my neck and stares down at me like I punched him in the gut. He's trying to hide the hurt, but I can still see it clear as day. I'm panting, trying to understand what's happening and worried I'm having a heart attack. Can you have a heart attack at twenty fucking five? "Steve, I didn't mean—"

"No. Yeah, okay. I uhm. I understand." He shuffles around, pulling up his pants and avoiding eye contact. I reach out for him, but he pulls his arm away. "Uh, I got a client in a few. I'll see you tomorrow for your session."

"Steve, come on, man."

"No, it's fine. It's cool. I get it, and I'm sorry. I shouldn't have done that."

"Stevie, look at me. Please?" He does, and it's like a stab in the heart because I can't tell him what I meant. I can't tell him what's wrong with me. "I didn't mean that. I can't… I'm trying, but I can't—"

"Whatever. I'll see you tomorrow, LaVoie."

He pushes past me and out the office door while I stand there watching, unable to get the right words to come out of my stupid mouth. I wait a few minutes so hopefully no one can piece together what we've been doing back here. I take deep breaths and force myself to relax enough to try to go after him.

When I finally get out to the reception desk, I see him cozying up to a bottle blonde with big boobs. He's got his hand on her ass and she's giggling at whatever he's saying. I have this urge deep in my gut to walk over there, push him against the wall, and show this whole fucking gym he's mine.

But he's not. Not in public. He might not even be mine in private anymore, and that's my own damn fault.

I shove the door open and walk out of the gym, bottling up a little more self-hatred as I remind myself I'm nothing more than a fuck up. Now, I might have fucked everything up.

It's been four days and I'm still pissed off enough to have a shitty skate. I take a shower and I'm ready to head home, eat an entire box of donuts, and cry during a few more depressing movies. It's how every day has been since the gym. We haven't started the new workout schedule yet between games because we're not talking to each other.

I'm hollow and broken, barely going through the motions. I've called my mom and my sister more times in the last four days than I have in five years. Mom said what happened was a panic attack and that if it happens again, I need to talk to someone. I told Devin about it because he's a nosey fucker and he had Chase give me the number of a couple of good shrinks, including the one he sees.

I'm toweling off my hair when I see Devin standing by our lockers, waiting for me. I tried avoiding him, too, but his locker is right next to mine. He's happy, like he always is, and I wish some of that would rub off on me, but that's not likely anytime soon. He throws an arm over my shoulder and slaps an envelope in front of me. It's got my name on it.

"Attendance is mandatory for all players who don't have a local family, or a better offer. I get that you're planning to head home for a day or two, but with your mom being sick, I figured I'd extend a just in case offer."

"What is it?"

"Christmas dinner, baby! My brother does a big ass spread for the team. It's a tradition!"

"How is it a tradition when you've only been on the team for two seasons?"

"Uh, because this is the second year we're doing it, so now it's a tradition! That's totally how it works, man." He slaps me on the back. "Dude, even Coach makes an appearance, and you kind of live in the house. If you don't head back to Boston, you can't exactly hide in the guest room the whole day. We'll drag you out."

"Yeah, well, like you said, hopefully I'll be in Boston." For the first time, I wish I could move out. I don't want to ask, but I know I have to. I look around the room to see who's here and make sure they're not in earshot, then I lean in. "Steve going?"

"If I say yes, are you more or less likely to make an appearance? Are you guys fighting?"

"I dunno. It doesn't matter."

"Well, the answer is probably no, if that helps. He should be off the grid in the mountains with Laurie. Don't worry, he's not gonna get on your ass for eating all the glorious food. I already plan on skipping the next day's workout, too. I puked last year. And how is he going to know when he's chilling in a fucking cabin?" He jokes.

"Yeah, okay. If Boston falls through, I'll be there. Not like I have anywhere else to go."

"Fuck yeah. Hey, when you come out tomorrow, will you do me a favor?" I stare at him, trying to figure out what the fuck he's talking about. Why would I be coming out and why tomorrow? Fuck, did I miss something? "Go out the left side door, not the right?"

"What?"

"Well, we lost the other night and I still think it's because the defense went out the right side of the locker room door. We normally go out on the left side. I think it jinxed us and we need to fix it before tomorrow night's game, man."

The laugh I let out makes him jump back a bit, so I slap him on the shoulder. It's almost a relief to laugh like that again. "Man, you goalies are so fucking weird. I'll go out whatever door you want me to, Hollywood. No problem."

HOLLYWOOD
Steve

CHAPTER 18
LOSE CONTROL

TEDDY SWIMS

SWEAT DRIPS down my forehead and my muscles feel like I've dipped them in lava as I run. I've got a podcast on, but I can't hear it over the sounds of my breathing and the screaming in my head. I'm not sure what I expected from Ethan, and I guess I pushed it too far. He was nervous about getting caught, sure, but I could have sworn we were good. Now, he isn't answering calls or texts and he's ghosting me for workouts. My watch alarm goes off, telling me I have an elevated heart rate. No shit. I've been running all out for nearly twenty minutes now, overthinking my entire life. It isn't a marathon. It's a fucking race against the demons in my head.

I finally jump off just before my knees give out. Since no one else is around, I let myself fall to the floor and enjoy the coolness against my back. I like running and it's something I'm good at. I even ran track and field when I was in high school, but running when pissed off is brutal. I'm not sure I've learned my lesson though, because I still want to call him again. If he doesn't answer, I'll call an ex and try to fuck Ethan out of my system when that's not what I even want.

I thought going cold turkey from the playboy lifestyle would kick my ass, but trying to quit Ethan is proving much harder. I should start a therapy group for single guys trying to claw their way out of being a dog. We can meet at the gym, I'll bring donuts. No, not donuts.

Hi, I'm Steve. I have a problem, and that's why there are no donuts.

Hi Steve.

So there's a guy I really like, a guy I want to try harder for, but he's pissing me off right now and being a fucking dick. I'm weak, and I'm worried I'm going to go back to what I do best. Fucking up. So if any of you wanna fuck in the shower till we both cry, meet me in five.

I wipe the sweat from my face onto my t-shirt, but it doesn't do much good since that's soaked in sweat, too. I get up and wipe down the mat and the machine before I head for the showers. I stop halfway there and walk back out to the front and lock up. The last thing I need right now is to be robbed after finally getting back into positive cash flow again. I flip the sign saying we're closed for the holiday and shut off the lights before I head back to the locker room. The hot water helps my muscles and I'm about to decide to head over to Chase's place for a dip in his hot tub. But I remember I can't do that.

As if she knows I'm on edge—maybe she feels my anger through the force like Luke and Leah—my phone vibrates on the shelf. I grope for it, trying to keep the soap out of my eyes and answer without looking at the caller I.D.

"Hello, brother dearest."

"Oh, fuck. What did I forget?"

"Nothing, I'm actually calling because tomorrow is national tree worship and gift giving day."

"Yeah?" I'm not sure why she thinks I need reminding of that. I mean, I forget important dates all the time, but not this one. We do the same thing every year. Go to Uncle Bob's cabin, cook the least Christmassy meal we can come up with, and play board games. We don't come back down the mountain until a week later, just in time for Chase to throw a New Year's party. It's relaxing and refreshing, but most importantly, it's just me and Laurie hanging out and decompressing like we used to. She has no idea how badly I need that this year.

"Don't be mad, but, uhm, can we kind of change it up this year?" I close my eyes and lean my head against the wall. So much for the twin force connection. *"I kind of agreed to go to Craig's house for dinner with his family. It's usually a you and me thing, but Steve, this is seriously a big step for Craig and me. Since you have Ethan, it could be good for all of us if we skip it this year to be with them."*

"Oh, yeah, cool." I try to play it like I don't care. I wonder if I should head back out and do another twenty minutes on the treadmill to get my mind off yet another thing going wrong in my life. "Uhm, I already had the service go open the cabin up and everything, so if you and Craig want to use it, that's cool."

"What are you not telling me?"

"Nothing. The cabin is a great idea, it will be…Craig will love it up there."

"Did you break up with Ethan?" I don't answer her. *"Steven!"*

"Fine!" I groan into the phone as I bang my head against the wall. "We got into a fight, and he hasn't talked to me in a week. Honestly, though, take the cabin. You can go up tomorrow night and have the place all to yourselves. It's stocked, it might as well be used. You'll have fun. Please? Please just go and have fun for me?"

I finally get her to agree, finish my shower, and get ready to go home. Home. Shit. I was supposed to be gone for a week, so I have no groceries and it's Christmas Eve. If there's a grocery store open, it's going to be a madhouse.

I pull my phone back out again.

Laurie just bailed on me, so no cabin this year.

COOP

Dude, that sucks. Get here at one tomorrow.
Earlier if you wanna help.

E's flight is at 6 am if you're still avoiding each
other.

I text Coop back and ask if there's anything I can do or bring, and he just says baggy pants.

The next morning, my stomach rumbles at me so loud it wakes me up. I grope around for my phone and head to the bathroom. As I take a leak, I flip through my phone looking for the flight number and see Ethan's flight is on time and he's probably already at the airport. I type out a message. Delete it. Type out a new message. Delete that one, too. It's probably for the best. It was fun while it lasted.

I shower and get dressed, and toss my phone into an overnight bag before heading out. I swing by a liquor store that's on the way and pick up a couple of the necessary staples— whiskey, tequila, and a few bottles of wine. I go to text Coop to ask if there's anything else I can grab, but my phone is still in the bag in the trunk of my car. I add a couple pints of ice cream into the mix because what breakup is complete without ice cream and wine?

When I get to the house, I see Jamie's jeep and, but also a ton of other cars. Before I can get to the door, Jamie comes running out. "Hey, Don't go in the front. Dev has a bunch of guys from the team over, so we've set up the game system in the garage instead and given them the full run of the house. Need a hand?"

"Nah."

"Uhm, Coop told me about you and Ethan—just don't give up. Okay?"

"What's that mean?"

"Don't give up on him. He's going through a lot, you've experienced that. We all have."

"No, it's better this way. I would have cheated on him and ruined his life, because that's what I do, Jaim."

"Don't do that. You're better than that, Steve. That's not who you are." Jamie is my cheerleader, he always has been. Which is hilarious since he's also a cranky dick most of the time. He reaches into the trunk and grabs the bottles and ice cream. "I get that it's how you cope, and we're just worried about you, man. All I'm saying is you should hold off on calling the exes over for a quick one-nighter. Give this time to breathe."

"What if it's too late for that?" I shrug as I close the trunk and we head around to the side door. Inside, I find Lexi and Coop playing a racing game and pushing each other around, and I instantly feel better. I'm here with my family. They're not my blood, but aside from Laurie, they're closer than anyone else I'm related to. I'm walking toward the door to take my stuff into the guest room, but before I get there, Coop jumps off the couch and runs over, cutting me off.

"Uhm, hey."

"What? Jamie and all the cars already told me the teams in there, I won't mess with them. I just wanna drop this stuff in the spare room so I can crash out later."

"You didn't get my texts, did you?" Coop stares at me and I'm getting the sneaking suspicion that he's hiding something from me. "I was in the dark, bro. His parents got the flu, so they canceled their plans. I didn't find out till this morning because Devin thought you'd be at the cabin."

I close my eyes. I can't get mad at Coop. I was the one who tossed the phone into the bag. It's a short drive and normally I wouldn't be getting calls today, anyhow. I nod, then shrug. "I'll put this stuff up in the loft then. Less of an issue if I crash up there. That okay?"

"I can bring it up."

"I'm good, Coop. Promise. Go back to your game."

I'm silent when I leave the garage, listening for the one voice I need to stay clear of. When I don't hear it, I hurry up the stairs, drop my bag on the couch, and take a peek out the window. I don't see him with the guys out there, so I'm in stealth mode again as I head back down the stairs. As I get to the hallway between the stairs and the garage, I hear something that makes me stop and clench my fists.

"Come on, Ethan, lighten up! I'm surprised your little boyfriend isn't here today."

"Shut the fuck up," Devin replies. They're around the corner in the kitchen so I can't tell who else is there, but I recognize the first voice as that prick Girard.

"No, no, Hollywood, I want Lala to know he can be straight with us. Oh wait, no, he can't."

"Dude, seriously? I will kick you the fuck out of my house."

"It's not even your house, douche, it's your brother's. Besides, everyone knows LaVoie is gay as fuck. I told you, I've got pictures!"

"Bullshit," Devin yells. "You probably photoshopped them to add to your private spank bank."

"Hey, Hollywood, while Ethan's getting pounded, do you fuck Steve's sister? I've always been curious if she still has her di—"

I come around the corner and have him pinned against the wall before he can finish that sentence. "Unless you were about to say something about my sister's dinosaur collection, disco ball, or dildo, I suggestion you shut the fuck up."

"Oh, so you are here," Girard quips, trying to look like the badass even though my hand is around his damn neck. "Nice of you to join us. So is this what LaVoie likes you to do? Choke him out while you come on his face?"

"You're a fucking idiot, Girard. Let him go, Steve." I nearly listen to Ethan, but then Girard opens his mouth again.

"So, Jensen, are you here to cruise for fresh meat, or pick up your sloppy leftovers?"

"Why, you looking for a date, Josh?" Devin hits back.

"Nah. Not looking to catch whatever these two fa—"

Before Girard can finish, I snarl in his face, "My life stays the fuck out of your mouth, you dickless little shit."

"Jensen, everything okay?" Coach asks as he walks in. I let go and step back.

"You should have let him sign with Vegas, Coach. He's an overrated windbag who can barely skate," I answer back, still staring at Girard, daring him to start anything so I can finish it.

"Yeah, I think about that every damn day, Jensen. Come on, Joshua. You and I need to have a talk about some things that HR has been on my ass about, anyhow. Let's go talk by the pool so I can throw you in when you get a hot head over it." Coach wraps an arm over Girard's shoulders and leads him out of the room.

I close my eyes to calm down and I'm about to leave when Devin cuts in front of me, pretending to reach for something. "Hey Steve, no cabin this year?" He smiles and then quickly switches to a frown. "Sorry about that asshat. Hey, why don't I go get you a beer to make up for it?" He leaves, snickering like it was a smooth ploy when a blind person could have seen through that bullshit. I glance around.

Sure enough, the room is empty except for Lala and I. I'll make Devin run extra laps for this shit. Ten miles should be a fair payback.

"Hey, uhm, Devin said you'd be out of town," Ethan says after a few moments. "Guess I was supposed to be, too."

"Laurie and Craig took the cabin, so it's better than eating take out alone at home." I shove my hands in my pockets and study the floor. It's easier than looking at him. "They said you'd be in Boston, Ethan, otherwise I would have just stayed home. I'll keep to the garage and stay out of your way."

"You know," he says as he takes a tentative step forward. "You only call me Ethan when you're annoyed or trying to act extra professional around someone else."

"Guess you should get used to it." He's left out the occasion that I call him that the most. I call him that in bed when he's got my face shoved into a pillow and giving me the best damn fuck of my life. "About the other day at the gym—"

"It was my fault. I came to your office, knowing what would happen. I said things I didn't mean, and I fucked up." There's a heavy sigh and, for whatever reason, it makes me feel worse. I'm pretty sure I can guess what's coming. "I thought maybe I just needed to take some time after that to get my shit together. Steve. I... I got scared, okay? That what you want to hear?"

"Sure, Ethan. Whatever." He reaches out, grabbing my arm, but I shake him loose.

"I'm sorry. I'm sorry, okay? I'm sorry about Girard being a complete asshole. I'm sorry I came to your damn office, and I'm sorry... I'm sorry we can't, we shouldn't—Fuck."

"Exactly. You're sorry, and we shouldn't." I push past him and into the garage, slamming the door behind me.

"Bro! What the fuck happened to lying low?" Coop yells, throwing his hands in the air. I keep walking past him, headed for the door outside. "Come on, man. You gotta help me out here! Where are you going?"

"Back home."

"No. Nope. Not today, you're not."

"Are you going to stop me, Coop?"

He steps between me and the door. "Are you gonna hit me, Jens?"

"I hate that fucking nickname."

"Yeah, but I love seeing you all pissed off about it. Sit your pretty little ass down, get fucking baked, let me beat you in a few games. We'll eat, we'll drink, you'll pass out."

"Don't you remember the last time I came over and got drunk at a party?"

He shakes his head and lowers his voice. "Don't *you* remember what it's like to be the weird kid out? How you tried like hell to blend in with the cool kids and act straight. Dude, all you wanted to do was yell from the roof of the building that you were madly in love with me." He smirks and I start to argue, but he gives me a look that shuts me up. "He's not out, Steve. He's in a career where being out can cost him everything and you very little. Cut him some slack, okay?"

"I get that!"

"Do you, buddy? Of all the people in this house, you should get this more than any of us. But it's taking you an awful long time to pick up the beat of his dance."

"What?"

"Shut up. That sounded so cool in my head."

Jamie joins us, which just pisses me off more. "What he's trying to say is, what if someone was trying to do this to Laurie? To guilt her into coming out, basically tell her that her feelings and her fears don't matter? The kid is doing the best he can, but those demons he's fighting are kicking his ass when you're not around."

Chase grabs the sides of my head and holds me, so I focus on him. "He's been a fucking miserable dick without you and, dude, he's having panic attacks. They're bad."

"Steve, he feels like shit and like this is all his fault. He has it in his head that he's unlovable and untouchable, and like he has no one to talk to about it."

"Sound familiar, numb nuts?"

"That's—no—that's different! That's not what—" I shout back, then cut myself off when the air get's suck out of the room and I feel dizzy. Fuck. Coop and Jamie just hit me where it counts, where they could guarantee I'd shut up and listen long enough to realize I'm a fucking idiot. "Shit. What the hell do I do?"

"Well, for starters? Flowers are always a good, safe bet."

Jaime shakes his head. "You could try saying those three words that he needs to hear right now."

"Jaim, I know you and Lex were saying it on like day one, but it's only been a month. It's a little early for I love—"

"I. Am. Sorry." Jamie smirks at me. "I guess I should have said a contraction and another word, but I didn't know you were that dense. *I'm sorry*, that's what you need to say."

"Also, he didn't say it to me until day five," Lexi clarifies. "When he ditched you losers to bring me pie and cheer me up."

"I didn't say it at the beach?" He shoots back at her.

"Nope. You started to, but you chickened out on me."

"Huh."

Jamie's one hundred percent right, and I just came up with either the perfect or the shittiest plan ever.

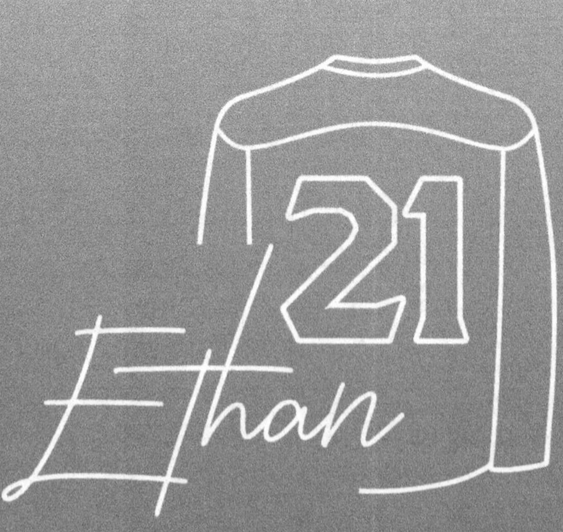

HOLLYWOOD
21
Ethan

CHAPTER 19
SOMEWHERE ONLY WE KNOW

LILY ALLEN

GOING through shit when you're playing a team sport is rough. It's not new to me. I played through deaths in the family, guys threatening to out me, and my father beating the shit out of me because I wasn't my older brother. I can—and have—played through things most pro athletes never have to play through. I don't wear it like a badge of honor or anything. I'm sure it's not exactly healthy, but learning to hide things, to bury them so deep that the people closest to me can't see them in my eyes—it's been a lifesaver. Just like burying the other me in the ice, I bury my problems.

But ice melts, and problems come to the surface. Right now, I don't have anywhere else to bury them but deeper inside myself. Chase and Devin are right; I need to see a therapist before I lose it on the ice.

Steve hasn't come out of the garage again, and after the team finishes dinner, I duck out to my room. I lock the door, put on some music, and crawl under my covers. I'm like an emotional twelve-year-old who found out the movie star she's in love with doesn't even realize she exists. Maybe now isn't the best time to have Taylor Swift on. I should have gone to Boston, or stayed in a hotel and caught up on some reading. Instead, I'm sulking in bed while the rest of the team continues their party like a team. I'm just not in the mood to deal with people, and my battery is dangerously low.

I'm not sure what I'm supposed to do, so I pick up the phone and do what I always do when I get this down.

"Hey! It's Dakota. If this is about the aliens again, I told you, I won't reveal my sources. Otherwise, leave me a message and I'll meet you at midnight at the docks. Trust no one!"

I smile right away, remembering the first time my dad heard that message. *What the hell are you talking about and who are you meeting at the docks? What docks?*

"Hey Kota, uhm, happy whatever pagan holiday this is for you. Sorry, I can't remember. I don't want to bother you, but I did want to hear your voice. I, uhm, still haven't made up with that guy yet, but he's here today. I tried to talk to him, but I locked up again and I don't understand why. I thought about going public, but I can't. Not while I'm in the middle of recovering my stats and respect as a player. You get that, right? I thought I could handle this relationship—the secrets and everything—but I can't. I want to hide him away so he's only mine; but I want to take him out on a real date, too. I dunno. It's all stupid and I'm just being dumb and rambling now. Fucking grown ass adult crying under the covers. Fuck. Anyway, there's a good chance I'll call you about this again later. I miss you. I miss you a fucking lot. Say hi to that prick brother of ours. I hope he's taking care of you. I love you, girlie."

I usually feel better after calling her and telling her about what's going on. Today, though, calling her might have made it all worse.

I think about calling mom, but I don't want to bother them if they're sick. I even think about calling my old man and telling him he was right all along. I'm a worthless piece of shit, ruining people's lives and getting in the way. Days like this, I find myself envying Aaron, my brother. He's the golden child. He fucked up his whole life, but Dad still thinks he's god's gift to hockey. Dad's still mad it's me here and not Aaron.

The day I called my father to tell him I made it to the pros was the last time I talked to him.

I didn't know they were taking sissy boys. Do they know? Maybe I should call 'em up. Tell them you're a queer. Maybe I'll save that for the sports broadcasts when they come to ask me how proud I am.

I close my eyes and try to meditate, blocking his voice out. Deep breath in. Hold it. Don't think about Steve. Exhale. Deep breath in. Hold it. Knock on the door. Of course.

"Unless you're Coach, fuck off." I wait for a snarky response from Devin or someone else, but there's silence, followed by a sound under the door. When I look, there's a piece of paper folded up with my name on it. I'm pretty sure only Steve is out of touch with reality enough to address a piece of paper before sliding it under a door. Like I wouldn't be able to tell it was for me or something. I stare at it for a while, not sure I want to get up for a letter I'm pretty sure I don't want to read.

"Fuck," I mumble to myself as I climb out of bed, tweaking my back a bit as I do. I hobble over to the letter like an eighty-year-old man, and it takes me three tries before I can bend over and get it. I really hope this is because I ate too much and not a flare up. When I open up the letter, there's just one word that I'm apparently supposed to understand. One word he thinks will get me back. I hate that he's right on both counts and with one word, the butterflies come to life.

Beach?

We've been talking about going for a while, and Steve knows a couple of beaches north of Los Angeles where we could avoid most of the crowds. I've said no every time because I can't get him to understand that two dudes don't go walking on an empty beach together when they're just friends. One person seeing us together could be one person too many. The longer I stare at the handwriting, the less I'm able to keep my emotions in check. I grab a baseball cap and put it on backwards before slipping my flip-flops on and heading to the front door. The cocky son of a bitch is leaning against the passenger door of his car like he's James fucking Dean while he looks at me over his sunglasses.

"You got my note?"

"Yeah, I had to wrestle it away from the three other guys in my room not named Ethan and show government issued proof of identification, but I got it."

He looks away, staring out over the lawn. "Wise ass."

"But you liked my ass." I should test the waters, take this slowly. But with the guys out back, I'm not sure we have long enough to stand out here for an emotional reconciliation like in the movies. "Didn't you?"

Without a word, he turns and opens the door. No gesture, no nod of the head, nothing but an open door. I bite my lip, shaking my head at how I'm making all of this easy for him. If Dakota taught me anything, it was never to let a guy off easy when he's the one who fucked up. She didn't tell me what to do if the guy is letting *me* off easy and it's *me* who's fucking up.

Before we were even out of the driveway, he took hold of my hand and hasn't let go since. We've been driving for an hour and neither of us has said a word, just holding on. He finally pulls off the freeway and takes us down this out of the way path that overlooks the ocean. The view is beautiful but also a little terrifying. He could kill me out here and no one would hear a thing over the waves crashing and the roar of the wind through the large rocks. He comes around the car and takes my hand again, leading me down a well-worn path to the water. We stand there for a long time, still not speaking, just holding hands and staring out over the ocean. I have a million things I want to say, but I'm letting the waves wash each of them out into the ocean. It leaves me with just one thing on my mind.

I want this.

"We were both wrong." He has to raise his voice so I can hear him, but it startles me after the extended silence. I nod slowly, but then I realize he's shaking his head like I'm not getting something. "I treated you unfairly. I did to you what people have tried to do to my sister her whole life. I fight those people any way I can, and then I fucking let myself become one. When I was younger, I fought with my fists. Now, it's my idiotic mouth. I tried to make you become something you're not. I don't want to out you, Lala. What I was asking for wasn't something I had any right to ask for."

I take my time to wrap my head around everything he's just said. "You're not the problem, Steve. You're out here trying so hard, while I'm the one finding every fucking excuse in the book. I'm the one trying to change you, trying to hide who and what you are. I was selfish."

"No, you weren't. I was. I'm so used to jumping around that I've forgotten how a relationship needs time apart as much as they take time together to work. I forgot how damn hard a relationship is. I don't have your experience. I didn't have to stay hidden in a closet or have that fear of someone coming for everything I love because of *who* I love. Not until now, anyhow. Thanks, Dad."

"I think I was more ready for you to cheat on me than for me to...to..."

"Be who you really are?" he cuts me off, saving me from

saying the words. I nod. "When I said you were wrong, I didn't mean about us, Sweets. You were wrong about the beach."

"I was wrong about…the beach?"

"You said two guys can't just hold hands on the beach or people will assume they're fucking."

"Not my exact words, but yeah. I get your point. It's a tree falling in the woods situation at the moment. If no one sees us, can anyone start assuming?"

"Ethan." He steps in front of me, taking my other hand. "I'm pretty sure you're my last hope. The last shot I have at making something real and connecting with someone I want to be with. But that's not right of me to put on your shoulders. I don't have any right trying to convince you to stay with me because my life will spiral when you're not in it anymore. I get that now, and it's not your fault. I thought you should know that I never wanted you to feel the way I made you feel."

"Happy?"

"I meant the panic attacks, but—wait, what?"

"I mean, you're an annoying asshole sometimes, but even then, I was still happy. *Am* still happy."

"Hey, you're the one who wouldn't answer the phone."

"And you stormed out of a conversation to grab some hot girl's ass to show me you didn't need me."

He nods. "Yeah, I'll admit to that, and that was fucked up. She was hot, and I was trying to piss you off. It was dumb. I do need you, though."

"Why are you such a prick?" I move to lean my head on his shoulder, but he stops me and presses my head to his.

"Why are you such a snarky asshole?"

The waves wash over our feet. The water is cool, but not as cold as I expected for this time of year. After a few more minutes, he leads me over to a nearby table and hops onto it, looking out over the ocean as he lets go of my hand. I miss its warmth.

"What can I do, Lala? What do I need to do to make this right?"

I step between his knees and turn his hat around backward so he can't hide from me. "Give me time?" He scoffs, ready to argue. "Not away from you, not time like that. It's not you, Steve. Well, not all of it, anyhow. Give me time to adjust. To learn how to step outside of the comfort zone and see how far I can go. Don't give up on me, even when I do. Because that's what I did. I gave up on me, not on us. Not on you."

The look of surprise on his face tells me so much.

"What about me? How can I make this up to you? How do I remind you that I want this, even though it scares the fucking hell out of me?"

"I'm not sure. Ethan, I wasn't always like this. I had a fiancé a couple of years ago. Losing them turned me into someone I don't even recognize anymore." He explains, resting his head on my chest as I rub his back. "They were everything to me, and when they left, there wasn't a hole big enough for me to crawl into. The weird thing is, after a week of depression, I got out of bed and went on with life. Not the life I had before, and certainly not the life I wanted—a new life. Jamie noticed first and tried to help, but he was in a bad spot, too. Coop didn't even notice until probably the fourth or fifth time we hung out and I disappeared on him for an hour or so. I thought he'd be pissed at me, instead he hopped on the ride right next to me. I regret doing that with him."

"Wait, you and Chase?"

"No, not like that. He's super very straight. He lost his girl in the worst way possible a couple of years ago and he still hasn't recovered. So when he saw me out there living life again after only a week or so, he wanted to try. He watched me, watched how I moved, walked, and talked. He's an actor. He studies human behavior and tries to imitate it every day of his life. This was no different."

"I didn't know he was like that. The player mentality."

"He's not. He sucks at it. Where I could fuck a different person every night—hell, every few hours—to get that high, he has a conscience. He didn't like treating women like that, and I shouldn't have, either. But I needed the fix; I needed to get numb all over again. Until I didn't. I made people hate me after we fucked. Coop sent them fucking flowers."

I lean closer and kiss his forehead, holding my lips against his warm skin for a few extra seconds to give him what he needs now. Acceptance. There's a hiccup noise and when I pull back, I find him trying to fight back the sobs. Cupping his face, I run my nose up Steve's and whisper, "I want you. I don't mean sexual shit. I mean, I do, but I don't. I'm scared to fuck up; I'm scared I'll chase you away because I'm a damn coward."

He chokes out a laugh.

"Hey, life fucking sucks sometimes. Right? People we think will be there forever leave when we need them most. I can't promise you I'll handle any of this the right way. I know I won't be able to because I can't even look in the mirror and admit what I am to myself. But each time I'm with you, I hate myself a little less. You make me feel safe. Even when you're doing something completely fucked up and reckless, I know you'd be by my side if I needed you. You're not a coward, Steve. We're both just, you know, scared."

"How are we gonna do this? Us?"

"One very tiny step at a time. Gotta learn to skate before you can walk."

He gives me a sideway stare. "That's, uhm, backward?"

"Clearly, you didn't grow up in a Canadian-Norwegian home."

"Ethan, if this thing works out, if we make it." He reaches his arms around me, pulling me against him. "Remind me never to leave you alone with our kids and skates."

"No chance, Jensen. I'll have them on the ice before you've even built the crib."

"We're good?"

"We're… okay. I don't think either of us can say we're good right now. Close, though." I kiss him, gentle, playful kisses like we're exploring each other, which we are. We will be for a while because that's how a relationship is built.

He squeezes my ass before pulling his mouth from mine with a grin. "You ever fucked in the back seat of a Dodge Charger?"

"Your pickup lines are…seriously, do these ever work? How did you fuck so many people with lines like that?"

His smirk morphs into a grin as his thumbs rub circles on my hips. He licks his lips and I can't fucking believe it.

"God, you're such an ass," I sigh, exasperated. "I can't believe that shit worked."

"Get in the fucking car, Ethan. I wanna fog the windows up and write our names on the glass."

HOLLYWOOD
Steve

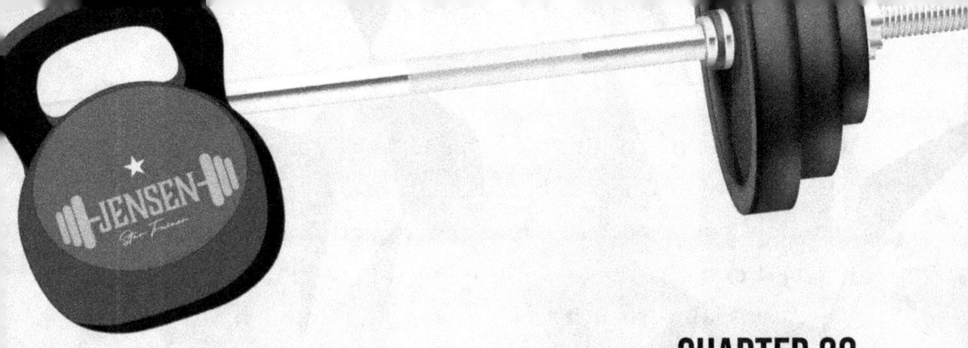

CHAPTER 20
BORN THIS WAY

LADY GAGA

"WE, well, we kind of got engaged."

My jaw hits the floor. I was absolutely not expecting that. "Kind of? Did you go to Vegas and get *un*-engaged or what?"

"Un-engaged?" Craig asks, still holding Laurie's hand as he smirks at me and plays with her ring. Oh, that fucker is getting some hours cleaning the men's locker room this week.

"Married—he means married, but he has trouble with words that mean commitment," Laurie says, rolling her eyes at me. She drops his hand and walks across the patio as she digs through her purse. When she pulls out the cigarette, I damn near walk over and slap it out of her hand.

"I thought you quit?"

"Yeah, but then, I un-quit!"

She tosses the pack over to me and I check inside. She's smoked three so far and I glance up at her for more information.

"I bought that the day we drove up to the cabin last month. After talking to Mom that night, I had one for obvious reasons. One a few days after we got back, before we talked to the lawyer for the first time. This is the third. Does the math add up?"

"Yeah." I run my hands through my hair and crash down on

the lounge chair. All I wanted was to come home, get high, and pass out. I wish Lala was back home already. I wouldn't even be here right now if he was. A bird goes by and I watch as it flies up to a nest in one of the few nearby trees. I used to love sitting out here, especially when it's cold like now. Although, it's been a while since I've taken the time to enjoy it since they built apartments in a vacant lot next door. The big ass, ugly building blocks what used to be a perfect view of the Hollywood sign. With the right binoculars, I could almost see Chase's house. That shit got me laid several times right here on this patio lounger. I'd give anything for that view back while I rail Ethan up here someday. The setting sun in his pretty hair and his skin glisten while I lick that spot that drives him wild.

"Earth to Steve?"

"Huh?" I watch Laurie put out her cigarette. Guess I'd been daydreaming for a while if she's already sucked down the whole thing.

"Christ. I asked you if you've talked to the lawyer about Mom and Dad yet. We're already scraping the barrel even with some funds being released, and it's getting tighter than I like— financially." I shake my head and she throws her hands in the air. "You said you were taking care of it. Where's your head right now?"

"I'm sorry, Laurie, but I'm still struggling to grasp what you just told me. Like, you two are serious right now about this whole marriage thing?"

"Why not?" She turns to Craig and in a sweet, soft voice she asks, "Baby, can you go get us all something to drink? This will probably take longer than it should." Craig leaves, kissing her head as he passes by and heads into the apartment.

"Why not?" I echo quietly so he can't hear me. "Uhm, oh, I

dunno. How about we start with the obvious? You've only been dating for like six months."

"Eight. And?" She crosses her arms while her laser eyes cut me in half. "Come on, your best friend got married in, what, four months?"

"Three, but that doesn't matter. He's fucking crazy. I mean, I'm happy for you and all, but you could wait until you've—"

"Died of old age? Steve, I've finished school, I've fixed my life, and aside from the Dad shit, I'm happy. What the fuck do I have left to wait for?" She leans forward, putting her hands on her knees. "What if it's what Mom and Dad need to come to their senses and recognize this isn't a phase?"

"See, that's what I'm worried about! What if you're doing this for the wrong reasons? Shit's been so damn crazy since October and with everything going on—Laur, are you sure about this?"

"Steve, two things. First, I'm capable of making my own decisions—good, bad, it doesn't matter. Second, there's this thing called divorce. If it doesn't work out, we go our separate ways."

"Those aren't cheap! They're not cigarettes you can burn through for a couple bucks."

"I wish cigarettes only cost a couple of bucks." She laughs, but I'm still serious. "Besides, this is Los Angeles. People get married and divorced in record time around here. I might as well live it up!"

Before I can respond, my phone is going off. The caller ID is a friend of mine who's working on the countersuit we filed against our parents, so I answer while Laurie just rolls her eyes at me. Someday, those eyes really are going to roll right out of her head.

"Mills! Please, save me from this conversation with some good news?"

"I can do that, pal."

"Okay, you're on speaker and Laurie is here with me, so don't tell her what I said about her."

"Great. So I did some digging into the financials of the gym, Laurie's school, everything you two have had your hands in over the last fifteen years. I looked it over and sent copies of anything important to your lawyer. To me, it looks like we have more than enough backup and paperwork and he should have your accounts fixed up in no time. It's still not all the money, but it's everything we can easily prove without a doubt is your income that you earned through working and the trust, not your father."

"Okay, how much?"

"Seventy percent. The rest is a little trickier. Your dad is smart, and he was a damn good lawyer before he was on the bench, so he's throwing everything he can at us to slow everything down. His whole plan of attack is simply to wear you both down until you're broke and he has to get what he wants."

"Yeah, but he doesn't own the gym. How can he take that money?" I get an idea and blurt out, "What if I sold it to Jamie or Chase right now?"

"Can't do that while there are open litigation cases. Steve, unless there's something I missed in the documents I sent over, what he did was illegal. It looks like he knows someone at the bank and that's who froze your accounts. When do you meet with your lawyer again?"

"Ten tomorrow."

"Good. He should have time to go through the paperwork and talk to you about the countersuit."

"He's meeting with Dad tomorrow afternoon," Laurie tells us. It's a surprise for me.

"Yeah, I was worried about that. Be ready to see your pops while you're still there. It sounds like he's coming in to sign some paperwork

and he's being a fucking snake about it. His meeting is well after yours, but I bet he's showing up to rattle you a bit."

"Thanks. Hey, while I have you on. Can you do some digging for me on a Craig Jo—" Laurie thwacks me in the arm and I laugh it off. "Kidding. Just fucking with Laurie. We'll talk to you later, Mills."

"Really?" Laurie deadpans after I hang up. "Having Mills run a background check on Craig, the guy who's been your employee and friend for how many years?"

"I was only joking." I stand up again, wrapping my arms around her and kissing the side of her head. "I'm happy for you and Craig, sis. I just had to play the brother role for a bit to give you a hard time."

"You're going to make him clean the bathrooms, aren't you?"

"Damn right he's cleaning the bathrooms."

"Men are so fucking stupid sometimes."

"I take it our father is here?" I say to our lawyer, Mark, who's waiting for us in the parking garage.

"He is. He wasn't supposed to come until later, after we had a chance to meet."

"Has Mom signed his deal yet?"

"No, not yet. She's here, though, and she's holding out. It's got him madder than a hornet on fire. He knows you've been snooping around on him, so he's been up there shouting about wanting to see everything we've found." He laughs and shakes his head. "When I said his lawyer can request the documents, he threatened to relocate my jaw for me."

"Well, that's pretty typical for our father, honestly. Sorry he threatened you, but glad you didn't back down from his threats." I look over to Laurie. She looks like she's gonna hurl. "What?"

"Everything?" She shrugs. "Why would Mom take our side on this? She's always followed whatever he told her to. She's like a Stepford wife. He tells her where to go, what to do, basically everything. Without Dad, she wouldn't have a clue what to do with herself."

"Delay tactic?" Mark suggests as he holds the elevator door open for us.

"He wouldn't use her like that." I answer. This mentality can be hard for people who aren't rich or from New England to get their heads around. It's a weird obsession with being this perfect housewife with a perfect home. It's not a traditional wife, and it's different from a stay at home mom—it has little to nothing to do with kids at all. This is some old school send your kids away and make sure you have a perfect house for the company mentality. "Years of psychological abuse made her what she is, but I guarantee he doesn't trust her with a plan beyond making sure the cook gets him dinner on time. Dad didn't marry Mom for her brains, and she's perfectly okay with that. It's how their marriage works, I guess. But she's not as dumb as she pretends to be. There's something else going on, maybe in our favor, maybe not, but I don't trust either of them."

Our father is standing just outside the door to the office, with Mom on a bench across the way. She's staring at the floor, wringing her hands, but he's standing tall. A looming dragon ready to protect his gold, but willing to sacrifice his own family to keep us away from his pockets. He steps in front of us, blocking the door and puffing out his chest like he's a badass. He's a bloated windbag at best.

"Mr. Jensen, we—"

"Judge."

"I'm sorry?"

"Judge Jensen, seeing as how I finished school, did my services to the courts, and earned the title. I assumed they were here to get this over with, but I can already see that's still not the case." He looks through us, not at us, taking a longer than necessary look at Laurie. I scoff in his face because I know what he's looking for. He thought Laurie would cave and Spencer would be here. "I see you've made your choice, no matter how fucking stupid it is. Steven, you have until noon tomorrow to clear your personal items out of the gym. Spencer, you have—"

"Laurie," I growl, stepping closer to him. "Her fucking name is Laurie, you prick."

"Laurie," her name oozes out of his mouth like sludge. "You have until the end of business today to come pick up your things from the office you abandoned three months ago. Your internship is over. Everything has already been boxed by the—"

"Internship?" Laurie snaps at him, not believing what she's hearing.

"Judge Jensen, I'm afraid we have a misunderstanding." I watch the lawyer's posture change like he's growing a spine right here in front of our eyes. "You see, we are rejecting your offer on the grounds that it violates the rights of Ms. Laurie Jensen. Also, on the basis that you have no way to prove your ownership claims to the gym. Now, as you are aware, we have asked your legal team to meet us here later to go over the requested proof and financial documents."

"Do you know who the hell I am? Your dumb ass wasn't even in diapers when I was trying cases of—"

"Oh, here we go," I cut him off, rolling my eyes in annoyance. This is what he does. Laurie knows it, too, so she goes and joins Mom on the bench. "You know what, Dad? No one is going to remember you for any of the shit you did in Boston, Hartford, Los Angeles, or anywhere else. You'll fucking die and people will see it in the paper and say *Hey, honey. Isn't this the fucking asshole that tried to blackmail his gay kids?*"

"Steve," the lawyer interrupts, but I've already said what I wanted. He turns back to my father. "Judge, you are an upstanding member of the community. There's no denying that. However, you're on the wrong side of history, and the wrong side of the courthouse. This isn't a criminal trial, yet. It's a waste of money and time. Now, we'll see you at your allotted appointment time. Until then, please step away from the door."

A smile spreads across my face and for the first time since all of this started, I feel damn good about our chances.

"What the hell are you smiling about, son?"

"Oh, I'm pretty sure you know already. Also, don't call me son." I shake my head and laugh. "I've been done with you for a long time, but stuck it out for mom. Write me out of your will, or mom's will, whatever you want. I don't care. In fact, if you kept me in it, I swear I will donate every single dime I get, every property, every fucking boat, all of it to trans rights in your honor. Your Honor."

His mouth twists up, and he balls his hands into fists, but I just stare him down. "Elaine, we're leaving. We'll be back. This is far from over."

"Mm, is it though?" I question sarcastically as Mom stands to leave with him. Neither of them turn to look at us again before they head down the hallway. "Mom, I'm a phone call away if you need anything. We love you."

"Do not speak to her!" my father turns on his heel and roars. "You're an embarrassment and an abomination. Both of you! This ridiculous idea you have in your heads has gone on long enough. We're done coddling you. You'll be begging for our forgiveness soon enough."

"Steve runs a successful business. I just passed the fucking bar exam. What more do you want from us?" Tears run down Laurie's face.

"I want my boys back!"

"Bullshit! You want your fucking legacy." My laughter is low and rumbles like a growl. "We're your legacy, and we'll make sure everyone knows it, you fucker. Die mad about it."

As my father storms off with my mother in tow, the lawyer shuffles us past the reception desk and into his private office, shutting the door behind him. "I should have had you two in sooner to coach you. Although, knowing you both, I doubt it would have changed much. Steve, if it happens again though, keep quiet."

"Good luck with that. You'll need to sew his mouth shut or knock him out," Laurie scoffs.

"She's not wrong. Besides, Dad only intimidates when he's coming up empty. Did you get the info from Mills?"

"I did. So, how do you two want to proceed?"

I look at Laurie. We haven't talked about this specific question much because we both already know exactly what needs to happen. It's the only way.

"We want them out of our lives. If Dad drops all of this and stops this idiotic bullshit, Steve and I will walk away from everything to do with them. However, if he keeps attacking us, uses my dead name again in public, or tries anything else, we're going to sue the fucking shit out of him." Laurie's cold as ice, slipping into her legal eagle mode. "Restraining orders, revised wills for both Steve and I, and all the other necessary documentation to remove any rights they have to us, including our healthcare decisions and our businesses."

"Absolutely. We're already working on the paperwork and backup for defamation, intent to cause emotional distress, and invasion of privacy. We've got solid evidence of financial crimes, among other things, and Mills is pretty sure he knows who the contact at the bank is." He sits and leans over on his desk. "Laurie, you also have a wrongful termination case. We've got plenty to work with, which is why I'm going to ask this next question, and it's very important. Is there something going on in your father's life right now that would have caused this? This all seems very out of character for him, or am I off base thinking that?"

"No, it's more likely that he's just letting the mask slip a little in his old age." I reply and the lawyer nods. "He wouldn't tell us if he was sick, but I could see this being the hill he wants to quite literally die on."

"Mark?" Laurie says as she adjusts her skirt—it's her nervous tick and reminds me a lot of our mom. "To be on the safe side, can you please draw up the necessary paperwork to be filed the minute that dickhead dies? To get out ahead of anything he has planned? Include us taking over control of our mother's estate, my father's share of the firm, and anything else I'm not thinking of."

"That's what I was about to suggest."

"Why wait?" I offer. "I want him to know we won before he shuffles off to hell."

HOLLYWOOD
21
Ethan

CHAPTER 21
ANTI-HERO

ARCTIC MONKEYS

SINCE WE MET, days have turned into weeks, weeks into months, and as the season goes on, Steve and I grow more comfortable with each other. Since Christmas, we've started going out a little more, but we've been careful where we go and how we interact with each other. We hold hands in the movie theater, but not until the lights have already gone out. We let our feet touch under the table at restaurants when we sit across from one another, but only the edge of one food each. It's little ways of showing affection that can be easily dismissed and each time we go out, it's like we get a fraction closer to something more. It's helped Steve feel more connected while keeping us out of the public eye. A win-win for us.

A few people I'm close to have noticed a change, but I pass it off as having found an excellent trainer who's working hard with me and turning me into a new man. So far, they're buying it, and it's not a lie because my performance on the ice has been nothing short of a highlight reel.

"Wake up, sleepyhead."

"What time is it?" Steve mumbles into the pillow as I kiss his shoulder.

"Uh, you don't want to know, but the sun is...well...it's coming up."

"Too early."

"You sound like Chase. Come on, I got up early and got breakfast. Your favorite cheat spot that's open this early."

"Norms!" He yells it half-heartedly and holds one hand up like that old TV show about a bar. My dad used to watch that all the time, and Steve shouts it every time we pass the restaurant. It cracks me up how much a guy who's into fitness and health loves a giant stack of good, old-fashioned pancakes and a side of hash browns from a diner like Norms. Then again, I've got a sweet tooth that would make Willy Wonka look like a rookie.

He stretches, but I'm standing too close to escape when he grabs me, pulling me into bed on top of him while covering my face and neck with sloppy morning kisses that have us both laughing. Steve is such a hard ass outside of this room. Even when we're at his house—and especially when we're at the gym. It's like my room is the only one where he can trust himself to be who he really is and doesn't have to put on a mask to impress anyone. I think the same goes for me, too.

"Breakfast is getting cold."

"I don't wanna go out there yet. I wanna lay here with you and have a sloppy, half-awake make-out session that leaves you with a thousand hickies before you leave me."

"Well, how about a compromise, since you can't leave me with any hickies? Breakfast is already here, dopey. Happy stupid cupid holiday, Stevie."

"Happy stupid cupid holiday to you, too, Lala. Come on, I'm gonna feed you breakfast before I suck your dick."

"Food and sex. Stevie's most favorite things in the world."

"And you." He pushes my hair out of my eyes and strokes my cheek with his thumb. No one has ever looked at me the way

Steve does, and damn, it's hard to look away from those blues. "Are you blushing?"

"Whatever," I push off of him and walk across the room where I present the breakfast spread I've laid out on the floor like a picnic.

I woke up early, knowing today was his day off and he'd sleep in for once. I thought it would give me free rein in the kitchen to make some coffee and something easier on my stomach before the flight. Chase was already in there before I was after he had another fight with his insomnia demons. He lost. I had to beg him not to cook for us, but in the end I did let him show me how to cut strawberries into roses. I brought in a bowl of twelve of those, and there's more in the fridge for Steve to eat while I'm gone.

We feed each other, making a mess of it because neither of us is exactly the dainty type, and we keep taking short breaks for making out. We also do the one thing we're still not very good at. We talk. I'm not sure if it's because we're both tired or something deeper, but there's something different in the air between us lately. It's not quite tension and just shy of electricity. It's like something is just hanging there, waiting for one of us to pull it down out of the air. It's three words we're both terrified of saying or hearing.

After eating a strawberry out of my mouth, Steve looks at me in a way that has me thinking he might break the bubble. He opens his mouth. Closes it. Opens it again, and I can almost hear the words come out.

"I—need a drink. Orange juice. Do you want a drink? I can make you something. Mimosa, or, you know, anything," he stammers as he gets up and heads for the door.

"Nah, I'm good." I hold up my half full coffee. Fuck, so close. My heart is drumming like Tommy fucking Lee is in my chest and hopped up on coke. I lean my head back against the wall and close my eyes, wondering if we should have just stayed in bed instead of going to all this trouble for a stupid, made up, bullshit holiday.

"Lala?" I breathe in quickly and open my eyes. I must have fallen asleep because Steve is back beside me and he's got a carafe of orange juice. "I just took all the oranges and made a shit ton in case you wanted some. I also grabbed the coffee pot so I could top you off."

"You already do that, Steve."

He laughs nervously and I'm not sure what's up, but it's probably just the day. "Not always, Sweets. Not always. Hey, uhm, I kind of got you something. We don't really do gifts and all, but I saw this, and I wanted to get it for you because you could wear it around and no one would know it was from me. I was going to get you a necklace thing, but you already wear that one and never take it off so—"

"Yeah, it's, uhm, got special meaning."

"Yeah, no, that's cool." He reaches into his duffle bag and pulls out a box, thrusting it out like it's a hot potato. "You don't have to wear it if you don't want. I mean, you could get rid of it. It's engraved though, so that might be weird, but, yeah. Open it."

I reach over, ignoring the box for a moment while I grab Steve's coffee cup and set it up on the dresser. He gives me a funny look and I laugh before I lean over and kiss him. "Decaf, baby. Switch to decaf."

"Whatever. Open it!" I love seeing him like this, playful and a bit nervous. Sometimes it's me being the shy one, sometimes it's him. We switch in more ways than just sex.

I pull the bow off, making sure I take my time because he's vibrating with excitement next to me. It's too big to be a ring, which is good. It's way too early for that shit. But it has the name of a jewelry store on it. I carefully lift the lid and I'm staring at an absolutely breathtaking watch.

"Steve, how much—"

"Do not finish that question. It's even in green, to match the team colors—and your eyes."

"You didn't have to do this, Stevie."

"Yeah, I know, but the gym is doing better, and this is like three and a half months' worth of gifts all in one. Okay, it's a little more than that, but who cares? Take it out, try it on."

I pull it out of the box and flip it over to read the engraving. "Glad you went with what felt good," I read aloud. "Huh. Yeah, no one's gonna know what the hell that means."

"I know, except us. Plus, you'll think about that day every time you put it on. About that first night when I had you up against the wall." He puffs his chest out, proud of himself.

"It's absolutely beautiful, baby. I love it."

He grabs my face and we're kissing again, but I pull away and stand up, confusing him even more. "Yeah, you think you're the only one who doesn't listen when we say don't do gifts, huh?" I open the top drawer of the dresser and pull out an envelope. "It's not as flashy, but, uhm, yeah."

I'm nervous as fuck as he opens the envelope and opens the letter inside. He reads it quickly, then flips to the next page.

"You hate it. Fuck. I feel like shit because I didn't—"

"Behind the home goalie? Behind Dev?"

"Uhm yeah. Shit, I didn't even think about the box seats. Those are so much better, fuck."

"Lala, they're not—" I go to reach for the paperwork and he pulls it away and grabs my hand. He stares at me, waiting for me to hold eye contact with him so I know he's serious. "You and those pretty green eyes are going to be the death of me, Lala. Please, sit back down."

The sigh is heavy and real. What the fuck was I thinking? "I'll, uhm, buy you some other stuff, too. I didn't know you were gonna go and buy a fucking watch and spend…so much."

"And yet, you still managed to one-up me." He throws his leg over me so he's sitting on my lap before he cups my face and pulls me to him, kissing my forehead and holding me there for a beat longer than normal. When he pulls back, I could swear his eyes were…wet.

"Stevie, what's the matter?"

"I gave you a watch. I drove to Rodeo at the second worst time of year, waited forever, and spent a bunch of money. In a year, I'll barely remember where I bought it or what I even had the engrave on the back. I'll likely buy you the same damn watch again, because I'll forget." He waves the piece of paper with the team logo on it as he continues. "You, on the other hand, spent brain power and emotion on this that makes me come off like a douche."

"Thanks, mom? Make sure you tack it to the fridge for me, yeah? Next to the drawing I made, that might be a llama, or might be an elephant. We can't tell."

"Ethan! You just asked me to spend time with you in public. Not just any time, either. Game time."

I stare at him, the lump in my throat threatening to choke me. I didn't think he'd understand. I was so sure he'd just see season tickets and automatically assume I went cheap or got him something lame. "Wait, you get it?"

"Yeah, I do! Because you'll be with Devin. So for two periods of hockey, I'm with you to celebrate the close calls, and for one period, I'm right there every time you score."

Those butterflies in my stomach? They just died, resurrected, and died again. This can't be my life. He actually understands why I got him the gift I did. He gets the meaning behind it.

"I mean, you're on the other side of the glass, but…yeah. That was kind of the idea. Emily, she does PR for the team. She nearly spoiled the surprise when she saw my name come up on the ticket package. She was going to call you because she thought there was a mistake. I told her it was a late birthday present, and she yelled at me for not asking for tickets."

"Sweetheart, my Sweets, that is some serious quality time together. I may have to split it up a little and do at least part of the game in the luxury box so Chase doesn't get lonely, but these are fucking amazing. Why two?"

"You know, you and your hot dates."

"Jerk," he pushes my arm and then starts threatening to tickle me while simultaneously grinding against me.

"No, I got it so Laurie could come with you. Or her and Craig can take those while you're busy or whatever. They're good for next season, too. Hopefully I don't get traded," I joke, but it is a possibility, no matter how good my season is going. "And we don't break up."

"We won't. Fuck, you keep getting better and better, you beautiful fucking man. Now, get on that bed and let me show you how much I love this fucking gift." As he moves to stand, I pull him back down, moving his hips back and forth. He raises an eyebrow and stares at me. "Lala?"

"Yeah, I think after you confessed to going the easy way on the gift, I'm gonna take a little extra from you. So, *you* get your ass on the bed, and I'll show *you* how fucking much I love y—the watch." I can't breathe. I can't fucking breathe. I couldn't stop it in time and he knows what I almost said. He's going to leave for sure now. Fuck. I grip his hips even tighter, hoping I can hold on if he bolts.

He leans forward as I screw my eyes shut and cringe. "Well? Come on, Daddy. Show me how much you love…the watch. Wear it while you spank my naughty, yet sexy, ass."

I let out a shaky breath. "You know the rules, sweetheart. Go get the jersey."

He gets up and runs over to the closet, dropping his boxers as he pulls my jersey out and slips it over his head. God fucking damn. He looks like one of those gorgeous Norwegian players that ends up on the covers of the magazines because he's too fucking hot to hide. The knot in my stomach tightens as I realize something else. This wanna-be Thor is mine. Nobody else's, just mine.

We're throwing ourselves into bed and running our hands all over each other in no time. I flip him on his stomach and have his ass sticking up in the air for me. That…is one perfect fucking ass. I rub his smooth, tan cheeks as he arches his back and gives me a porn-star level whine as he rocks back and forth.

"Fuck me, Daddy. You got a Daddy kink, E? Come on, what's your fantasy?"

"It's a pretty specific one, and no, not Daddy stuff." I squeeze the lube on my dick and make sure I'm good and ready before I spit in his ass and run my thumb around the puckered ring. "It involves hot blonde personal trainers, and teaching them not to be cocky little fucking brats."

I pull the belt out from under the blanket and I swear to god that man starts to salivate. "Oh, and you wanted to talk about kinks, huh? Now, keep your baby blues right here on me. Or else."

"What if I want the or else option with my happy meal?"

"Then maybe next time, I'll just tie you up and put a fucking gag in your dumb ass whore mouth. We can call it my early birthday present—your silence."

"Oh fuck, please, do not stop talking to me like that, Daddy."

"You hate your father, and you're gonna call me Daddy?"

"Daddy is a state of mind, Lala. That's what Lord Pedro says." He wags his ass and giggles. "Hey, it's not about our dad-related issues when it's in bed, so fuck me like you own me, Daddy."

I rub the leather over his skin and he bites his lip as I line my cock up. We've both switched ever since our first time together. I'm a bottom more often than he is, but oh, when he lets me have my turn? I turn this six foot three, two hundred and some pounds of muscle into a blathering idiot, and he loves every minute of it. I toss the belt up toward his hands and he stares at it, then looks back at me. All I do is wink, and he's moving as fast as he can to wrap it around his neck and give me the other end of the belt.

"Good job, Stevie. Now, eyes up, shoulders down, and don't you dare come before I tell you?" I pull tight on the belt around his neck while I plunge into him. The half scream, half moan that roars out of him can't be mistaken for anything but bliss, and I'm right there with him. Seeing that big ass twenty-one on his back just makes him even more mine. And I love reminding him of that, too.

"God damn, Stevie. I'm never gonna get over my jersey on you. You like wearing it, huh? Like being mine?"

"Yes! Oh…oh fuck. Yes, Daddy." Steve howls as I smack his ass. "I'm yours. My ass is yours, FUCK!"

"Look at me, Stevie, and tell me who you belong to."

He looks over his shoulder with those blown out eyes, bruised lips, and a pout that could easily push me over the edge most days. It makes my heart skip a beat, but not my hips—they're moving faster as I pull on the belt again.

"I'm yours, Ethan. I—I lo—I need you!" He claws at the

sheets and we make a chorus together of moans, whimpers, and grunts until we're both spent and I collapse on top of him. I don't care that we're both a mess. I wrap my arms around him and splay my hand over his chest.

"You're the best thing that's ever happened to me, Stevie. The one bright star in a void of nothingness." I nuzzle into the crook of his neck, listening to us both trying to catch our breath. "I need you, too."

They aren't the words I want to say, the words my heart wants to scream, but we're not rushing this and I'm taking his lead on that. We both know that need is just a placeholder for the word that will come someday. We both understand that, when the time is right and we can take our walls down and feel safe outside this room, we'll use the right word. But for now, need will do.

"I wish you had a normal job so I could tell you not to leave tonight."

"I wish I could call in, but I don't think sick for my incredible, wonderful, absolutely amazing boyfriend is really a great excuse in the pros. Even if you did offer to dress up like a pretty little nurse for me."

"Better than being sick *of* me." He turns his head to the side so I can kiss him while we lay there. We're not the most romantic couple in the world and I wonder, if we were public, if that would be different. If we'd try to be more like society expects of a couple. I hope not. There's something special about what we've got because there's no one to impress, no standard to meet. We're just doing what feels right. Doing what feels good. "I'll order that nurse costume while you're gone."

HOLLYWOOD
Steve

CHAPTER 22
WHERE IS MY MIND?

PIXIES

WHEN I WAKE UP, his pretty blonde head is the first thing I see, and I can't help but smile. This feels right. More than any of my one-night stands, more than even my fiancé, I want this to last. Five months of this guy and I can't imagine my life without him, even though that scares the fuck out of me. He got in around three this morning and came right to bed, curling up on top of me as he mumbled and fell right to sleep. I wish I could lie here with him forever, but I need to get to work. I reach out, running my hand up the back of his head and massaging his scalp.

"M'rnm," he grumbles into my chest.

"Is that the best good morning you've got?" I ask, surrounding him with my arms and kissing the top of his messy hair. "I missed you."

"Mhmm, missed you. Don't go t'work."

"Gotta work, Sweets. But I'll lay here with you for a bit."

"M'kay."

"Lala?" I whisper and he mumbles again before he pulls my arm from around him, laces his fingers between mine, and holds our hands to his chest. "I...I think my dad is dying."

"What?" His head rolls to the side and his body follows. The instant he's on his back, I pounce, climbing on top of him and going right for his neck. He says something under his breath and before I can kiss him, he pushes me out of reach.

"Stevie, you can't drop that on me and go right into making out!"

"Why not?"

"Seriously?" He stares at me, unblinking. "Sometimes I forget that you're the older one in this relationship and not the idiot twenty something year old."

"Yeah, well, sometimes I forget that you're not in your sixties with how cranky you are."

"You are such an asshole."

"Yep, and you love it. And by it, I mean me." I kiss him, he kisses me back, deeper and desperate. "And my asshole."

"You…are twelve. Get out of my bed."

"Nooo! I'm not as innocent as I seem—just have a look at my ID, officer. Oh man, we should get some handcuffs and—"

"No, Stevie. I'm too fucking tired for this shit. Now, what the hell was that about your dad?"

I crash down on top of him like a giant starfish and he grunts and calls me names. We lay there together for a while. This is why I'm getting better at talking to Ethan—he listens in a non-judgmental way. Chase listens, but he knows too much about me already. Jamie listens sometimes, but most of the time he's pretty sure I've lost my mind no matter what I'm saying. That's not his fault, because I've always been a bit of a rambler and not one to stay on track in conversations. Ethan doesn't rush me, doesn't try to cut me off to remind me of something I did in the past, and doesn't try to explain my problems.

"I'm not upset about it, if that matters and means I can go back to sucking your face—or something else." I wink and waggle my eyebrows, but he just rolls his eyes and covers his face.

"Because you've accepted it or because you and your dad's relationship can't be fixed?" He asks, hands still over his eyes as he rubs his face. "Remember, I've only met him once over donuts."

"With any luck, you'll never meet him again." I rest my chin on his chest and he looks down at me. "You have pretty eyes, and you have this cute dimple on your chin when I frustrate you. It's right here."

He swats my hand away and tries hard not to laugh. Once, when Jamie's wife Alexis asked us how our relationship was going, he told her it was like some of the greatest in history. Then listed off duos like Bert and Ernie or the Odd Couple. He wasn't wrong.

"Okay, okay. So, you know my sister is…different, right?"

"Like, smarter, cooler, and far better dressed than you?"

"You forgot better looking, but also no, none of that. Anyway, my dad wants her to be someone she's not. He wants her to give up everything that makes her Laurie. He's still mad about moving to California to give her a chance at a new start."

"I know what that's like. When did you move here?"

"High school. Our junior year."

"So you've been here, fuck. How long is that? I can't math before coffee."

"Like twenty years. Laurie wanted to transition. We even talked about coming out here on our own, but our uncle convinced my dad to start a branch out here. I even found him the perfect spot. The promise of big bucks was more important than the mental well being of his kids." I draw shapes on his arms and chest as I talk.

"So he has an issue with Laurie, and not with you?"

"Fuck, he thinks this is a phase, too. He probably expects me to get over it, find a good wife, make babies, and get a damn job."

"Oh, he and my dad would get along great. Maybe we should tell them we're practicing hard on that baby making part, but it just isn't taking."

I laugh and kiss a trail up to his mouth, catching his bottom lip between my teeth and pulling gently. "Do you think I should be upset because someone like that might be dying?"

"Trust me, I'm not saying that at all. I just wasn't expecting you'd wake me up with that instead of how you usually wake me up. Family sucks sometimes."

"Mmhmm, but I suck better."

"There's the Stevie I...know."

He wants to say it. Hell, I want to say it too, but we haven't gotten there yet.

"Yeah, well, we've cut them out of our lives, and they've cut us out of theirs. Actually, instead of cutting anyone off, it's more like we're both managing different teams in a cage match to the death between lawyers. Hopefully that will all be over soon and we'll come out on top. Alright, I've aired my dirty laundry, so what have you got?"

"Broad strokes or specifics?"

The past hasn't exactly been an open topic for either of us because of the amount of open scars we both still have. Part of me felt like I've always known him since, in a way, I grew up around his brothers and his family. You couldn't play or even like hockey in Massachusetts and not know who the LaVoie family was. We never played on the same teams, and I don't remember meeting them other than in line to shake hands at the end of games. I still heard so much about them and their dad, though. It was unavoidable. They were legends before everything went sideways. I didn't exactly keep up with them when I stopped playing hockey.

I quit halfway through my freshman year. I was too busy protecting my sister from bullies to care about sports. Of course, now I understand that not playing hockey was a luxury I had that no one in Ethan's family could even entertain.

I remember his older brother, Aaron, was a year younger than me. He was standoffish and shy, but not exactly known as a nice guy. When he got on the ice, he turned into a fucking beast. I remember another brother who got into fights both off-ice and on, but he dropped off my radar fast. We were already in California by the time the third brother was making waves.

"Whatever you need to tell me right now, in this moment, to help you."

"Guess I should give you the whole deal." He puts his hands behind his head and closes his eyes. "Aaron got in his car accident on the way to his wedding. A kid died, and Dad paid to cover it up. It ended his career, because he was high as fuck on painkillers after an injury the week before. Now he coaches travel hockey and does some hockey school coaching."

"Shit, that's harsh."

"Next up is Briar. Right after high school, Briar and his friends took a trip to Mexico and met up with a guy who offered them ten grand each to smuggle drugs for him. They agreed, and then they took some samples as additional payment. They found their car three weeks later in Louisiana. They said he didn't feel a thing, but I think that was to keep my mom from flipping out. That's when she left. She blamed dad. The last one was Cole. He was older than me by six years and was constantly crying out for help, always getting into trouble. Dad sent him away to some kind of fucked up bootcamp, said it was to help him. He lasted two weeks before he stole a car and ran it into a tree. He was better than Aaron on the ice, and a better man than any of us off the ice, given the chance. Dad never bothered to take the time to understand him."

"If this was a contest, I'd say my family is all peaches and cream next to yours." He brushes a hand through my hair, tousling what little there is. "Sweets, you're not them, okay? You're not cursed, your family is, well, kind of fucked when it comes to getting in the big leagues."

"Sure, that's it. What are you going to do about your dad?"

"Hey, I mean it." I lean down till we're nose to nose. "You're not your brothers. It's like they got all the bad, and you took all the grumpy and called it even."

His eyes close and I want to will them back open so I can stare into that green galaxy again. He surprises me when he reaches around me and pulls me closer, kissing me hard. I should call him grumpy more often if this is what it gets me. His hand is in my boxers and I'm moaning into each kiss, but I think he's crying. I pull my face back and glance down at him and he looks away, pulling his hands out with a sigh.

"Lala, what's just happened?"

"I just needed you to shut up for a little while, and I figured that was the fastest way to distract you." He looks lost and sad, so I bear hug him and roll us over so he's on top of me, but I don't let go. I hold him, feeling the dripping tears on my bare skin as he fights hard not to break down in front of me. I stroke his hair and keep my damn mouth shut.

"When was the last time you talked to anyone about all this?"

"Never," he sniffles.

"Do you need to talk about it more or less right now?"

"I need to call my sister."

"Okay, where's your phone?" I find it on the nightstand and

grab it for him, watching him hit the speed dial and hearing the voicemail message. His whole body lets go as he melts into my arms. I hear the loud beep and watch him hang up and call again two more times. He listens to the message all the way through every time before he tosses the phone to the side of the bed. "Ethan?"

"I still call her. I leave her messages sometimes, too. My parents don't know I kept her phone, but I did so that no one would shut it off. I pay the bill to keep it active, so she'll always be there for me, like she promised."

"What are you talking about? Why didn't you leave her a message?"

"The night of my first college game, I checked the stands a hundred times. I knew exactly where she was supposed to be sitting because I was the one who gave her the seats. My coach found out what happened during the second intermission, but my dad caught him before he could come and tell me. Dad told him to keep me in, to not tell me until the game was over because hockey was more important."

"She's...not around anymore, is she?" He shakes his shaggy head and I have to wipe away my own tears from his pain. I vaguely remember headlines about his two brothers and something about a scandal with his dad, but I had no idea he even had a sister until recently. "Were...were you guys close?"

"Yeah. She was two years older than me, but people always thought we were twins. It was a car accident. The car my stepdad and I rebuilt for her as a birthday present. She was side swiped by a drunk driver on the way to the game. I've always felt like it was my fault. Like if she hadn't been in that car and headed to my game, she'd still be around."

"It's not your fault, Lala. Sometimes, life just fucking sucks."

"I, uhm, I didn't miss a game, but I wasn't playing well.

Coach figured out that my dad was forcing me to be out there on the ice instead of grieving like I should have been." He sniffles and I rub his arms, trying to soothe him. Reliving this shit is never easy. "Coach benched me and had a talk with my dad. He thought that might take some of the pressure off and maybe Dad would back off. That didn't go well, instead it made everything worse. I had to sit in the back of the church during her fucking funeral to hide the black eye and the limp."

I kiss the top of his head. "I'm so sorry, Ethan."

"I used to get a season ticket for whatever team I was playing for. College, minor leagues, pro, it didn't matter. One seat. It was in my contract and no one questioned it, even when no one ever sat there."

"Behind the goal? Ethan, look at me." He picks his head up and his eyes are red. "Is that why you got two seats?"

"The night I got hurt, there was a lady sitting in Dakota's seat. It looked so much like her. It's why I wasn't ready for the hit. I swore I saw her. I asked for the tapes and everyone thought it was to see the accident, but I needed to find out who was there. I wanted answers to understand why they did that. I wanted to know why they had to sit there. I wanted to scream at her for doing that to me. In reality, I wanted closure from my sister's death. Problem was, there was no one in the seat. The therapist I saw for a while said it was likely a reflection and someone else nearby, a trick of the eye. That's part of why I stopped going to therapy."

"What do you think it was?"

"Her telling me the worst was yet to come. She would have liked you."

I tuck my finger under his chin, lifting it up again. "I think she was there exactly when you needed. Telling you she had always been there, always there watching you. Telling you everything was going to be alright. And she's gonna be in that seat next to me, cheering you on for the rest of the season."

He's quiet for a while, his steady breathing almost lulling me back to sleep, but his long eyelashes tickle just enough to keep me awake every time he blinks. The tears have stopped for now, but he's been through. His demons are still right there with him, ready and waiting to grab his feet and pull him under. Soft taps on the door have us both looking up and me thinking we need to spend more nights at my place where we don't get interrupted so damn much.

"Are you two decent?"

"Yeah," Ethan shouts back to Devin as he rolls off me and wipes at his eyes. I give him a pout and he gives me a peck on the cheek. No matter what we do together, his softest, smallest gestures are what make me blush and wake the long dormant butterflies. It's like he's got a key and his own private entrance right into my soul, and I hope he never leaves.

"Hey, Chase made breakfast for everyone. We figured you guys were probably tired, so I brought it in for you." Devin carries in a tray with enough food for an army.

"He okay?" Ethans asks as he nods to the tray.

"Yeah. I mean, he is now. The cooking helps. He and Pongo are leaving in a bit to see the shrink."

"I'm gonna go talk to him," I say, kissing the side of Ethan's head and pouring a cup of coffee from the French press. He stops me before I go, taking off his necklace that he's always wearing and putting it over my head.

"Lala I—"

"It's good. Leave it. She'd want that." I kiss his forehead and make my way to the kitchen. We can argue about wearing the necklace later.

"Pants in my kitchen, dickhead!" is the first thing Chase says as I walk in. He may not be feeling much better, but he's at least back enough to give me shit.

"I'm wearing boxers! Besides, I'm just in here to say hello to my best friend!" I grab him in a hug that he fights like always, giving him an exaggerated kiss on the cheek. "Good morning, sexy. Thanks for breakfast. How long have you been up?"

"Oh, you know, like four? It's cool, I'm good now. We have breakfast, lunch is in the oven, and I tried my hand at cookies because Doc said to try baking."

"How'd that go?" I ask, arms still wrapped around his waist.

"I'm gonna save those for him."

"That bad?"

"Hockey pucks would taste better. Anything new from your dad?"

"Not a peep. He's got nothing, and I'm sure he's heard through others about Laurie's engagement. That has to have him fuming even more. Racist, homophobic fucker. The job offer she got from his competition can't taste too good either."

"Don't worry about it, dude. Besides, Jamie's dad was more of a father to us than our own. Especially yours. Remember how you had to go to Jamie's house to get dressed for prom because you were wearing that hideous rainbow suit? I mean, your plan was brilliant, and we didn't have to beat anyone up for messing with Laurie, but it was still ugly as fuck."

"Yeah, you're right. Did I tell you I told Dad to die mad about us back in January? You should have seen how red his face got. So fucking perfect. Now, he might actually be dying."

"Not all superheroes wear capes, buddy. Oh hey, I got tickets to a St. Patrick's day burlesque slash speakeasy pop-up thing. You know, drinking, hot chicks, hot dude, drag shows. I could use the distraction and my stunt coordinator went last night and said it was fucking amazing. You guys should come."

"Yeah, we don't really do public events like that together. Too risky. At least until he retires."

"That's a long way off, man. But lucky for you, my co-star rented the place out, so there's no real public there. It's just us weirdo movie people and our friends. Come on, it will be fun." He nudges me in the ribs with an elbow and sings, "One word, big guy. Kilts."

"Okay, okay. I'll ask Lala."

"You two are good together."

"Slow your roll, bro. It's still early. I haven't had the chance to really fuck it up yet."

"Almost five months? That's a big deal and a change from the last, what, two years? Let's hope it stays that way. Now, get your horny ass off me and go put on some fucking pants!"

HOLLYWOOD
21
Ethan

CHAPTER 23
VAMPIRE

OLIVIA RODRIGO

CHASE INVITED us out for the night to some kind of party tonight, down off the strip. He swore to us that it was more of an industry thing and no one was even allowed cameras inside. It sounded fun, and after months of hiding, I even liked the idea of getting out for a bit with Steve and his friends. I'm hoping it ends up being the right time to invite Steve on a trip back home to meet my mom. And also to tell him that the trainer is suggesting I see a therapist. The muscle spasms have come back, but not as bad, and he thinks part of it could be stress. Maybe keeping Steve a secret is finally extracting its toll on me, but I'm not too worried about it. I may suggest he go too.

I want tonight to be fun, especially since Steve has more than earned a little playtime since we've been together. Chase ordered us a van and since it was all friends, Steve and I got to have a few moments of small PDA. The smile on his face every time we kissed was nothing shy of euphoric, and it had my butterflies in knots.

The place was more crowded than I had anticipated, and everywhere I looked were Hollywood A-listers, so I was a little start struck at first. I pointed people out to Steve and he'd tell me a story about how much of a dick they were to him or what they did at Chase's parties. He also told me which ones he'd enjoyed sleeping with the most. I think I kept my jealousy mostly inside. Mostly.

When the jealousy did rear up, Steve would remind me that I am also somewhat famous and I'm the only dick he's come back for seconds with. I guess that's supposed to be a compliment, but it's hard to focus on that when so many people are coming up and talking to Steve. Hell, one propositioned him right in front of me, and why shouldn't they? We're not together.

There are plenty of distractions though—Irish dancing, Highland games, and so much green beer people are going to piss green for a week. Steve's eating every second of it up with his Irish accent so horrible, he's got ancestors rolling over in graves right now. I told him to knock it off, but he's in his own little world and stoned out of his mind.

We lose Chase and have to hunt him down and pry this very drunk PA that used to work with him off his face. After that, we all decide we need a little break and head to an area where a variety show is taking place. We find a table just in time for the drag show to start, and it's fucking amazing. A few of the drag performers I'd seen before online or on different television shows, so it's next level to see them performing in person. I wish we were allowed phones in here so I could get pictures, but given the crowd, I can see why they banned the phones.

There are a ton of comedy acts and a few burlesque numbers sprinkled in between. One of the queens, Electra Stardust, does a burlesque dance that has Steve drooling. I'm pretty sure he's about to climb on top of the table and start wolf whistling, given the chance. We watched a couple of her videos online earlier when he found out she would be here, and I get it—she's beautiful. If I had the courage, I'd walk up after her show and thank her for the incredible blowjob I got earlier tonight. She doesn't need to hear about Steve and me watching her videos in bed together, though.

I could let stuff like that bother me, but I don't. Steve and I are different in a lot of ways, and who we find attractive is one of them. Besides, either way, he's going home with me tonight, and it won't be her nursing his hangover in the morning. Love is weird. So weird that I think tonight's the night I'm going to tell him I love him. That's why I want him to meet my mom and step-dad. I've even cleared it with Coach for a night off to handle some family stuff and then meet the team in Boston. I've got the whole thing planned as a surprise for my mom and I've been buzzing with nerves all damn night.

"You should talk to her!" I hear Chase say to Steve as each of them pop another edible. Neither one is capable of opening their eyes all the way at this point, so I'm not sure how they're even watching the show.

"I'm gonna go get another drink, and those two a couple of bottled waters. Anyone want anything?" I offer to the table.

"There's a waiter somewhere," Alexis says as she looks around and shrugs. "Okay, there was. Wanna hand?"

"Aww, you're leaving me?" Jamie whines as she climbs off his lap.

"Yeah, pretty boy. You're on babysitting duty for those two idiots."

He pulls her down and kisses her hard, telling her to hurry back. It's disgustingly cute. I look at Steve, tempted to do the same to him, but now isn't the time.

"So, is this your first night out on the town together?" Alexis asks as we get to the bar. I go to flag down the bartender, but he looks super busy, but we're in no hurry. He also looks familiar, but I can't place him.

"Yeah, sort of. We've gone to a few movies, a couple smaller restaurants, places where we can be seen without bringing up questions."

"I haven't known Steve for long. Shit, I've barely known him a year, but he's so different now than when I first met him. Jamie says this is more like how he used to be before everything in his life was turned upside down." She pats my arm assuringly. "He's still a pain in the ass, no pun intended, but at least he's not hooking up in bathrooms or whatever anymore. You guys are cute."

I like Jamie and Alexis. They're fun and open-minded people, but that's pretty normal for a couple of artists. They met and got married all in just a few months, but when you meet them, it makes sense. They're completely and madly in love with each other. Some days, I'm a bit jealous of what they have together.

"Oh, he still hooks up in bathrooms, but now it's with me instead of someone he just met."

"Hey, what can I get—Wait, I recognize you." The bartender says as he wiped down the section in front of us.

"You've probably been saying that a lot tonight with this crowd," I answer, shouting over the music.

"No...GOT IT! Goose! The Halloween party at Chase Cooper's place!" He grins and leans forward. "The one with the pretty eyes and the nice voice that disappeared on me half way through the night."

The memory flashes in my mind, but it's hazy. I remember a bartender, and looking at this guy, there's a solid chance my drunk ass might have hit on him a little. Or vice versa. So much happened that night and most of it has been reduced to a blur, but I do vaguely remember this guy.

"Bar by the pool?"

"Yeah, that was me!" He nods toward our table. "That big dude ever make up with his girlfriend?"

I laugh because I can't help it, but I also can't tell him that by the end of the night, the big dude was hooking up with me. Of course, now that I'm remembering that party, I remember hitting on this bartender. I think Steve might have even been a little jealous of him, too.

"Nah." I lean forward with a smile. "But she did drive her car through the front of his business that night."

"Ouch!"

"Yeah, it worked out, though. He's doing much better, and she got rehab out of it."

"Oh, see, a happy ending for everyone. How about you?"

"He," Lexi cuts in, draping her arm over me, "is sadly taken. Well, he's not sad about it. They're fucking brilliantly cute together."

"Well good! So you got your happy ending, too." He laughs and flings the towel over his shoulder. "So, what can I get the two of you?"

We order for the table, leave him a very good tip, and head back. Steve and Chase are still focused on the stage since Electra is up there again, and I doubt either of them even knows we left. I nudge Steve's leg under the table and slide a bottle of water in front of him and another in front of Chase. I don't get an acknowledgment, but they're having fun, so I leave it.

A few minutes later, Electra leaves the stage and I'm finishing off my drink, chatting with Jamie and Alexis about the split the last queen had done. There's a loud noise and the three of us all jerk our heads in that direction. I'm not sure what we expected, but all we find is Steve staring at me with fire in his eyes.

"What the fuck?!"

I glance around, expecting something bad like a fight or, hell, I wouldn't have been surprised to see Kennedy standing there. But it's just Steve, and it's me he's staring at. "What, the water? I figured you could stand a break from all the—"

"Are you fucking serious right now?"

"That I got you a water instead of a drink? Yeah, I asked and you—"

He looks over my shoulder at the bar and something I haven't seen takes over in Steve's eyes. A storm of fury and full-blown rage. "Him? You're chasing him?"

"Isn't that Marco? The bartender?" Chase asks. "Dude, he works like all my parties. Chill out."

"The party? That's what he fucking means, isn't it? That's what this is all about?" He's keeping his voice down for now, but people around us are keying into the tension as his anger boils over. "You fucked him first, didn't you?"

"You're drunk, Steve. I don't know—"

"You're preaching to me about not keeping secrets while you're fucking a prick like him behind my back? And you're just gonna flaunt it in my face?" He's a fire-breathing dragon and I'm a deer trapped against a cliff side. "Go on, *Lala*, go back behind the bar and suck his dick while I'm not looking, then tell me not to step out on your high and mighty ass."

"Steve, calm down. None of that is happening." Jamie tries, but Steve's rage has overtaken him. He goes to put a hand on Steve's shoulder, but Steve pushes him away.

"No, I want a fucking answer." He grabs the napkin that was under my drink and holds it up.

Looking for a new Maverick to your Goose? 310-555-1718

"How long, Ethan? How long have you two been fucking behind my back? Have you been fucking him since the god damn party?" Now his voice is raised, and other tables start to notice something is going on.

"Woah! Woah!" Chase holds his hands out. "Bro, he's not—"

"Shut up, Coop! Answer me, Ethan!"

"I didn't even know he wrote that, Steve. Why would he give me his number if I'm fucking him, you idiot?"

"I'm only an idiot for believing you'd be any fucking different."

Without another word, Steve gets up and storms off to the bar. Chase goes after him with Jamie following close behind to make sure he doesn't do anything stupid. Meanwhile, I just sit there staring at the napkin that Steve slammed down and left on the table. Devin and Dani stumble back from one of the other rooms, their smiles and giggles fading as they read the room. Alexis tells them what happened, but it doesn't seem real. Devin is talking to me, trying to get me to answer him, but I can't focus on the words. They're just garbled noises.

Jamie comes back a few minutes later, alone. He assures me Steve is just drunk and high and being stupid, but that's not what's happening. I'm pretty sure I know what's happening and there might not be anything I can do about it.

"He bit the poor guy's head off. I feel bad for him, really." Jamie explains to Lexi. "He recognized Ethan from the party, Steve, too. How was the poor kid supposed to know they were together?" Jamie takes his seat, but his eyes stay on me and I only see one thing. Pity. Even he knows this isn't good.

"Where is he?" I'm doing everything I can to fight the panic creeping into my vision and choking my airway. "I should talk to him."

"He and Coop took a walk. It'll be okay, Ethan. He's just being stupid."

"If they're not back soon, we'll head back to the bus and meet them there. It might be time to call it a night." Dani recommends as she drops Devin's hand and looks around, worried.

My stomach churns, and I'm pretty sure I'm about to throw up. I grab Steve's water and drink half the bottle, trying to keep everything in my stomach where it belongs, but it doesn't help. I need to get out of here, but there are four people at the table who will stop me, and I don't have a car.

"Yeah. Uhm, I'm gonna go hit the head." It's the easiest way to get out of here without any of them trying to get me to stay or following me. I can make it to the restroom, puke my brains out, get my phone back, call a cab, and head home. I think we already caused enough of a scene out here, and I don't want any trouble for us or for Chase and his friends. Not when I'm the cause of it. Steve can sleep it off on the sofa and we'll talk through this in the morning.

I hope.

The bathroom is dark and there's fake graffiti covering the walls with cheesy St. Paddy's day messages and dirty limericks. I'm glad it isn't February. I don't think I could handle graffiti walls telling me they love me when my boyfriend and I haven't even said it yet. After tonight, there's a chance we never will. I splash water on my face and stare at the reflection. Even through all the tragedy I've dealt with, I don't think I've ever seen myself this terrified before.

"What the hell do I do, Kota? I'm so fucked, aren't I?"

I duck down a back hall that leads to the outside alleyway, hidden from the party. I've got my hands in my pockets and my head down, not wanting to disturb the homeless guy sleeping up ahead, or the couple making out against the wall. I can't get it out of my mind that this is worse than the arguments we've had before. Then comes the thought that Steve's been looking for a way out and tonight, he found one.

He's told me this is what he'll do. He's warned me about the sabotage and how he sets fire to relationships just so he can get out of them faster. How he panics and runs to the nearest warm body. I told him I wouldn't blame him if that happened. I told him we'd get through it.

But what if he doesn't want to come back? We can't go out, and if we do, we can't act like we're going out. I expected too much from him and I should have known better. Now, he's found an exit, and he's running for it as fast as he can. I don't think I can blame him for that.

There's a moan from the couple, and my stomach lurches. What if I'm right? What if this was it? What if—

"I thought you said your boyfriend was here?"

"Shh, just let me make you feel good, baby."

I stop and look over my shoulder, even though I don't want to. Twenty more feet and I would have been around the corner and I wouldn't have heard them. Twenty more feet and my blood wouldn't be rushing so fast I can hear it. Twenty more fucking feet and I could have held on to the tiny string of hope that just snapped in half. I know what I'm going to see. I think I knew before I even walked by them.

He's pinned her chest against the wall and has her skirt hiked up. If they're not in the middle of fucking, they're about to be. I don't say a word, just take off the watch he gave me and throw it at his feet.

"Dude, who the fu—" He stares down at the watch. I'm not sure what I expect from him—an apology, probably some fucked up sarcastic bullshit. But when he looks up, and that anger is still in his eyes, it reminds me of my father and I want to throw up again. I want to run away, like I couldn't do as a child. Instead, I just stand there, tears in my eyes.

"You know him?" The girl says. Except she's not just a girl, she's from the drag show. Electra Stardust.

"Yeah. Yeah, I know him. He's my cheating boyfriend. Probably fucks every guy he can when he leaves on his fucking road trips. Do you know who he is, baby? He's fucking famous."

"From, like a movie?" She slurs, high on something or drunk out of her mind. Maybe both.

"No, baby, that is Ethan LaVoie. Star player for the Parrots. For five months, I've been so damn good to him. I haven't even looked at anyone else. You know, earlier tonight, I sucked his cock while I was thinking about you. Guess this was fate, huh?" He spins her around and holds her in front of him. She can barely stand, but he isn't much better. "You wanna fuck him, baby? Come on, Electra, he'll get on his knees for you and tell you he's yours."

"Y-you didn't, did you? You didn't picture her earlier." I ask, my voice cracking under the pressure. This is revenge for the women I slept with while pretending I was with a man so I could get off. Just so I could pass as normal. "Please, Steve."

"You fucked him!"

"No, I didn't."

"Bullshit, Ethan! Why don't you get on your knees and suck her dick like you suck Marco's?"

"I didn't sign up for a menage, baby," Electra slurs, but he doesn't listen to her.

"Fuck you, Ethan. Fuck your stupid rules and your *oh but my career* bullshit. You never cared about me. You never care about what I wanted or what I needed."

"Oh, cause you never fucking once looked at a woman right in front of me? Never once hit on them right in front of my face when you knew I couldn't be what you wanted? Is that it, Steve? Was all of this a fucking joke, just like your fucking father thought it was?"

"How many times did you cheat on me, Ethan? How many guys did you fuck when you went out with the team? Is that why Girard came to the house? Are you two fucking on those long, lonely road trips?"

I suddenly lose the will to fight him. I turn my back on him and I hear Chase and Jamie running down the alleyway, trying to figure out what's going on as I round the corner. I don't stop at the bus. I don't even stop at the cabs that are lined up and down Sunset, waiting to catch a fare. I just keep walking, not even caring where I'm going or where I'll end up. I'm not sure how long I've been walking since I have no watch and no phone, but I find a metro station and head down the stairs. I have a TAP card in my wallet, not that the train will get me closer to home, but it gives me somewhere to hide for a few hours.

I find a spot in the back and stare out the dirty window as Los Angeles passes by as an unrecognizable blur. The last five months play on repeat in my mind as I ride. Destination? Anywhere but here.

He never wanted me. It was all a sick fucking joke. He'll probably out me now. Everything is over. Everything.

I can tell it's late when a new announcement plays telling me this is the last train of the night, so I take it to end one more time. It's strange to see Los Angeles at night. People think the party never stops when it comes to Hollywood. But the tourists go back to their hotels and the homeless people shuffle back to their encampments. Parties move off into the hills or out into the valley. The only thing to keep me company are the lights that still dance on the wet streets. I guess it rained while I was in the tunnel. I look up at a marquis and realize I'm in front of the El

Capitan theater, and if Hollywood Boulevard is this dead, it has to be after two. I should be tired. The way I was sitting on the train for so long, I should be sore as hell. But all I am is numb. I turn in the direction that will take me to Chase's so I can get my things. All I want now is to go home, but I don't even have one anymore.

HOLLYWOOD
Steve

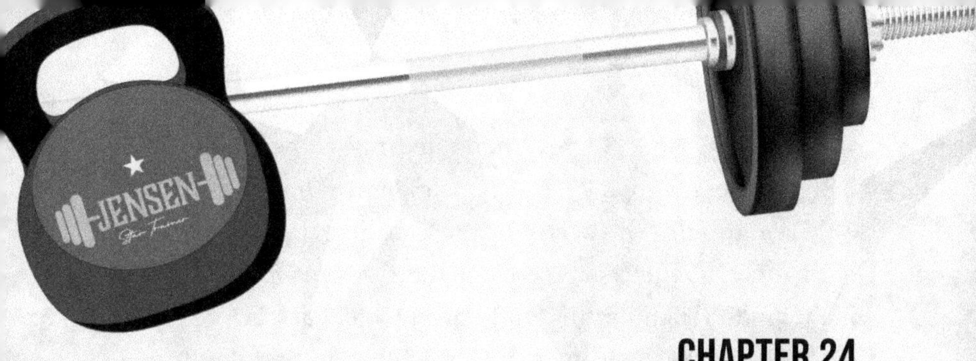

CHAPTER 24
ALIBI

ELLA HENDERSON (FEAT. RUDIMENTAL)

I'M ABOUT to run after Ethan when two strong hands grab me and slam me into the wall. I'm ready to fight anyone I can get my hands on. I don't give a fuck who has a hold of me right now —they're going down. Suddenly, Electra screams and I see my best friend for a split second before my fist connects with his face.

This is not good.

"Son of a bitch!" Coop yells as he and Jamie pin my arms to the wall in case I try to swing again. "You fucking dickhead! You punched me! In the damn face! I left you alone for two fucking seconds and you're trying to break my god damn nose?"

"What happened, Steve? Where's Lala goi—" Jamie turns to search the area and that's when he makes eye contact with Electra. "Jesus. Are you fucking kidding me right now, Steve?"

"Hey." Electra holds her hands up and starts backing away as she explains. "I don't know him. I met him backstage. He came onto me, asked me if I wanted to get high and fuck. That's it. If you guys wanna fuck him up, that's your deal, but leave me out of it."

"The guy that just left. What happened?"

"Fuck off, Jamie!" I yell, then I find myself begging. "Electra, baby, please. It's cool. It's just a misunderstanding."

"The guy threw a watch at muscles here, and they yelled at each other about cheating. Something about sports. I dunno, man. I'm too high for this, and I need to get back before my next set." She picks her purse up from the ground, pulls out a cigarette, and lights it. The action reminds me of Laurie and now all I can think about is how much she's going to hate me for being a fucking idiot.

What the fuck have I done?

"I fucked up, Coop," I say to Coop as he checks his face again to make sure he's not bleeding. "I fucked up, bad. I did exactly what you said not to do."

"Punch me in the fucking face?"

"No, I...Ethan saw us!" I can't breathe, hyperventilating, as I search around in a panic.

"Wait, he saw you with the drag queen?" Coop grabs me by the shoulders when I don't answer and my eyes meet his. He has to hold me against the wall to keep me from collapsing into a heap of sobs on the ground.

"I'm gonna go try to find Lala," Jamie says before the first sob wracks my entire body.

"Oh fuck, Coop. Coop, I fucked up so bad."

Jamie comes running back a few minutes later, but no one is with him. "I'm gonna go get everyone. I don't know where he went and the bus driver said he hadn't seen him. He's got no phone and no car."

The bus ride to the event was loud and echoed with laughter and happiness. The ride back to Coop's is silent and serious. It's all my fault. Jamie and Devin stayed behind to walk the area around the club and see if they could find Ethan. Coop told Alexis he's taking me home, getting his car, and he's going to drive around and try to find him. None of them will even look at me, and every time I glance up at Coop, I only see the ice pack he's holding to his cheek.

I was sure I'd hit rock bottom when Skylar walked out on me. That's what forced me to drag myself out of bed and start over. I built giant walls, stopped caring about people's feelings, and moved on because I believed that would keep me safe from slipping. I was wrong. Hello, rock bottom. We meet again.

"No, he has his wallet. So at least he has money on him." Alexis whispers to Dani. "I should tell Jamie to check the metro. He could have walked up to the rail line or caught a bus."

"Shit, that means he could be anywhere. The rail is a hell of a walk, but I guess it's possible." Dani says—she's never learned to whisper. "Not a great place to be tonight, with all the drunk assholes getting wasted. Higher chances he gets mugged. But he's not a woman, and he's short, but feisty. Like my sister."

"Don't talk like that, Dani. He's gonna be fine. He's a fucking pro athlete." Coop answers with a little more bite than his usual style. "You two should lay off the crime dramas. And he's not that short."

"I mean, not as short as my sister, but he's not as tall as you and Devin. Then again, you guys are kind of giant, and so is Xander. I just hang out with a lot of tall men." It's like she can't stop talking, but I don't mind since the silence is deafening. "Tall guys are cool though, and I mean… Fuck. Devin and I made out in the bathroom."

"Jesus fucking Christ, are you serious?" Chase tries to keep his voice down, but fails. "What the hell was in the drinks tonight?"

"It might have been more than make out."

"Okay, that's…for another time. Does Ethan know anywhere around here? Have any friends that he would go to?" Alexis asks. I don't hear an answer, so I assume Coop either nodded or shook his head. I couldn't even answer that question. Some boyfriend I am—was. "Well, I'll stay at the house in case he comes back. I'll text you guys as soon as he does, so you can stop looking."

"Do you think he'd walk it?" Dani asks "Like, all the way back to the house?"

"It's over two hours to walk from here. It has to be. He's in shape, though, so he could do that pretty easily." Coop replies. After that, they all go silent again. Probably imagining the same thing I am. LA isn't the safest place on a normal night, let alone a drunken holiday weekend. There are good streets, and there are bad streets, like anywhere else, but there's a lot of robbery. He's a good looking, young white kid that's out randomly walking the streets of LA alone.

I should be out there looking for him. I should be out there begging him to take me back. I glance down at his phone, turning the screen on. No missed calls or texts. No notifications at all. I enter his code and find a picture I didn't even notice him taking. It's from the beach, from where I wrote our initials on the window of my car after we fogged the windows up. The picture only shows part of our initials and the beach through the window, but I recognize it all.

What the fuck have I done?

A siren screams past us, heading in the opposite direction, and the lump in my throat nearly chokes me. When we get to the house, Coop has to grab my arm and pull me off the bus because I'm not even on autopilot anymore. I've shut down to a level so low, I'm unaware of what's going on around me. As the bus pulls away, I jerk my arm free and run to the sidewalk, throwing up in the grass. I keep my head down, watching Coop's shoes come closer.

"Hey, buddy, let's get you inside. I'll call Laurie and have her come get you."

"No. No, I need to stay. Please, let me stay. I just want to know he's okay."

"I mean, he's not. I'll text when he's back, and I'll check in on you tomorrow morning." Coop's never been one to skirt the issues or coddle me. No matter how shitty I feel, if I deserve it, he'll make sure I stay shitty until I've learned my lesson.

"Please?"

"Alright. I'll put you in my room on one condition. When he gets home, you leave him the fuck alone. Got it? So help me, I will deck your bitch ass if you so much as glance at him tonight. You need to sober the fuck up and give him space. Got it?"

"I think I'm already working on that."

"If you puke in my room, I will disown you for at least a month."

I haven't even bothered to lie down and try to sleep this off because that will be pointless. I've been sitting on the floor next to Coop's bed with Lulu curled up next to me for the last three hours watching the clock. Watching every single minute tick by. I didn't know I could hate myself anymore than I already did, but now I've learned that I can. I'm learning all kinds of new limits I wasn't aware of tonight. There's a soft knock on the door and Alexis comes in, sitting on the floor next to me and taking my hand.

"Xander picked up Dani to drive around looking for him. He'll be okay."

"No. He won't. Physically, sure, but I ripped his heart out, lit it on fire, and tossed it in the trash."

"I mean, making out with a smoking hot drag queen when you're blazed out of your mind might be forgivable on some levels. I'm guessing you said shit you can't take back?"

"So much shit I can't take back. If Jamie ever said that shit to you—screamed at you and accused you of cheating—would you even want to go back to him?"

"Well, there'd be a lot of factors I'd have to consider. But I'm not gonna lie to you. If he screamed at me and said I was cheating after I caught him up against a wall with a hot as fuck drag queen? I'm not sure there's enough therapy in the world to get me over that. But that's probably because Jamie isn't gay, so that's a whole level to unpack in itself and some seriously deep-seated issues that…aren't at all what you're asking me about."

"Fuck me, this isn't helping."

"Sorry, I'm not super good at this. I'd forgive him if he was bi and hooking up with her, I think. If that helps you feel any better?"

"My dad hates me for being gay. He hates that Laurie is trans. He hates us so much, but right now, I hate myself more than even he hates me. I hate myself more than I hate my fucking dad."

"Oh, I understand that feeling! Well, he was my stepdad, but I sure as fuck hated him. Hated myself for a while there, too. You guys got me out of that—Jamie, Chase, and you. It's possible that right now, hating yourself is a good thing? That sounds fucked up, but it means you understand how big of a mistake you made. He might forgive you when he sees that."

There's a flicker of headlights coming into the driveway and Alexis pops up from the floor to check out the window. I count the doors as they shut. One. Two. Three. Four. Five. Coop, Jamie,

Devin, Dani, and Xander. I hold my breath for a sixth door, but it doesn't come and Alexis shakes her head to confirm it.

"Go get some sleep, Lexi," Jamie whispers to his wife, and I understand what Coop was saying months ago. I do envy them, but I'm only admitting it to myself now. I envy how perfect they are, even though they're anything but. I envy that they beat the odds and didn't give up on each other. I gave up based on a rumor my own head started and didn't waste a fucking minute going back to my old ways.

Jamie walks over to the front window, glancing outside, then looks back at Coop.

"Hey, why don't you go upstairs and get some sleep," Coop says to me as I lean against the wall, staring at the front door, willing it to open. I don't move. "Steve, if he comes in the door and you're standing here like a kicked guard dog, he's gonna shut the door and walk right the fuck back out. Go upstairs."

"Is he…is he out there now?"

"Don't do this, Steve," Jamie chimes in. "Go upstairs with Lexi and get some sleep."

"After what I did, you trust me with your Alexis?"

"You already know that if you touch my wife, I'll rip your dick off. Stop being an asshole and go upstairs."

I push off the wall and walk to the window, but I don't see a damn thing out there. I'm just about to turn away when I see something move by the road. It's probably a coyote or a bear. Great, now I have that to worry about.

"Come on, Steve. Leave him alone."

I turn to Coop and stare at him for the first time since this all happened. "I'm gonna go outside and sit on the stairs. I'm sorry I punched you in the face. I don't know what the fuck got into me or why I'm like this. I don't know what to do, but I don't want to leave him alone out there."

"Stay here." Alexis offers. "I'll go take him a blanket and some water, see if I can talk him into coming inside. If not, I'll sit with him so he's not alone, and he's not with one of you testosterone and booze filled dickheads. I don't mean you, Jamie."

"I can—"

"No, Steve. You can't." Chase holds me back. "Go upstairs and sit in purgatory until he has time to decide what he wants. You can't force this."

"Give him space and time, Steve." Alexis says as Jamie hands her a blanket and heads for the door. "With space and time, he just might miss you enough to know you didn't mean it."

"What if I did?"

"Baby steps, sweetie. For both of you."

I've been staring at the ceiling of the loft for an eternity, even though the clock is telling me it's only been an hour. I hear shuffling downstairs, then Chase coming up to his room and shutting the door. I can't sleep, but I also can't move, frozen in a cage of fear that I made.

My mind is cruel and spiteful, making me imagine things that aren't there. Footsteps softly climbing the stairs and breathing that sounds so familiar from all the night I've fallen asleep to its sound. The sniffle and shuffle of a blanket are so real sounding, I almost glance up.

"I—I'm leaving for Boston tomorrow."

I'm too scared to sit up.

"Dani is going to get your stuff out of our...my room while I'm gone and pack up my things for me."

I finally sit up and look at him, but he's not looking at me. His face is streaked with tears and I've never seen him so pale, but I can't think of a damn thing to say that will make this better.

"Give her the necklace back, please." He turns to leave and I jump up, standing there and staring at him. "Don't. Just...don't."

With that, he disappears down the stairs and I run into Chase's room, throwing up in the bathroom while I sob.

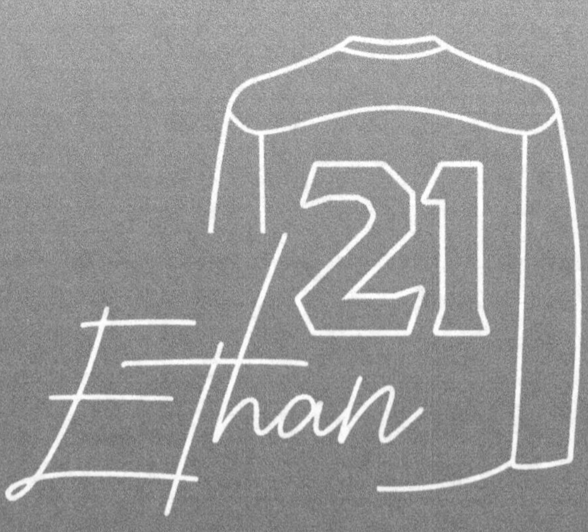

HOLLYWOOD
21
Ethan

CHAPTER 25
BLK CLD

XYLØ

I'VE BEEN STANDING outside the door for at least forty-five minutes, but I haven't knocked yet. I'm scared to knock because as much as I want the advice and understanding right now, I don't want the lecture or the *I told you so* looks she's about to give me. I end up not having to knock because Charlie opens it with a bag full of trash and a shocked look on his face when he sees me.

"Ethan? What are you doing here? Is everything okay?" He drops the bag, not caring if it rips open, and grabs my arms, checking me for head injuries, I guess. "Christ, you're freezing!"

"Is…is Mom home?"

"Yeah. Yeah, she's in the living room. She was about to turn the game on. Ethan, what are you doing here? Get inside, son!" He shoves me in the door to the kitchen and quickly closes it behind me.

The warmth inside has me realizing just how cold it is outside. I guess I'm lucky I didn't get frostbite standing out there. The kitchen smells delicious, which reminds me I haven't eaten all day. I can't keep much of anything down lately, but considering my depression diet has been candy, donuts, and sugary cereal, it's not surprising. A black and white cat hops down from his perch on top of the fridge and circles my feet twice before rubbing against me. "Hey Bax, how are you doing, old man?"

"Charlie, did you feed Baxter?" Mom asks as she comes into the kitchen. Her head down, sorting through the day's mail, so she doesn't see me at first. "I need to give him his med— ETHAN!" She jumps, dropping the mail on the floor before she runs over. In a flurry, she brushes the snow off my jacket and grabs my face.

"Hi, Mom."

"Baby, your lips are blue, how long were you out there?! Get in here, we've got the fireplace going and the game—Ethan, why aren't you at the game?"

"I, uhm, I got a night off. I asked Coach, and he said yes, so I was… I was…I was gonna bring—" my voice cracks and the tears start again. I can't hold any of this in anymore. She hugs me close and rocks me back and forth, rubbing my back and whispering words that should be comforting, but I can't even hear them over the sobs. "I—I fucked up. Steve fucked up. It's… I think it's my fault, mom. I don't… I don't know what to do."

She leads me into the living room, sitting me down on the couch and pulls off my wet coat and sweater. She grabs the biggest knit blanket she has and wraps me up like a burrito or something. Crouching in front of me, she cups my face every few minutes, making sure I'm warming up while I stare blindly into the carpet. It's the first time I've been able to break down since it happened, the first time I've allowed myself to let it out, because I didn't trust myself around anyone else. There's no one I trust to be vulnerable with when I'm in California, but then again, hockey players aren't raised to be vulnerable. We're supposed to be rugged and rough. We're supposed to be these strong, otherworldly superheroes, like from Chase's movies. We're just fucking humans.

Charlie brings out a pot of tea, saying it will help me relax and warm up from the inside. I stare into the cup for the longest time before my mom puts her hands on my legs and I meet her eyes. They're green, like mine. Dakota and I were the only two to get the green eyes, while everyone else got Dad's blue eyes. She's wearing my jersey, and when I look over at Charlie, so is he.

"I should be able to handle this on my own like a fucking adult, but—"

"Did you and Steve split up?" Charlie asks, pity and softness in his voice. I nod, then I shrug, because I'm still not sure exactly what happened. It all happened so fast.

"Oh Lala, sweetheart, I'm so sorry. It's no wonder you're a mess. You didn't go through this when you were younger, like most people do. Your father never let you, so of course you don't know how to handle it. How would you? God, I wish I could have taken you two with me when I left. My sweet, sensitive angels." She rests her hand on my cheek, trying to assure me that everything will be okay.

I tell them about Steve and about how close I was to saying those three little words to him. I tell them about how I planned this trip weeks ago to be the one I introduced Steve to the family. Then I tell them about the fight, leaving out some of the details they don't need to hear—like finding Steve with Electra. Every word makes me hurt more and feel shittier—reliving that night over. The more I talk, the more walls I put back up, this time with a sturdier foundation. I can't risk letting anyone in again.

"Ethan, you're barely twenty-six, and you've had more pain in your life than most people. You've lost three siblings and went through a horribly painful childhood emotionally and physically. I blame myself for that."

"No, mom, you tried. Dad wouldn't let you take us, and he would have run you through the mud, or worse."

"I could have fought harder, but I had hoped that with Aaron's career, your father would be too busy to come down on you kids. There was a good chance your sister would take care of you, since she always did, even when you were born. When you lost her, you lost your best friend, and you never had the chance to grieve for her—or your brothers." My mom is crying now, which has my tears falling again, too. "Your father made you think the only thing in this world worth a damn was hockey. You're talented, Ethan, and I'm so proud of how far you've gone and how hard you've fought, but there's so much more to life."

"You told me, mom. You told me what would happen and I… I didn't believe you. Or I didn't listen. I don't know. It's my fault, though. I made him hide who we were and he…he…"

"Ethan," Charlie says softly as he sits next to me. "At your age, I was still working at a grocery market, trying to figure out what life was all about. I didn't have four years of professional anything under my belt or as many zeros in my checks as you've seen. Anyway, there was a girl that used to come into the store every day. I had such a crush on her, and one day, I worked up the nerve and asked her out. She turned me down."

"Good thing, too. Otherwise, you would have never met me." My mom smiles, trying to lighten the mood.

"That's true, but first I locked myself in my flat for a week, convinced the world was over and I'd never find anyone who'd take me." Charlie hands me a box of tissues. "What I'm trying to say is, Ethan, at your age, everything feels a thousand times stronger than it really is because everything is so damn new. Like your mother said, you should have had your first breakup when you were a teenager, but your shyte father never let you live life outside of a damned hockey rink. He shuttered you in and stunted your emotions. He treated you like a machine, not a child that needed to explore and experience the world."

"Great," I mumble. "So I'm over-reacting. Just like I figured."

"No, dear, you're finally letting some of those bottled up feelings come out. Come on, I'll get you some dinner, make up the bed, and tomorrow, we're going to go see a friend of mine. Someone I've wanted to introduce you to for a while now, but was too afraid to."

"Who?"

"Don't worry about that. How does a big bowl of Yankee Pot Roast sound?"

My stomach grumbles, begging for food, but all I can think about is making that for Steve. "I'll pass. I can sleep on the couch so you don't have to—"

"You will do no such thing. Come on, I'll make you some toast and draw you a hot bath so you can warm up at the very least. We got heaters installed last year—they're absolutely brilliant."

The tub reminds me a little of Chase's hot tub, but without the bubbles and the amazing view. It's weird wondering if I'll ever go back there again, but the odds are high considering every time I open the app to find a place of my own, I get frustrated and break down crying. I understand what my mom was trying to tell me earlier, and it helped put some things into perspective. I was mad at myself because it was only five months, and I shouldn't be this broken up about it. But for someone like me, someone whose longest relationship gets counted in days and weeks, not months, being with someone for five months was like being with them for five years.

The part I'm struggling with most is Steve didn't fight. He wanted to fight that night, in that he wanted to punch me in the face rather than talk about it and use his fucking brain. But after, when I told him I was leaving, he just...let me go. Not a word. That's eating at me the hardest. If he'd done that, if he'd tried, I could forgive him. Not instant forgiveness. He'd have to work his ass off to make it up to me and we'd need to have a real talk about therapy. Although, I can't even pick up the phone and call a therapist, so I'm not sure how that would have gone, anyhow.

But did I fight? Did I give up on us, too? Sitting here and replaying our time in my mind, maybe he didn't fight because I wasn't fighting for us either. I told my mom Steve was worth fighting for and worth the risk, but when the time came, maybe I didn't do enough, either. I knew who he was going into the relationship, and there's a chance I held him back too much.

I reach over and pick my phone up off the stack of towels my mom left me, hoping I can check scores and stop dwelling on Steve for at least a few minutes. It's the first time in three days I've turned it on, and as soon as it gets a signal, a message comes through from early yesterday when I was at the hotel.

CHASE

Hey kid, Dani is here packing up your stuff, but I want you to know you don't have to leave. Dev and I will work out at the gym so you have your space, and he who I will not name won't be over when you're home. Hang in there. I'm here if you need to talk.

I stare at the message, a weird feeling in my gut that I can't place gets stronger as I read it again. Before I can read it a third time, more messages buzz in and I damn near drop the phone in the water.

Buzz.

ALEXIS

Hey kiddo, Jamie and I just finished building the bed in our spare room. Let us know if you want to come crash here for a few days. It's not as fancy, but we're closer to work and I promise I won't try to cook.

Buzz.

ALEXIS

Hey, we went to see you this morning, but Dev said you're in Boston?! You're coming back, right? We miss you. Jamie and I have been through some pretty rough shit, and if you ever need a shoulder to cry on, or just someone to talk to, we're here. You're part of the family now, even if we are a little dysfunctional at times.

Buzz.

DEVIN

Bro, this fucking rookie keeps trying to sit next to me. In your spot. NOT COOL.

Buzz.

JAMIE

Why didn't I have your number? Hey, don't worry about Steve, we'll take care of him. We're also here for you, too. I'll even go punch Steve in the face if you need me to. Call any of us if you need anything.

Buzz.

> **DEVIN**
>
> Fuck, now he's saying he's gonna sit next to me on the plane so we can watch a movie he thinks I've never seen because he hasn't figured out I'm related to Chase.

Buzz.

> **DEVIN**
>
> If you don't come back soon, I'm moving him into the other guest bedroom, so you have to deal with him when you come back.

It doesn't take a genius to decipher that's Devin's way of saying he misses me—on ice and off. I haven't exactly been up for hanging out lately, so he and I haven't talked outside of practice.

Buzz.

> **DEVIN**
>
> Uhm, when you're in a better headspace, can I talk to you about something? About Dani? I think I made out with her the other night and I don't remember, and now she's pissed off at me. Hit me up, bro.

I'm about to shut the phone off when it buzzes one more time, this time with a different notification.

> 1 New Voicemail from: Pumpkin Spice

I gave Steve that nickname on my phone so no one would realize who it was. Also because he wouldn't stop singing fucking Spice Girls songs in the gym one day while drinking down like three pumpkin spice lattes. I want to laugh at the memory, then remember him yelling at me. I take a deep breath, close my eyes, and hit play.

"Sorry I called you ten times before leaving a message," his voice is softer than I've ever heard it, all his wit and cockiness gone. *"I know I have no right to ask this, but, uhm, can we talk? Before you hang up and ignore the rest of this, I made an appointment with a psychiatrist in a few days so I can try to get my shit together. I know they aren't miracle workers, and it would take a miracle to fix me, but I'm... I'm trying. I know I fucked up, but, well, you told me that there was a chance you'd forgive me if that happened. I'm really hoping you'll give me that chance if you're ever ready. Good luck in your game tomorrow night, Sweets. Don't let me and my dumb ass hold you back. You're an amazing player. And you're an even better person."*

"MOTHERFUCKAHHH!" Devin screams as he runs down the hall, clomping like a horse in his skates. He slams into me and lifts me into the air before spinning me around. "Fuck, I missed you, asshole!"

"Dude, I was gone for one game. Put me down."

"Correction, you were gone for one game and three practices! This damn new kid is like a tick, and I can't burn the fucker off of my ass!"

"Great visual. Thanks for that. Here, it's from mom." I hand him a box and he shakes it as his eyes grow wide. "They were in Canada last week and picked these up for you."

"I love your mom so fucking much! If she wasn't married, I'd totally propose to her. She's here, right?"

"Sort of. They dropped me off and they'll be back later for the game. Like always. Don't eat all of those before we hit the ice.

You're already hopped up like a jack rabbit and you'll puke on the bench."

"Dude, do not stand between a Canadian and their maple sugar candies! Come on, I need to finish getting dressed."

"I got your messages." I say as we walk toward the guest team locker room. "I didn't see them till last night. You and Dani?"

"Uh, yeah. Apparently, we didn't just make out. It's…weird between us right now." He rips the wrapping off the box and shoves it into his pants, since he has no pockets. "I guess we were pretty wasted that night. I thought she was messing with me, but she's not. She's serious."

"Okay." I hold open the door to the locker room as he shovels three candies into his mouth and his eyes roll back. "So what's the issue? Xander?"

"Well, yeah, he's one, but he's not *the* issue. I'm freaking out." He drops down hard onto the bench and makes sure no one is listening. "We fucked in a bathroom, dude. What if she's you know…what if I got her…"

"Oh. OH!" Sometimes the idea of pregnancy is fully foreign to me, since I've never actually had to worry about it. It's one of the perks of being gay, no surprise pregnancies.

Remind me not to leave you alone with our kids and skates.

Great, now there's a chance that on the worst night of my life, my best friend knocked up one of his friends and my mind is playing back a conversation Steve and I had about kids. We'd talked about it, about adopting sometime after I retire. I've got a bad back, so the chances that I'll be playing in my forties are slim. Yet another way he was willing to be there for me, to wait for me. I have to decide soon if I can risk my career for this, for him. Because if I try this again, we can't stay a secret.

"Okay, Dev. Let's get through this road trip, and we'll figure it out when we get back home, okay?"

"She's telling Xander about it tonight, since Chase and I aren't home. You know, just in case he loses his shit and wants to come beat someone's ass for banging his girl."

"What happened to the open relationship triangle thing?"

"Dani and Xander are stupid complicated. They always have been." He waits, but I can sense he's still staring at me. "Uhm, so what are you gonna do about Steve?"

"I don't know. I had a talk with a therapist today, one my mom knows. I've got a lot to think about, a lot of decisions I need to figure out before I even tackle what's going to happen with Steve and I."

"Is there a chance?"

"That's a damn good question, Hollywood. I don't have the answer yet."

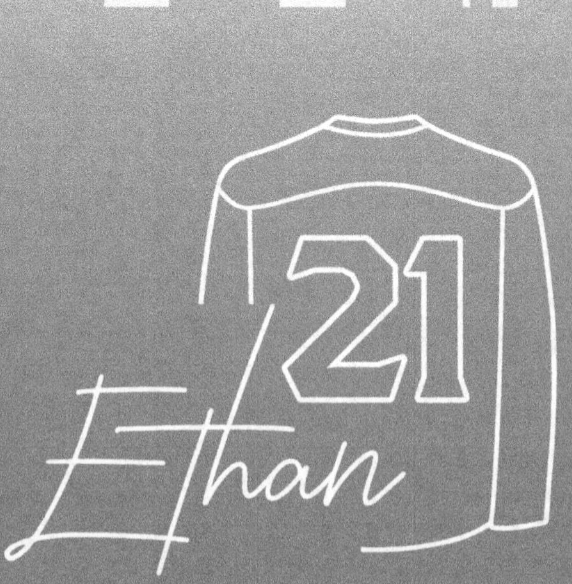

HOLLYWOOD
21
Ethan

I'M NOT OK

H.E.R.

THE SHOWER WATER TASTES SALTY. It's how I can tell I'm still crying, even though I'm numb. A grown ass man crying in his fucking shower is perfectly healthy and normal. Or that's what the shrink told me the other day.

She also reminded me that I had every red flag waved in my face like it was ten car pile up at the Daytona 500—and I tried to drive right through it. The hardest part isn't the way it happened or how it ended, it's that it ended at all. It's been two weeks of a wild roller coaster ride, but that night is as fresh as if it happened yesterday. I only have one step left, and it's a big one. I'm not ready for that step yet because I'm scared, so I'm doing everything I can to blow it off or blow my life up.

"Lala?" For a second I think it's Steve and my heart slams into my chest so hard it hurts. "Hey, you gonna be ready in ten?"

Devin. I'm hit with both relief and sadness. I'm too into my emotions right now, and that's not going to work with the game in a few hours. "No. I'll drive myself. Sorry, man."

"No worries. See you at the rink."

I check the time. I have less than four hours to get my shit together and play this game. This is a big one, a game we can't afford to lose if we want to go to the playoffs. Vegas is becoming a rival, and the blood is already bad, so I have to watch my back, too. They'll take runs at me because they'll know about my past and my injury. Some people call hockey a gentleman's game, but that's bullshit and the genuine fans know it. We're a bunch of fucking sharks out there waiting to smell the blood in the water. We're vicious, the hits are brutal, and the fights are real. Being too far in my head could get me or a teammate injured. It could leave Devin open to hits and bad goals, and I can't have that on my watch.

I shake the water out of my hair and straighten up. The tweak in my back is finally gone, so the hot water must have helped. I towel off, fix my hair, and grab my things. Out of habit, I reach for my watch, stopping myself and shaking my head.

"Get your shit together, LaVoie."

"I missed you, girl. Don't worry, I'm coming back tonight. Your dad and your uncle threatened me, so I'm not going anywhere for a while." She wags the short nub of a tail she has, which is more like wiggling her whole butt. It makes me crack a smile, which is the first step to getting out of my head.

The drive to the rink is a blur of boredom and traffic, and it takes longer than normal. This is why Devin likes to leave earlier. He understands Los Angeles traffic better than I do, but now that I have a car again, it's nice to go through my own pre-game rituals. Someday, I'll bring the playlists back, but I'm not there yet. The shrink said to take my time, so I'm trying.

I'm the last player there and most of the guys are in the locker room dicking around before Coach comes in and gives us our pep talk. My locker is next to Devin's, but I don't see him around anywhere. That's unusual for him since he has about two full hours worth of rituals to go through that involve everything just shy of calling in a priest to bless his gear. I have no doubt in my mind that he would, though, if he thought it would help his game.

I go through my dressing rituals—we all have them—and when I'm done, I sit on the bench with my head in my hands. As I sit there, I try willing the right part of me to be trapped under the ice tonight. I've been playing on autopilot since St. Patrick's weekend, and my stats have been suffering enough to bother me. Coach claims it's a slump, but in the back of my mind, I think he's figured out what happened. I shake my head and focus again. I need the player to come out. I need the sad, gay puppy to go the fuck away. I'm terrified the opposite is what's going to happen. Something heavy crashes down on the bench next to me and I recognize Devin's pre-game mumbling, so I don't bother to look up.

"I, uhm, Chase told me about last night."

"Not now, D." My stats are also suffering because I've been getting drunk every night so I can sleep. Last night, I got into a bar fight. Luckily, the bouncer was a fan, and I signed a hat for him so he wouldn't call the cops. I haven't told the shrink that yet, so I'm sure that will be an hour of super fun times. I'm not like that, irresponsible and hot headed. Chase reminded me of that when he saw me stumble into the house, still drunk. For the first time in my life, I had a real big brother talk. He reminded me that I have a support system, then he smacked me on the back of the head for not using it.

"Yeah, no." He shuffles around, kicking his legs out and bringing them back in. He's nervous, that's why he's being so quiet. "I just wanted to tell you that I've got your back tonight."

"What?"

"I just, you know, got your back. On the ice."

I finally lean back to stare at him, and that's when I see the stitches on his cheek. "Jesus, what the fuck happened to you?"

"Huh? Oh, that? Yeah, I kind of clocked Steve yesterday at the gym."

"He hit you back?"

"No. I wish! I mean, I told people it was a gym accident, which it kind of was. I swung on him. He didn't move like I thought he would, and it threw off my balance. I landed the punch, and then got punched back by a dumbbell."

"You what?"

"Shut up. You heard me. I fell on a damn dumbbell. It was stupid, but he can't do that kind of shit. Not during the season. There are fucking rules, man. He needs to fix this so we can make the playoffs!"

"Dev?" He turns and looks at me. If this guy isn't the human embodiment of a golden retriever, I don't know what is. "There's nothing he can fix, and you're a fucking dumbbell. But thanks."

"Yeah, no problem." He shifts nervously and crosses his arms, which in his equipment more or less looks like he's hugging himself. "Oh, I talked to Dani last night. We're good. Crisis averted!"

"Good, that's great. Honestly, I figured Xander gave you the black eye for knocking her up."

"Dude, he would have done way worse than that if I had." He laughs, then gets serious again. "So, uh, don't check the stands tonight, okay?"

"What do you mean?"

"The box. Chase is coming tonight, and that usually means, well, Steve and Jamie are probably going to be here, too. They're up in Sam's luxury box."

And there it is. That was exactly the kick in the ass I needed. I feel the pain and sadness slide away, replaced with determination and focus. I can't let him see the weakness he's caused me. I won't let him get that satisfaction. My head is fully in the game now. All because I'm pissed off. I grab Dev's head and pull it to me, kissing the side. "Thanks, buddy. You're a fucking lifesaver."

The horn for the second period blows seconds before Vegas shoots a cannon right under Dev's glove. Saved by the damn bell. It's tied at one each, both goals scored on power plays. The hits have already sent two of ours and one of theirs into the locker rooms early, but luckily, it looks like our guys will be back on the ice for the second. Coach gives his talk and we get our rundowns of what went wrong, what went right, and what we need to do in the last period. When he's done, our equipment manager comes over with my stick in his hand.

"Hey, Lala. I need to trade out your stick." He points to a crack, which is common in these sticks, and tells me we can't tape it up, which I already know. I shrug and expect him to leave, but he doesn't. "Uhm, there's another problem."

"Fuck, what did I do now?"

"I can't find your backups."

"What?"

"We had them two days ago. I know they came off the bus, but I can't find them anywhere."

I take the stick from his hand and check at the broken piece more closely. Composite sticks tend to shatter when you're about to take a damn shot and hit it just wrong. Usually, there's no warning. When I ask if he's ever seen one break like this, he shakes his head. I lift my eyes and meet Girard's as he stares at me with a smirk. I hand the stick back and follow the manager out to the row of sticks against the wall. Just like he said, my sticks are nowhere to be seen. Sticks might all appear the same to an outsider, and in a pinch, we can trade out. The issue is, I'm a fucking righty and I'm short. I'm not the shortest in the league, but on the team, I am. And statistically, there are more lefties in hockey. I have no idea why, but I'm a righty because that's what was handed down to me. Normally, that's still not an issue because there should be a handful of other guys who are also right-handed. This team? There's three of us, and every other one of those guys is over six feet tall before skates. I'm double fucked.

"What's going on?" Coach asks as he comes out of the locker room and sees me standing there staring at the wall.

"Nothing," I mumble, not fully realizing who I'm talking to.

"Uh huh, sure." He turns to Greg. "What's really wrong?"

"His stick is broken, and we can't find his backups."

"You can't find what now? How the hell did you lose sticks? Who else is missing sticks?"

"That's the thing, it's just Lala's. Usually, his are easy to spot in the lineup, no offense, Lala. But we've looked everywhere."

An angry bear would run if he heard the growl that just came out of Coach. He storms back into the locker room and yelling spills out into the hallway, so I book it back in. He's about two inches from Girard's face, and Girard is backing up into his locker while sputtering out a litany of excuses that are just making Coach more pissed off.

"You're benched. Get the fuck out of my locker room!"

"You can't do that! You don't even have proof!"

I glance over at Devin, then back to Coach, half expecting me to be tossed out, too, given the week I've had. Instead, he storms over to me, snatching the broken stick from my hand before addressing the whole team.

"This is not a fucking toy. This rink is not a fucking

playground. They may call this a game, but it is not a fucking game. If any of that needs to be explained to you further, take off the damn jersey, hand it in to Greg, and get the hell out of my locker room. We'll mail your final check. Is that clear?"

The team mumbles a barely audible response.

"I'm going to ask once. If I get an answer, you won't be benched tonight. If I do not get an answer, and I find out you helped Girard the moron over there, you'll be off the damn team. Question one, where the hell are Lala's sticks?"

Bourque is the first to make eye contact with me, and his face says he thinks Coach is speaking in Spanish. He rolls his eyes and stands with a rage I've never seen from him. Girard goes pale as Bourque takes my broken stick from Coach and then stands on top of one of the benches. Sure enough, he fishes three of my sticks from the top back side of the lockers. Tossing the old one in a can for broken sticks, he hands me the rest.

"He told me he tossed his car keys up there when I caught him. Said he was using your stick to get them, since it was closer, even made a big show of putting it back. Must have been how it got fucked up, too." He turns and glares at Girard, and in the thickest Canadian accent ever, he yells, "You're an asshole and a shit player. You're a disgrace to the fucking game and a fuckup. You don't deserve the C, and you don't even fucking listen to Metallica."

Girard's chest puffs out as he stands, grabs the jersey behind him, and throws it in a nearby trash can. "Fuck all of you. By the way, your little buddy, Lala? Yeah, he's a fucking princess that takes it up the ass from Steve Jensen every fucking chance he gets."

"Fuck you!" I yell, and he steps toward me.

"My dad invited me out to a round of golf with Judge Jensen. He told me all about your little fuckboi."

I don't even get to react as the entire team stands and moves between him and me, staring him down like he's injured prey and they're a pack of rabid wolves. Yuri Nitushvek, the biggest guy on the team, walks through them all like he's Moses and goes nose to nose with Girard, which he has to bend over to do. "I don't give a shit if he's fucking an octopus in his spare time. He's a better player with a broken back than you'll ever be or have ever been. You come into our home and you defile it with your nonsense? That could have cost us the game! Now, Coach told you to get out, so get the FUCK out!"

Devin leans over to me and whispers, "I've never even heard that guy say more than five words in English before tonight, and those were yes, no, hockey, Coach, and taco."

Girard grabs his clothes and storms out of the locker room. We all know he won't get very far with his skates still on, but at least he's gone. I'm not sure how to react to what just happened, because in my mind, it was me leaving. I was completely convinced that Coach was going to kick my ass off the team the second he learned about me being gay, but I don't think he cares. I don't think any of them care—in the good way.

Tyler Michaud, a guy I've known for a few years, walks over to me and puts his hands on my shoulders. He's another big guy, at least six-five without the skates. He's built like a defenseman in the NFL, but he's one of our fastest forwards and leading goal scorer at the moment. "Lala, I mean this as a teammate and a friend. If any more of these mother fuckers come at you, I'll take care of it. Personally."

"Nah, you gotta wait in line, Ty," Devin chimes in with a giant grin. "Goalie gets first swing. Mostly because I live with him."

"Okay, okay!" Coach settles everyone down. "We got two more periods of hockey left. Bourque, I'm designating you captain. I'll get Greg to switch it out on your jerseys for the next game. Use this, people. Use the rage and get the fuck back in this game. That's all I've got."

"Dude, did he just *Palpatine* us?" One of the rookies asks and gets a sweaty shirt thrown at him for it as the guys grab their gear and get ready to head back out.

I swing around and start digging through my locker. Fuck! I left my damn phone in the car. I spin again, looking at the countdown clock for the next period. There's only a few minutes left.

"Dev, do you have your phone?"

"No. I leave that in the car, like always." He stares at me for a second and I see the lightbulb turn on over his head. "Shit! Seriously? You're doing this now? In the middle of a game?"

"Jesus, how the fuck is anyone supposed to get a hold of us?!" He stares at me, unsure how to help. "And yes, I'm doing this now because I'm fucking crazy, okay? The momentum shift, Girard outing me like he just fucking did, fuck, I want him back, Hollywood. I want to win this game, but I want to know that after we win, he'll be there waiting for me."

"Bro, I don't want to be the bad guy, but what if—"

"Then I'll fucking fight harder."

"Okay, valid hockey answer. What about the office phone?"

"I don't know his fucking number, dude! Wait, do you?" He shakes his head. Of course he doesn't, we were raised with cell phones and never needed to memorize numbers. I run out the door looking for anything I can use to get his attention. Instead, I do one better and run smack into the PR lady, Emily.

"Woah, slow down there, big guy. Actually, you're exactly who I wanted to talk to. What the hell happened in there? I heard yelling and Girard is in the security room cussing up a storm and using your name in ways I didn't know anyone could. Kind of amazing wordsmithing, if I'm being honest."

"Uhm, can I explain later? Because I need a huge favor. I need to get someone a very specific and very important message."

"That's kind of my specialty, sugar."

HOLLYWOOD
Steve

CHAPTER 27
BACK TO YOU

LOST FREQUENCIES, ELLEY DUHÉ

BEING HERE tonight was probably the biggest mistake I could have made. No, the biggest mistake was going out two weeks ago. Tonight is just a continued study of my idiocy. Coop, Jamie, and Jamie's boss, Sam, have been chatting away all night, having a great time, laughing and drinking. I, on the other hand, have been sulking in the front row of the box seats by myself, like a privileged, sad puppy. I should have stayed home and caught a movie.

Every time they announce his name or someone around us says it, it's punch right to the fucking nuts. Not the gut, the damn nuts. I fucked up and I have no idea how I'm ever going to crawl out of the hole I dug. I'm not sure if I can crawl out.

I find myself checking the seats behind the net where I've been sitting for the last month's worth of games. Laurie and Craig are down there today, and have been for the last few weeks. She's even called to check up on Ethan and make sure he's okay with them being there, because she knows I can't. She still has this hope that we reconcile and try this again, but I'm not sure I could, or he would. They say insanity is doing the same thing over and over and expecting a different outcome, and if you break the last five months down, that's all we were doing. Try, fight, try again without changing anything, fight more until it gradually escalates into me setting the relationship on fire.

I'm barely even aware that it's intermission as a team full of kids floods the ice to play a short scrimmage game to entertain the masses. I didn't realize a bunch of Mini Mites would be what pushed me over the edge, but it is. My brain conjures up images of Lala and me with kids, teaching them how to skate. They'd skate better than some of these kids, that's for sure. Clearly, they learned how to walk before they learned how to skate. Fuck.

I stand up, excusing myself as I head out of the box and down the hallway. I don't have a destination in mind. I just need some time and space. I find a corner tucked away from the main hall right by the big windows and I stop there, leaning against a column to hide myself even more. It's a beautiful view, the sun in the last stages of setting just like it was on the beach a few weeks ago. We'd gone at least five times since December; it's been cold enough to keep people away from the already secluded spot. I'm not sure I can ever go back there without breaking down. How do a few weeks change everything in my life so fucking much? I shiver, but I'm not sure if it's because of the cool air coming off the rink or my body telling me I'm the world's biggest idiot.

"Steve?" Coop's voice echoes down the hallway. I wipe my eyes and take a deep breath before I step out from my hiding spot so he can find me. He takes one look at me and his shoulders slump to match mine. "Talk to me, Stevie."

"I'm fine."

"And I'm the queen of Brooklyn. Talk to me."

I don't even have to search for the words, I just have to force them out of my mouth. "I feel like I've gone back to the day Skylar left me and I'm…I'm scared."

"Hey, if you and Ethan don't work out, you just don't work out. You can get through this."

"Again? No, I'm not sure I can, Coop. I've got nowhere else to go except right back into the shit I was doing before. I'll break right through the lowest low and find a new low where I can wallow." I shake my head, dropping it so he can't see the tears. Coop's seen me cry, but right now, I don't want the sympathy bullshit. "Chase, I'm scared. I'm scared I'm going to go back to that and I'm gonna get worse, and I won't be able to climb out of it this time."

"I mean, death by getting laid every night can't be all that bad, can it?"

"Fuck, man! I'm trying to—"

"I get it, dude. I'm trying to tell you that maybe you're thinking about it the wrong way. Maybe you can use this as a growth experience. You fucked up, and I could be wrong, but there's a chance he'll come around. You could make it up to him and show him you've, I dunno, changed?"

"I wouldn't take me back, that's for sure."

"That's a lie and you know it. You're like what's his name from the Clarice movie staring into the mirror saying he'd fuck himself. Only, you're probably more Jay and Silent Bob about it." He sighs when I don't at least chuckle. He knows I love that stupid bit. "You've got other things to be happy about. You've got your gym back, for one. You and Laurie are out there kicking your dad's ass all around California while he tries to scrounge up lawyers who can put up with him. That's a win!"

"I get what you're doing, and it's not gonna work."

"Hey, come on, man. If it's this bad, let's go home. I'm sorry I pushed you to come here tonight." He wants to say more. I can see it in his face, but he's not. My guess is he brought me here and there's some kind of plan to get Ethan and me to talk to one another after the game. It won't work, but these two idiots will try, and that's why I love them.

"I'm fine. It's a big game for Dev. We should stay."

"You sure?" I nod and he throws his arm over my shoulder and pulls me in for a hug before we walk back. As we get closer, I see someone going into the suite and I wonder if I was wrong about staying. When I'm stuck in a miserable frame of mind around my friends, I don't care, but I'd rather not be that way around strangers. And I've been doing that enough already at the gym. Sam didn't say anything about inviting anyone else, though. Not that I remember.

We get to the door and it bursts open just as I reach for the handle. Luckily, I step back before it can slam into my nose. She's short with dark, curly hair, somehow familiar, but I can't place it. She's wearing a name tag, and that's something of a relief. I read the job title and I'm confused as to why is the team's public relations head in our box? Then I remember who I'm with.

"I'll meet you inside, Coop," I sigh, nodding to Chase as she stares up at me. I move to skirt around her so I can go back to moping some more when she reaches out, grabbing my arm. If I were in a better mood, I'd laugh at the extra squeeze and the cute smirk that followed, but tonight is definitely not the night.

"I'm not here for Mr. Cooper. I was asked to drop this off. I was told it was important, and you'd understand, even though I said no one would understand a shirt, but whatever. Here. A shirt!" She's snarky, but enthusiastic about it.

When I glance down at what she's holding out, I see it's not just any shirt. My heart is fully lodged in my throat and I've forgotten how to breathe as I stare down at the jersey she's holding out in front of me. He even folded it for full impact and I can't stop myself from running my fingers over the green and gold letters that spell out his name. This has to be a joke.

"Who sent this?"

"I mean, I think it's pretty obvious."

"Is it? Because I think it's obviously a fucking cruel joke." I snap back and Coop smacks my arm. "Just tell me who sent it. Girard? I swear to god I'll—"

"Mr. LaVoie sent it—I told him no one would understand a shirt."

I turn to Coop because I can't form the words to tell her that I do understand a shirt. I understand this shirt and what it means. So does Coop. Ethan is offering me a second chance. No, he's offering *us* a second chance. Coop smirks and claps me on the back.

"Go get him, Tiger."

I pull the jersey on as I run down the stairs two at a time because there's no way I'm waiting on an elevator right now. When I hit the ground, I glance through one of the tunnels and check the scoreboard. I've got about two minutes left, and I'm on the wrong damn side of the ice.

Fuck it.

I take off down the hall, dodging bodies until I can't anymore, then ducking in and out of the tunnels. I watch the second Zamboni pull through the doors and off the ice as I run down the steps. The players come out of the tunnel as I slam into the glass to stop myself, but I don't see him. More players come out, some staying on the bench, others skating around, ready to start the next period. Finally, I spot him, but when he steps out of the tunnel, he looks toward the luxury box—of course he does.

"ETHAN! LAVOIE!" I yell, but I'm too close to the glass now and the way sound travels around these boards means I'm just another fan yelling his name. His head drops and Devin pats him on the shoulder. I try again, but this time, I'm determined to get his damn attention. "SWEETS!"

His head snaps so fast he must have whiplash. There's a smile that grows bigger when he sees I'm wearing his sweater. He steps onto the ice and skates in front of me. He stares for a minute, like he's not sure I'm real and I worry I've overstepped. First it's his hand on the glass, and I hold mine up, too. Then he presses his helmet to the glass, and I mirror the action while I mouth the words he wanted so desperately to hear. *I love you, Lala.*

"I love you, too, Stevie. Come see me after the game?" He says just loud enough for me to hear over the crowd. I hadn't noticed how loud it got, so lost in this guy in front of me. What the hell are we doing?

We both turn to find they've got us on the scoreboard screens and the crowd is cheering us on. I damn near fall flat on my ass. I expect Ethan to be upset, but instead, he's smiling from ear to ear. He used to be terrified of what would happen if the fans and team found out about us. But here we are, professing our feelings toward each other in an extremely public way in front of a packed house and his teammates. I have no idea what happened in the locker room during intermission, but I owe someone. Big.

I don't want to leave the glass, but I have to let him get on with the game.

"Go win this."

"I already won, Stevie," he says with a wink before sliding away to slap Devin's pads with his stick. I stay there, staring at him until just before puck drop. We can't stop looking at each other, and I know his butterflies have to be going as crazy as mine right now.

As he lines up, he tucks his stick under his arm, makes a heart shape with his gloves, and nods up to the box as he tells me to get the hell back to my seats.

The trek back to the box takes a lot longer since I'm not running, and I have to stop a few times to check what's going on in the game anytime I hear Lala's name. When I open the door, I'm greeted with cheers, hugs, and high-fives from the guys, each of them trying to hand me a beer and show me the pictures they took while I was down there. Nothing seems real.

"Hey," Jamie grabs me by the shoulders so I face him. "I'm proud of you, Stevie. I'm proud, and I'm so fucking happy."

He pulls me in, hugging me so hard I feel the bridge between as it repairs itself. When we pull back, we've both got tears in our eyes. "Hey, it's not like we're getting married or something."

"Not yet," Jamie teases while I roll my eyes. "Dude, I know that look in your eyes—and his—and that's only a matter of time, my friend."

"Oh, thank the hockey gods!" Coop shouts. "So I'll be seeing more of you at the house again, I take it?"

"No, uhm, I think I'm going to ask him to come live with me once we get this all sorted out." They all stop, even Sam, and stare at me. I glance down to make sure an alien isn't bursting out of my chest and confirm it's just my heart. "What?"

"Move in? With you?" Chase asks, his face teetering between excitement and concern. "Did you hit your head while you were running down there, Stevie?"

"No!"

"You're serious right now?" Jamie follows up and I roll my eyes again.

"Yes, I'm serious!" I fold my arms over my chest. "Do you assholes think I can't handle that or something?"

"No, I mean, we just—" before Chase can finish his explanation, Jamie is pulling out his wallet and handing him a twenty. "It's nothing."

"You had a bet on this?"

"More like a pool," Jamie replies. "I had you moving into Chase's house."

Chase scratches his head, trying to play it off like nothing happened, and heads back to the seats to watch the game. Jamie shrugs and follows him, leaving Sam and me behind.

"Jamie's right. I might not be as close to you as I am with the two of them, but your eyes are telling me all I need to know. It's the same way I look at my wife every time I walk into the house."

"Yeah? How long have you been married?"

"Thirty years." He slaps me on the back and heads to his seat.

The rest of the game is so intense, we barely sit down again. Cheers and shouts from the fans make me smile every time they show Lala on the big screen, and it's a lot. My guy is on fire. Going into the third period, he's got two goals and an assist, the team is up by four goals, and Devin has become a fucking impenetrable wall, not letting anything by him since the first period.

With minutes left, the other team pulls their goalie. The seconds tick down and the fans are all holding their breath while Devin puts on a damn clinic. Kick saves, blocker saves, nothing is getting by him. One gets close, but Lala dives in front of the shot, blocking it with his body—it scares the hell out of me to watch. He gets up and I glance at the clock, forty seconds. There's another close shot that echoes off the posts and right to Lala. He flicks it down the ice and the other team goes screaming after it, diving forward to keep it out of the next. The red light comes on and the entire building erupts because there's no way they can catch up now. Hats pour out onto the ice and the team is jumping all over Lala, celebrating the game and the hat trick.

In the box, we're all hugging and jumping up and down like a bunch of lunatics. We join the rest of the crowd as we all scream, "We're going to the fucking playoffs!"

HOLLYWOOD
Steve

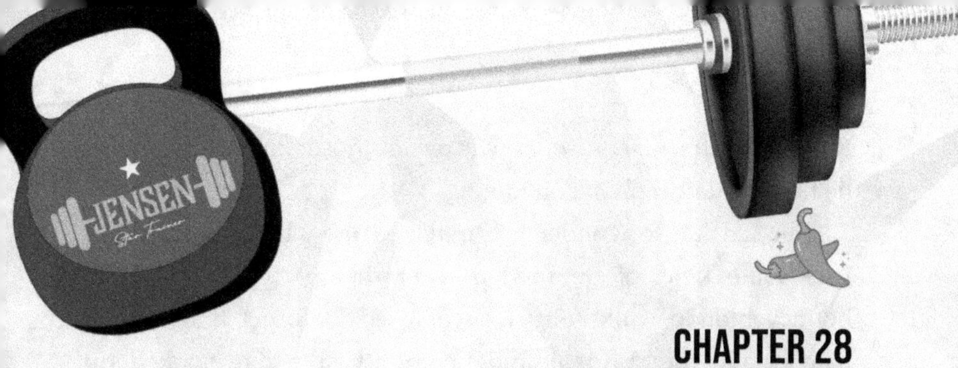

CHAPTER 28
KICKSTARTER MY HEART

MÖTLEY CRÜE

I'M BOUNCING on my toes as I wait outside in the cold—partially to keep warm, partially because my brain is buzzing like a hive full of bees. When Chase offered to give me a ride home to wait for Ethan there, I passed because I wanted to wait. Now I've been standing out here for over an hour, watching the visiting team pack up and leave while the Parrots take their time coming out of the rink one or two at a time.

After the win, the swarm of reporters descended on Ethan before he left the ice. A few I recognize from sports broadcasts, but after our little intermission show, we've apparently gone viral, and that sent even more reporters to the rink to try to catch him. They're looking for me, too, but I've got a good hiding spot, and I have credentials to be back here in the player's parking lot.

I turned my phone off because all the notifications were getting a little much to handle, and also because Ethan and Devin both keep their phones in their cars during games so they don't get distracted. There was a time when I used to bug him about the phones because that means I couldn't reach him during the game, and he reminded me that I was the distraction.

Rude, but cute. Of course, now is one of those times when I wish he had the damn phone on him.

I'm starting to wonder if I imagined the whole thing, like it was some kind of depression fever dream, when this cute, bouncy blonde walks out. I never used to forget that hockey teams have cheerleaders, and I'm pretty sure I've hooked up with a couple from this squad in the past. When she spots me, she starts jogging toward me and I panic, worried I'm screwing this up already. I'm praying she doesn't know me and that Lala doesn't come out thinking I've called her over here. My back hits the wall and I realize I have nowhere to run, just as she reaches me and hands me a piece of paper.

"Uhm, no thanks. I've got someone."

"Oh, sorry, it's not my number. You are Steve, right?"

I look down at the paper and find Ethan's name scrawled on it in my handwriting, so I take it and nod as she bops off to her car. If this is how freaked out I'm going to get over a cute girl even looking at me now, maybe Lala and I really do have a chance. The paper is folded a million times, and I can tell he's folded and unfolded it over and over. *Beach?* It doesn't really make sense that he'd send her out to give me my own note back, but then again, it's not like I have a door he could slide it under.

Maybe it's a trap. What if this whole thing is a setup to humiliate me, which I would absolutely deserve? I don't think it is, though. He kept a stupid note with his name and one word on it. He probably had this shoved in his wallet because there couldn't be pictures of us in there, so this was the next best thing. It's making my heart flutter, but my stomach sinks. How could I have done this to him, to the one person I really loved? A sharp whistle pulls me out of my head and I turn toward it, expecting the press looking for our story or security telling me I don't belong here. Instead, I find the most beautiful man in the entire world leaning against an SUV the same way I was leaning against my car that day.

"Need a ride?"

"Can't, I'm waiting for someone."

"Yeah? Who's that? I might know him."

"Short guy, plays hockey. He's a bit of a wise-ass, but I need to find him." I make my way toward him. "See, I messed up. I got drunk and let my fear and my dick take over. I said some shit that he didn't deserve to hear, and I need to beg for his forgiveness."

His hands are in his pockets and his hat is down low. I can smell the soap and fresh shower on him, making my head spin a little. I'm elated he's giving me a chance and terrified I'll mess it up again. I don't deserve this, I get that, but here we are.

"Yeah, I've seen him around. You sure you want that guy? He's a bit of a fuck-up, and his shrink does this thing where she just stares at him for long periods of time, not sure what the fuck to say."

I laugh, inching closer. "Mine does that, too. But my guy isn't a fuck-up at all. He just has a world of hurt and confusion on his shoulders that he didn't ask for. I just want to ask him for a chance to take some of that weight off. Help him carry the load while I spend the rest of my life proving to him that I...that I love him and I'm so fucking sorry."

"So, there are these books that a friend of mine—her name is Alexis—she lends them to me because I like to read. They're dirtier than those magazines you find behind the counter at gas stations and shit. They've got this idea in some of them called 'found family' that seemed so weird to me." His fingertips touch my hand and my body shivers. When his head tilts up and I see those green eyes, my stomach flips and all I want to do is kiss him. "I didn't understand what that was. I mean, why would someone need to find a family? Then... I found one I didn't realize I was looking for."

"I'm sorry, Ethan. I recognize that's not enough, and it will never be enough to—"

He grabs my face and pulls me in. It's like one of those kisses in sappy movies, minus the rain and heartfelt music. When he breaks the kiss, he runs his nose up mine. "Steve, people fuck things up in life. I want our second chance, or our fiftieth chance, whatever this is. You're not perfect, and I don't want you to be, but I want you. I want my forever to be with you by my side and in my bed."

"I love you. I should have said it sooner. I should have said it every fucking day."

"*Over there! There they are!*" The shouts come with camera flashes right behind them as a wave of reporters and paparazzi collide and head right for us.

"Shit, let's go!" Ethan pulls the door open for me before running around to the driver's side. He climbs in and starts the car, giving me a smirk and a grin. "Beach?"

"Do you even know how to drive?"

"Fuck you, Steve! Yes, I can drive just fine, thank you. I just fucking hate driving!" He shifts into gear and takes off before the press can reach us, but there are pictures and videos of tonight that we won't be able to run from. As he pulls out of the lot, he takes my hand, bringing it up to his lips and kissing my knuckles. We drive like that for a while, him holding my hand to his lips every so often, but neither of us saying a word. A few minutes later, he pulls into a gas station and parks by the side of the building.

"What are you doing?"

"Well, I need to set the GPS because I have no clue where we're going, and I figured we should grab a few things."

"You're here for candy, aren't you, Sweets?"

"Baby, I gotta be honest—I'm starving! But I figured we could pick up a couple of beers and see what else they've got. Come on."

The store is brightly lit and there is a wall of craft beer selections like I've never seen. Lala has my hand and isn't letting go while I look around at the paintings on the wall and a giant button that clearly says not to touch it. I pull him over toward it and kiss him hard as I slam the button. The security camera footage could make someone a lot of money if they find the right website to sell it to.

"Jerk," he laughs as we pull away. I missed that laugh so much. "Alright, let's get whatever else we might need to watch the sunrise together."

"Lala, the sunrise doesn't happen for like five hours. What the fuck are we doing at a deserted beach for five hours?"

"Fogging up the windows and writing our names on them? There are a lot of windows on an SUV, Stevie."

"YES! Oh fuck, Daddy, harder!" I yell as Lala sends me rocketing over the edge. The way this kid fucks is just another reason I love him.

That's still weird to say.

"Almost.. Almo—oh, god. Oh Jesus!" I reach back and pull his hair as he bites down on my shoulder, coming between whimpers and groans.

"Yeah, I'd definitely describe that as a religious experience," I say with a grin as I collapse to the floor of the cargo space with him on top of me. He nuzzles against me as we listen to the ocean; his tongue traces our names on my shoulders where I'll likely have teeth marks. "You know, now that you've shown me what making up with you is like, how am I *not* supposed to fuck up on purpose now?"

"Shut up, dickhead. You're ruining the moment." His arm moves under me as he wraps around me, biting at my ear with a giggle. He's not done with me yet—I hope he never is.

Our clothes are scattered everywhere, and it's too dark to see anything. I can almost admit that this might have been better than fucking in my car. Almost.

"Please, just find better ways to piss me off that don't involve your hand around anyone else's dick but mine, okay?"

"Eth, we're gonna be okay, right?"

"Pumpkin, nothing about us is okay." He grabs a blanket from somewhere behind us and I wonder if he knew this is where tonight would lead as he drapes it over us. "We're going to be a tiny boat in a raging storm of chaos, especially now that we're public. Okay will never describe us, but I'm good with that so long as we're us."

"That sounds like more of your mom's logic."

"Mmm, she's a smart woman. Fuck, I can't stop kissing you. Stop bringing up my mom!"

"Wait, so who was the blonde chick? With the note?"

"Margot?"

"Was she, like, a test?"

"A test for wha—Oh! No. No, I ran into her in the hallway while she was headed out. Margot has three kids and a very happy marriage. I'm not messing with that to test your resolve." He squeezes my nipple hard. "Why? Didn't you pass?"

"No, we fucked in the alley. Yes, I passed!"

"Good boy, let's get you a reward then, yeah?" He goes after my neck as his hand wraps around my thigh, moving it to the side and granting him access to my cock. He teases at me as he sucks hard on my neck, bringing out whimpers and whispers. I feel the familiar pressure building inside me again—but it's him.

"Sweets, are you…Dude, you just finished like five minutes ago! How are you already getting hard again?"

"Are you complaining?"

"No!"

"Good. Then get those hands back on the window and call me *Daddy* again."

"Wait!" I reach out and grab his wrist, and for a second he looks scared, like I'll change my mind. "Ethan, move in with me?"

"What?"

"I mean it, move in with me. It's not the swanky Cooper hotel and spa, but…I want you and me to be together."

"Steve, I'm half hard inside of you right now and that's when you ask me to move in?" He shakes his head and laughs before leaning over to kiss me hard. "My stuff is ready to go when you are, Pumpkin."

"Are you talking about the move or your cock?"

"Yes," he sighs, then gives me that no-nonsense look. "When the time comes, do *NOT* propose to me while we're fucking. You got that?"

"I make no promises." I reach back and cup his face, grinning. "Now ruin me, Daddy. Again."

HOLLYWOOD
21
Ethan

EPILOGUE- MORE THAN A FEELING

BOSTON

"SWEETS! We're gonna be late, baby. I don't want to die today. We have enough dead bodies going into the ground today."

"Relax," I hum as I come out of the bathroom and spin around, making sure he approves of the suite. "We've got time and Laurie said she'd only behead you if we held the wedding up because we were fucking."

He strides across the room—which I should have been expecting—and pins me against the wall. "You think she'll still kill me when she sees how fucking good you look in this suit? Cause I think she'll understand I couldn't resist."

"We gotta go, pumpkin."

"Pumpkin? Still?"

"Yeah, well, you're going to turn into a pumpkin if you order another one of those fucking coffees."

"Oh, you do not want to come between this man and his pumpkin spice. I don't care how good your ass looks or how big your dick is."

"Oh, you care. You care very much about both of those things, *Pumpkin*."

I finally get him off me and we grab the rest of our things and head down to the car. It's been weird living with Steve instead of Chase and Devin, but he's really worked hard to make sure I didn't just feel like a guest. What he's struggling to understand is how I don't care where we are, or how much stuff we each have—it's home so long as he's there with me. I have finally convinced him to look at houses to move into so I can stop freaking out over the neighbors hearing us through the walls. We've got a house closer to Pasadena, and only a few blocks away from Jamie and Alexis, that we're pretty close to agreeing on.

"Okay, wait, did you bring directions?" Steve asks, checking his phone and then reaching over for mine. I swat his hand away and plug my phone in so he can use the GPS. He's supportive in every way I could never imagine, but he's about as organized as a squirrel on crack. Luckily, I'm a stickler for detail, so it's yet another way we complement each other. I hold his hand as he takes a deep breath and backs out of his spot. "Shit. I don't know if I'm ready for this, Lala."

"You are. Laurie knows you are."

"It's just, I dunno, weird. Like, I didn't expect either of us to get married. I thought it would always just be the two of us against the world."

I bring his hand up, gently kissing each of his knuckles. "How about we get used to the four of us against the world?"

"You're so cheesy sometimes. I love you."

"I love you, too. Pumpkin."

"Do you know some people are calling Laurie a witch because she's having her wedding the same day of Dad's funeral? Like she penciled it in when she booked the venue three months ago."

"Remind me never to piss your sister off. I'd hate to see what she'd do to top this." I straighten his tie and kiss his cheek when we stop for a red light. "Also, they might be calling her a witch because she's getting married the day of his funeral, *and* since she took over the law firm, so a lot of the big shots are here to impress her rather than there to respect him. That's cold."

"Whatever, jerk."

"Hey, I mean it with all the love in my heart that isn't reserved for you already."

"So cheesy."

"Whatever! It's fucking impressive, and I think she'd make a great mafia don with moves like that. I need her on retainer in case I ever decide to do anything illegal."

"Oh, we're gonna do so many illegal things to each other. No one will be able to stop us."

"We're fine…in some states."

"Sweets, there is nothing fine about what you did to me after you tied me up last night. That level of pleasure is a damn crime, even if we were in fucking Vegas."

"Now who's being cheesy?"

Laurie's wedding has been phenomenal. Pink roses fill the hall and she's a fucking knockout in that dress. She's surrounded herself with people who love her and care about her happiness, and it shows in her confidence and that smile when she glances over at her new husband. Craig is giving her the strength and love to come out to more people as trans, and that's helped since she took over the law firm a week ago with their uncle's help. Steve walks her down the aisle, crying the whole way, then steps off to her side and joins her wedding party. He glances over at me from time to time as he winks and mouths he loves me. After the ceremony, the group and I all head to the reception hall in the next building to meet up with the wedding party.

Jamie and Lexi haven't stopped holding hands the entire ceremony, Dani keeps poking Xander and threatening to propose to him at her next concert, and Chase and Devin keep looking at Steve and I like they're expecting something. I've already told them we're not getting engaged, especially not today, but they don't believe me. To be fair, I did bring the ring just in case.

We're sitting around the table, waiting for the wedding party and having drinks when Steve sneaks up behind me and covers my eyes. "Come with me if you want to live," he says in the worst Arnold impression ever before dragging me out of the room and down a hallway.

"Steve, they're about to—"

"Yeah, I know. It's the most fucking boring part of the wedding and nobody wants me giving a damn speech anyhow. So I wanted to take a walk. Don't worry, we'll be back before they cut the cake or anything like that. I'm not a total dick." We slip down another hallway and he stops, looking around like he's lost. "Ha! Found it."

"Found what?"

"Stop asking questions," he says as he leads me into a small room, locking the door behind him. "Laurie told me I'm not allowed to let today get to my head and ask you…something stupid. So instead, I'm going to keep my mind, and my hands, very occupied for a bit. I mean, if you're okay with it."

"Stevie, what the fuck are you—" He's on me in an instant, backing me against another wall and caging me in, his knee between my legs, pulling out whimpers and moans while he kisses me. I'd be lying if I hadn't been wanting this since we started it this morning and didn't get to finish, but I expected we'd have sex at the hotel when everything was over. He makes short work of my belt, pants, and boxers, then spins me around, grinding against my ass as his hand slides up my shirt.

"Fuck, I need you so bad, Lala. Please? Please tell me I can have you?"

"One condition."

"Anything," he moans, staring down at my ass as he lifts my shirt out of the way.

"You don't step on my toes later when I go to ask you the stupid question you're not allowed to ask me." He freezes, then slowly lifts his head and looks at me. I'm staring right into those big, beautiful pools of blue. "I, uhm, figured we could keep it quiet for a few weeks. Let Laurie have her moment before we come crashing in."

"Ethan, are you saying—"

"Right now, I'm just asking you to not ask me. That's all. Because I don't really want to say more than that while my fucking pants are on the ground and the tent in your pants is rubbing against my ass. That okay?"

He nods and then digs in his pocket because, while he might not be prepared for a lot of things in life, Steve is always prepared to have sex. I yell out when he picks me up and carries me across the room bridal style, dropping me down onto a bench. We're eye to eye and I'm not sure what to do because, of all the ways we've fucked, we've never done it face to face. I hear his zipper, then the snap of the lid opening. I suck in a quick breath as my head rocks back.

"I wanna see you, Ethan. I want to see the man I'm going to spend the rest of my fucking life with. I wanna watch you lose your mind for me every night. I want—"

I pull his shoulders down and kiss him hard as he pushes inside me. My fingers grip his hair so tight, I worry I'm hurting him, but he doesn't stop kissing me, and doesn't stop moving his hips. His hands wrap around my legs, pushing them apart as he sets his rhythm, taking me apart piece by piece. My other hand reaches around him, groping at his shirt until I can get it untucked. His muscles flex at my fingertips as I hold him to me, wrapping my legs around him, trying to push him deeper. I can't get enough.

"Harder, Stevie. Show me you love me. Show me how bad you need me." I'm clawing at him, begging for more, for all of him. "I love you, Stevie! Oh Christ, I love you!"

"I'm gonna show you every damn day, Lala. Show you I love you. I'll take care of you, baby. I'll suck your pretty cock after every game. I'll watch you bounce on mine while we watch movies. I'm gonna fuck you so much. Everyone will know you're mine. Tonight, oh fuck, baby, tonight I'm gonna ride you so hard everyone at this wedding will know I'm yours."

I reach up and grab his face. "Shut up and come for me, Stevie." Stevie whimpers as our tongues slide over one another and I feel how close he is by the way he tenses up. He's got tells and I'm getting to know each and everyone, but this one, the whimper, is the one that gets me every time. "Fill me up, Stevie. Make me yours."

"I wanna rip your shirt off so fucking bad right now, Sweets. Make a total mess of you."

"I thought you didn't want to die today?"

My name echoes off the walls of the mostly empty room when Steve goes past the point of no return. It takes everything I've got to not follow him over the edge, and when he's done, he pulls out quickly so he can finish me off before I ruin both our suits. It doesn't take long—I'm coming as soon as I hit the back of his throat. Now the room echoes with his name and every damn swear word in my vocabulary.

When he's done making sure he hasn't missed a drop, he sits

back and leans against the other arm of the couch as he stares at me. I must look like I got hit by a tornado the way we just went at it. Meanwhile, Steve still looks like a million bucks and his tie isn't even out of place. I close my eyes and catch my breath, not worried that I'm lounging around at a wedding with no pants like I'm Donald Duck or something.

"Hey, Lala?" I pick my head up and find Steve with his head against the back of the couch, staring at me like I'm his whole world, and then some. "I get that it's the beginning of the season and things are going to be crazy, but during the All-Star break, how about we go away for a while? Take a couple days in Boston and then Paris or Germany, somewhere fun. I mean, that's if you don't make the All-Stars, which you will, I'm sure you will. Never mind."

"Steve, if I make the All-Star team—"

"We can cancel the trip and I'll go to the All-Star game and watch you. Yeah, that's fine."

"I will politely decline that invitation on the grounds that I will be in Italy, giving the team time to redo my jersey, so it has the right name on it. Yours."

"Italy, huh? I like the sounds of that."

"Good, because I might have already booked the whole trip already." I sit up and caress his face before I kiss his forehead. "Now, we have to get back to this wedding, stop talking about our wedding, and maybe start figuring out what our name is going to be."

"LaVonsen."

"Not Jensen-LaVoie?"

"No. You're not the only one who's been making plans behind people's backs. Now, come here and kiss me like you mean it before I decide to go for round two while your pants are still down."

The Hollywoodland Series
will continue with
Chase & Ren in
Love the Stars Fondly

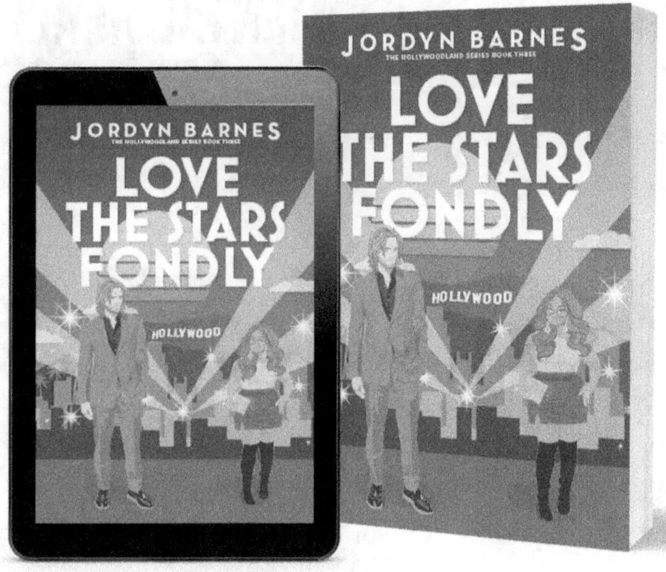

JORDYN BARNES
THE HOLLYWOODLAND SERIES BOOK THREE
LOVE
THE STARS
FONDLY
HOLLYWOOD

MENTAL HEALTH RESOURCES

IT'S OKAY TO NOT BE OKAY.

This book deals with several instances of mental health issues and struggles seen frequently in the LGBTQIA+ community. If you or someone you know is struggling, the following are free and confidential resources to help.

Suicide and Crisis Hotline
www.988lifeline.org | Call or text 988

National Domestic Violence Hotline
www.thehotline.org
1-800-799-7233 | Text **LOVEIS** to 22522

Prevention & Treatment of Child Abuse
www.childhelp.org/hotline/
1-800-4AChild (1-800-422-4453) | Text 1-800-422-4453

From hrc.org:

Transgender Community
translifeline.org | 877-565-8860

LGBTQ+ Youth

www.lgbthotline.org/youth-talkline | 1-800-246-7743

www.thetrevorproject.org/get-help-now
1-866-488-7386 | Text START to 678-678

All Ages
www.lgbthotline.org/national-hotline
1-888-843-4564

For more information on Mental Health:
National Institute of Mental Health (educational)
www.nimh.nih.gov | Chat: infocenter.nimh.nih.gov
1-866-615-6464

For International Mental Health resources:
dbtselfhelp.com/resources/international-resources

ACKNOWLEDGMENTS

If you ran to the internet to look up the band Revolver from the Halloween Party chapter, may I please refer you to the beautiful duet of Babydoll & Dollhouse by the incredible Thea Lawrence. Thank you so much for letting me be a part of your universe.

I'd like to start out by thanking everyone who read and enjoyed book one, Let Me Love You Anyway. If you haven't read it yet, and you've made it this far… Go read it!

Okay, starting from the top with my Alpha and Beta readers, you all were fantastic! You gave me so much input and really helped me get this book in shape. It's not easy going from a novella to a full book without changing a release date, but we did it! So thank you for everything.

Danielle, Emily, and Jennifer, seriously, this book wouldn't exist without you all helping me along the way and encouraging me to keep going with this silliness.

Also, Insert Trope Here PR, my street team, and all of you who share my social media marketing.

To my family, you are all awesome! Super special shoutout to my Mom, because she's awesome. If you come to a signing event, you'll probably meet her. Yes, she reads these.

To the parrots of Pasadena, long may you reign, you feathered menaces!

These business don't sponsor me, or even know I exist, however, they do appear in this story:
The Cheese Store of Beverly Hills- Beverly Hills, CA
Fat Sal's- Hollywood, CA (& other locations)
Trejo's Coffee & Donuts- Hollywood, CA
AMC Burbank- beautiful downtown Burbonk! (IYKYK) Also, yes, there are *THREE*, all under a half mile from each other.
Norms- Multiple Locations (I've never actually been, but they're everywhere!)
Arroyo Shell Gas Station- Pasadena, and yes, there is a giant button that says don't touch.

ABOUT JORDYN

Giving Broken Characters
Their Happily Ever Afters.

Jordyn Barnes is an author, graphic designer, nerd, & elder goth. She loves Halloween, creepy things, morally grey characters, and writing about the flawed and beautifully broken people she creates in her mind palace. When she's not writing or reading, she's rearranging the growing collection dedicated to her favorite Disney Princess: Bucky Barnes/Winter Soldier. She also enjoys Marvel movies/shows, true crime everything, and, occasionally, sports. She's a long time Disney adult who relates most strongly with Madam Mim's dislike of sunshine while envying her forest hag lifestyle.

For updates on upcoming releases, join Jordyn's mailing list at jordynbarnes.com. Don't forget to follow her on social media and Goodreads as well:

instagram.com/jordyn.writes.and.reads

tiktok.com/@Jordyn.writes.words

facebook.com/jordynbarnesauthor

goodreads.com/jordynbarnes

amazon.com/author/jordynbarnes

THE HOLLYWOODLAND BOOK SERIES

Let Me Love You Anyway

Faith in Fools

Love the Stars Fondly

Never to Suffer

In the Hatred of a Minute

Dream Only by Night

www.ingramcontent.com/pod-product-compliance
Lightning Source LLC
Chambersburg PA
CBHW070612300726
48975CB00006B/1789